I0653138

INHERITANCE OF
CRISES AND
DYSFUNCTION

A Novel
(Updated Edition)

James J. Maiwurm

Copyright 2024 by Maiwurm Publications, LLC

All rights reserved. This book or any portion thereof may not be reproduced or used in any manner whatsoever without the express written permission of the publisher except for the use of brief quotation in a book review.

Inquiries and Book Orders should be addressed to:

www.maiwurmpubs.com
Email: james.maiwurm@gmail.com
Phone: 2022566669

ISBN: 979-8-89175-146-0 (sc)
ISBN: 979-8-89175-141-5 (ebk)

America's Broken Politics, Public Health, Global Reputation, and Economy Face a New Administration

"Inheritance of Crises and Dysfunction" by James J. Maiwurm tells the story of America that awaits on the horizon and what led to its cracked foundation.

WASHINGTON D.C.- Masks continue as part of daily life, and a new administration is tasked with rebuilding a broken nation. "Inheritance of Crises and Dysfunction" by James J. Maiwurm is political fiction that launches readers into Inauguration Day 2021 in rural Virginia, where the COVID-19 pandemic and a recession have set farmers and small business owners into a life of financial instability and disarray. With roots in history, current events, and human nature, the novel provides valuable insight into foreign and domestic politics. At the same time, the protagonist's personal story also highlights the pain of losing a spouse and moving, the mixed emotions associated with contemplating retirement, and the psychological need to remain relevant and connected as one grows older.

The book follows Salt, a recent widower and retired lawyer whose career included stints with the U.S. Government. Just when Salt begins settling into his new life away from the noise of D.C., an old acquaintance who is about to become Secretary of State calls him back into the line of fire at the White House, where he is persuaded to take on a covert diplomatic role. Salt's hesitant acceptance ignites a chase around the world for sensitive meetings with key allies to begin repositioning America for productive leadership.

"This plot is an instance where fiction is truly no stranger than reality," Maiwurm said. "The book is designed to provide reader-friendly insight into both urgent domestic issues and the consequences of American's shrinking influence in the world."

"[The book's] ultimate message is one of hope. It postulates that, when politics are stripped away, Americans have a great deal in common, and that with patience and honest communication, the country's wounds can be healed so that a stronger nation can emerge," a Clarion reviewer wrote about the book.

"Inheritance of Crises and Dysfunction" is sure to intrigue readers with interest in the current state of America as the novel highlights struggles that lie ahead while also educating readers on topics such as government subsidies, the Black Lives Matter movement, Coronavirus, and economic instability so they can be better prepared to vote and handle what Maiwurm believes is on the horizon.

"Inheritance of Crises and Dysfunction"

By **James J. Maiwurm**
ISBN: 9781663204660 (softcover); 9781663204684 (hardcover); 9781663204677 (electronic)
Available at Amazon and Barnes & Noble

About the author

James J. Maiwurm is Chairman Emeritus Retired of one of the world's largest global law firms who in 2012 was named one of the top ten most innovative law firm managing partners by Law 360. Maiwurm grew up in small-town America, where he met his high school sweetheart whom he later married, earned a degree in history at the College of Wooster in Ohio, attended the University of Michigan Law School, and several years later had two children. For the past 30 years, Maiwurm has resided in the Washington D.C. area.

Contact:
LAVIDGE - Phoenix
Kayla Rutledge 480-648-7450 krutledw@lavidge.com

This is a work of fiction. Names, characters, places, and incidents are products of the author's imagination or are used fictitiously and are not to be construed as real. Any resemblance to actual events, locales, organizations, or persons, living or dead, is entirely coincidental.

Acknowledgments

For the most wonderful partner and spouse possible, a grand and fun family, the first responders and others who wear uniforms, Ukraine, the minority members of the special US congressional committee on January 6th and to dear friends Joe and Tex.

Inheritance of Crises and Dysfunction; Principal Characters (none of the names is intended to be real)

Cast Glossary

Salt	Staunton Pepper
Margie Hatcher	Friend of Salt in Carterville
(Marie) Louise Roseaux	CIA—on loan to the project
Eleanor Holmes	UK PM
John Watson	UK Foreign Secretary
Peter Banks	UK contact
Ray (Rene) Marchand	Salt's Canada friend
Gretchen Grant	US State Dept
Anthony Pope	Former US President
Walter Williams	State Dept in DC
President Evans	New President
Ed Jordan	US Embassy London
Carterville	A small town near Salt's farm
Martin Weber	German Foreign Office
Yoder family	Former farm tenants
Anja Besecke	German Foreign Minister

Jack Davis	Stone's current farm tenant
Ashkan Gilani	Iranian negotiation lead
Georgie	Barber #1 owns shop
Mary and George Anderson	Mary is a Bank President, and George is an entrepreneur and teacher
Alan Greene and partner Angelo	College President
Bob and Betty Reardon	GM dealer with 4 kids
Homer	Barber #2
Ellen	Barber #3
Steve	Farmer
Roy	Owns clothing store
Warren	Works at a hardware store
Don	Retired and hunter, NRA
Helen's Place	Local Diner
Stuart Bacon	Secretary of State Candidate (asst. Alex)
Max	Loquacious talker at the Fair

Contents

Foreward

As stated elsewhere, this is a work of fiction. It is not the product of scholarship. The book does not rely on substantive expert input from others. It is based mainly on one citizen's personal forward-looking perceptions of the news and developments surrounding the 2016 and 2000 presidential elections, the 2022 mid-term elections, some state elections, and imagination as to how 2024 may play out and affect the well-being of our children and grandchildren. This is like looking at history through the rearview mirror, knowing it will catch up with us.

I am not a futurist, but I do believe that—at least on our good days—we can learn from the past when setting a course for our own futures, even when an examination of the past demonstrates unacceptable inequities and some downright craziness. Perhaps some might use this book as an opportunity to look at the future through their own lens, i.e., a form of personal projected fiction, and using their own assumed conditions. And then when at a safe place (i.e., a place that is not yet evolved from reality), beginning to think about whether more and different outcomes are needed and whether we can muster the concern and huge collective body of work and – yes, compromise necessary to bring about much-needed changes in attitudes and results.

For the avoidance of doubt, this book is about the need for "more power to the middle," a renewed sharing of values that, except perhaps for the Civil War and the Reconstruction Era, have enabled us to strive harder to achieve the many goals we share, even though that sharing is not yet fair or fully endorsed by an overwhelming number of our fellow citizens. Our experiment at governance has been ongoing through the efforts of a majority—but admittedly not all—of our citizens for more than 200 years. Others are watching, and we no longer have time to think we are experimenting.

Do you hear and see them? Politics aside, on matters such as the climate, the red lights are blinking, the ugly-sounding horn is blaring, and a computer-generated voice is saying to us, "NOW HEAR THIS, NOW

HEAR THIS, this is a real emergency, not a drill. Get in the lifeboats. We are sorry if there are no lifeboats or places to go in them, but our more senior generations hope you have enjoyed your visit to Earth; they certainly have."

The first version of this book "started" on Inauguration day 2021 and continued into 2022. That period was dominated in many respects by a master puppeteer, President Donald Trump, who essentially was, and in many respects still is, the news in terms of foreign and domestic policy, diplomacy, cross-border relations, litigation and responding to global/political friends, enemies, and threats. By all means, remember Helsinki and President Trump's refusal to have others in the room when he spoke with Mr. Putin for a lengthy period and later embarrassed our senior intelligence officials by suggesting that Mr. Putin was more credible than our own experts. And, of course, there are January 6, tax breaks for those least in need, climate change, Black Lives Matter, supply chain issues, famine, the development of cult-like followings of some authoritarians (why is Orwell's 1984 a best seller, and which authoritarian state do you want to live in?), Ukraine, immigration, abortion, North Korea, the Supreme Court, the handling of secret intelligence materials in a resort, a delayed and politicized reaction to COVID-19 and variants, how we left Afghanistan, Iran, Russia, Saudi Arabia/Yemen, China/Taiwan, concerns about the staying power of US-style democracy, Venezuela, inflation, mass shootings, institutionalized racism, crime, automatic weapons, clean energy and a shortage of strong and charismatic leaders of all colors, shapes, and sizes.

Based on this array of issues, does our government focus more on the country or the parties (or getting re-elected)? How can there be so many unanimous single-party votes on significant issues in which none, or a tiny handful, vote with the other party (i.e., of, by, and for the people)? Maybe the problem is that we act like an aristocracy, asleep like Rip Van Winkle, who is said to have slept through the American Revolution, waiting for some good news about our new republic to wake him up.

Maybe we need to vote for good people who will exercise their own judgment. And not so much that of our Rip Van Winkles.

None of this is breaking news, but this aggregation of things creates an inheritance of crises and dysfunction—at home and abroad, and in red and blue states and regions, that deserves a view with perspective. In its own awkward way, we hope this book will provide some perspective and generate some thoughts about how and why others (within different regions and cultures of the US, both foreign and domestic, some with extreme views) react as they do to our leadership and followers. We need to do more of standing in others' shoes.

Disarray notwithstanding, all good people in the world want essentially the same things: physical security; financial stability; good health; and that our children do as well or better (broadly defined) than we did. To this end, all of us want to make a difference in this world. President Trump and some other domestic and world leaders surely have. It is now time for the rest of us to put our mark—the mark of moderates with the courage to stand up and the sense to migrate to and hold the middle--on the betterment of this world. And to be comfortable that most of our fellow citizens will join this effort— partly because although we might disagree, we will listen, respect, and compromise.

To borrow some phraseology from James Carville, "it's the grandkids, stupid". Our children and grandchildren deserve better than an inheritance of crises and dysfunction. In that regard, this is an excellent time to modify our political wills.

Prologue

I n 1765, there evolved a secretive group of provocateurs in the American colonies, heavily weighted toward Massachusetts, who were offended by British taxes ("taxation without representation") and other policies. King George III may or may not have been either decent or humorless, but he could not have been pleased with his faraway colonists. He never visited the colonies. And communications were made much more difficult by the lack of a vehicle such as a telegram, much less first-class mail, telephone, fax, or the Internet. Twenty-four-hour news cycles are distracting; 30-day news cycles would be more than an inconvenience. One wonders, if we had town criers today, that would imply a Fox news crier and one for MSNBC and each of several other networks? Our short news cycle is a mixed blessing, to be sure, but at least in the case of the United Kingdom and the American colonists, better communications might have been helpful. (However, picture the newspaper columns that would have been generated by communicators such as Thomas Paine, Alexander Hamilton, and Benjamin Franklin. Even the great Rush Limbaugh might have been vexed.)

The membership of this group of colonists, known as the Sons of Liberty, was limited to those who could be trusted and respected for their care, thoughts, discussions, and actions. But today, they would be called partisan; they had minds of their own. The membership included the likes of cousins Samuel and John Adams, Paul Revere, John Hancock, Joseph Warren, Benjamin Rush, Charles Wilson Peale, Alexander Hamilton, Hayn Salomon, Benedict Arnold, and Samuel Chase. They were not cut out of the same cloth or one mind politically, with some being "Federalists" wanting a strong central government and others preferring a more diffuse power distribution.

From the British perspective, they were the equivalent of our ungrateful domestic white terrorists. To many of the colonists, they were heroes. Others were not so happy with this highly progressive group. A triggering event took place on December 17, 1763, when a group of the Sons of Liberty dressed as Mohawk Indians moved tea from one of several ships in the Boston Harbor owned by the East India Tea Company (its tea a local and UK favorite) and unceremoniously dumped it in the harbor. An early case of evidence tampering? After the English Stamp Tax was imposed on the colonies in 1765, the group crystallized and became increasingly determined. The colonists were learning how to weaponize the colonial equivalent of defensive tariffs and trade sanctions.

Relations continued to deteriorate, with unrest ultimately giving rise to the Boston Massacre on March 5, 1769, when a group of nine British soldiers fired into a crowd of 300-400 colonists. The parties would have been using one-shot muskets, not assault rifles. A number of the locals were hurt. Ironically, John Adams was importuned to defend (successfully) the British soldiers. Was this an ancestor of police brutality cases?

One of many dates that could be used as signaling the start of the Revolutionary War was April 18, 1775, the morning after Paul Revere rode from Boston to Lexington and Concord—faster than the fastest town crier-- warning, "the British are coming." The Declaration of Independence was signed on July 4, 1776.

After several years of negotiations and confusion, the Articles of Confederation were adopted in 1781. But the Articles were engineered to protect the independence and sovereignty of the states. (Sounds a bit like some of the arguments made today about things like abortion and the power of the states.) Taxation was not among the new government's powers. Over time the states realized that they needed more governmental infrastructure. The Constitutional Convention met from May 25 until September 17, 1787, when the necessary states consented to the draft. The Constitution was ratified effective March 4, 1789. All elements of the Federal model were not disposed of. When Benjamin Franklin was asked about what form of government we had after the Convention, he is said to have responded, "a Republic Madame, if we can keep it."

That question should be ringing in our ears today. Indeed, January 6, with participation by groups such as the Oath Takers, Proud Boys, and perhaps today's versions of the Sons of Liberty (there are some) who made appearances at the US Capitol on January 6, 2022, is proof positive that among some of our citizens, the questions grappled with in 1787 are still alive Also, see some of the recent decisions of our reconstituted Supreme Court.

The American Revolution and its resulting constitutional governance were indeed revolutionary in the sense that they led to a democratic structure like no other but were also imperfect products of compromises. Democracy assumes voting rights. As originally adopted, white males did OK under the Constitution. Women and slaves, not so much. How about voting power? One man, one vote, for whites. But how would the number of members of the US House of Representatives be determined? Originally that count included in the formula two-thirds of the male slaves in the state—even though the vote was not passed through to the slaves. The number of senators? Two per state, no matter the considerable population differences. And most things needed to be passed by both the Senate and the House, thus giving a disproportionate vote to lesser populated states. This no doubt served a practical political purpose in 1787, but now gives "roadblock" power to a minority. Lincoln's Emancipation Proclamation (January 1, 1863) went a long way in the direction of effecting a change here, but the formal elimination of the two-thirds of slaves provision came with the 14th Amendment in 1868.

The current Electoral College provisions are also far from perfect. Under current law, the states determine how their electors will vote. The states' power as to the Electoral College was confirmed under the 15th Amendment (1870). The number of electors for each state equals the number of House members plus Senators. Score, smaller populated states. It is fair to conclude that the original Constitution discriminated against non-white males and women and was more than fair to the lesser-populated states. A lot has changed, but some of what we're going through now have their genesis at where we started with our Constitution and the compromises necessary to achieve adoption. Thus, the smaller states (in terms of the white male population) were protected by the core of the Constitution's structure.

This is a part of the background (recognized or not) to the white male chants in Charlottesville ("you will not replace us"). White males have lost voting power, and some no doubt feel the inevitability of a browner and blacker and more Asian America, but that is a fundamental element of a democracy. There was a time when white male Americans lost ground to the Irish, Italians and Jews, and women. Things were not entirely smooth, but there was no civil war. And heaven knows that institutionalized racism has served—and continues to serve--as an ugly brake on the pace and content of logical and necessary change. It is not surprising that many members of our organized domestic terror groups have white skin and hair that is greyer and greyer, or, dare we say, white.

The United States has had to deal with crises and dysfunction involving internal and external forces ever since it was founded. Some of us remember the 1960s, Vietnam, and the horrific assassinations of Martin Luther King, Jr. and Bobby Kennedy, and riots on campuses, in major cities, and at the national political party conventions.

We again sail in troubled waters. May we continue to achieve more fair resolutions and, when necessary, have the courage to construct, protect and preserve a prudent and truly fair middle path.

Chapter 1

Transitions

[December 2020]

In the middle of December 2020, Staunton Pepper, or "Salt" as he was known by anyone who knew him at all, had hauled another load of stuff from his townhouse in the District of Columbia (not quite Georgetown, but close) and was unloading it in the house on his family farm in Northern Virginia, near the foot of the Blue Ridge mountains. Unloading was all he was doing. The maximum available effort was figuring out whether he could stack yet another box on a pile that looked like it was already leaning. Reminded him of the days when his young nephew stacked wooden blocks on top of one another until they fell. Salt planned to stay at the farm for one night and then leave the next afternoon to visit some friends and a couple of relatives over the holidays, and he was to meet the moving van at the farmhouse in the afternoon on January 2. They were late (not a huge surprise) but were able to complete unloading by the end of the next day, a Sunday. But the days were all morphing together. Salt had no idea what was headed his way.

The weather? —about what you'd expect at that time of year and near the mountains: gray, damp, and chilly. The only thing not depressing about the morning was that President Anthony Pope was about to leave office. After a close, divisive, and uninspiring but somewhat frightening election, President Evans had emerged the winner. He did win—right? Evans presented as progressive enough to attract a sufficient number of millennials and minority voters but not so progressive as to alienate most moderates and suburbanites.

He accepted and promoted the need for different approaches to challenges such as the morphing COVID-19 pandemic and the related recession-type slowdown that remained scourges, won the popular vote, and managed not to lose in places where the Electoral College could have—

once again—overcome the popular voting results. From Evans' standpoint, things could be changed through the Internet, and he used some of that material in his remarks.

President Evans and his team were not the only group preparing for the inauguration in the middle of December 2020.

Chapter 2

Sons of Liberty Kick-Off
[January 5, 2021]

On a cold, dark, and clear starry evening on the 5th of December, in a worn and windowless barn not that far from Salt's farm— with what was left of one of those familiar "Chew Mail Pouch" ads painted on one side of the building—another meeting was about to start. "Samuel" presided and opened with a prayer, and the group joined in a hearty, if not talent-borne, rendition of the Battle Hymn of the Republic. "Samuel" called the meeting of the Sons of Liberty of Northern Virginia to order, asked a couple of the boys to throw some more wood in the stove, and then got things underway. The meeting was well attended, with none of the leaders (all of whom, like Samuel, used a first name adopted from one of the original Sons of Liberty) absent. Everyone knew that this was a big f . . .ing deal. There was only one absentee—some kind of a mystery man – "Alexander" (Hamilton)—referred to in ways that suggested that he was not a "regular" but perhaps a funding source. Many wore versions of the colonial tri-corner hat, a few coonskin caps, and red MAGA hats. Lots of flags, including the yellow "Don't Tread on Me."

The group was a mixture of a few Baby Boomers and more Gen X and Gen Y types. Some women, but mostly men. Hair length and greasiness, all over the spectrum (barbers would not make a living on this crew), lots of grey and white hair, no slacks, but lots of jeans and a few bib overalls, some with guns, some with knives, and a few who pretty clearly did not need a weapon. There would be a short attention span as a group, so Samuel was insistent on getting going before the beer kegs rolled out. The Sons were going to have to decide—individually and as a group—whether to shit or get off the pot.

Samuel explained that, consistent with the group's prior consensus, he had been in contact with Hamilton and with other similar groups around the colonies that were planning to accept President Pope's invitation (or was it an "order"?) to participate in the January 6 demonstration at the U.S. Capitol complex following a speech by President Pope. This was sure to get everyone's blood moving. It sounded like Samuel knew his way around some of the Internet's dark corners and used some of that material in his remarks.

Excitement filled the air, and the meeting took on the flavor of a pep rally, with high fives all around and plenty of cheering. Samuel cautioned that detailed plans were not being distributed because of the danger of leaks, though the Internet was full of chat about the event that was clearly building to a crescendo. He said it would be obvious what they should do when they got to the Capitol. They should dress for the temperature, come armed with whatever weapons they were comfortable with, the longer, the better, and if they ever needed to, should form a protective cocoon around President Pope. "Bring a photo of your ID of some kind in case you get arrested, not anything you could not burn, and wear a hat you could pull way down with a broad brim that would make it hard to get your picture from the top of a building." It seemed as though Samuel had a degree in "been there, done that."

Everyone agreed ("you bet your ass") that President Pope had actually won the election but had been cheated in more ways than folks could even describe. The judges in cases related to the vote were losers and all on the take, and standard processes could not be followed. Samuel detailed his calls and meetings (carefully arranged so there would be no—and he meant "no"— electronic evidence) with leaders of similar groups about what they intended to do in response to the call from President Pope for a big crowd that would send the ultra-progressives running for the hills and result in the reversal of the election results ("damn right"). For once, the lawyers had dreamed up a foolproof way to get things fixed and deal with the Vice President at the same time. All the Sons and others, like the Oath Keepers and the Proud Boys, needed to do was show up, display some honest-to-God grit for a change, and handle any troublemakers. No more bullshit and enough with the fast- talking, do nothing lawyers, who seemed only to sweat through their makeup, get thrown out of court on their asses, and then holler, "wait till we get their asses in the court of appeals." . . . "Enough."

After some minimal discussion, someone rolled out a keg of beer and said, "I think it's time to vote to save our country and the President tomorrow and wet our whistles tonight." There was a responsive chorus of mixed profanity that could only mean yes. John said they should meet back at the barn in the morning at 6:00 am and go to DC together. Samuel added, "no girlfriends; if you have needs, get laid tonight."

Chapter 3

Getting to Know Margie
[January 4, 2021]

S alt's trip to visit the relatives and friends was healing to some extent, for a good time was had by all: other than those deeply missing a lost spouse. It was possible to share another's happiness and satisfaction and be glad for them without sharing that empty feeling under a thick skin.

Pepper was a lawyer by training, not very handy, lacking practical organizational skills, and still adjusting to his wife's death six months earlier, during the initial stages of the COVID-19 crisis. He had even moved some of her things—some without knowing it. To make things worse, he wasn't a label person. Neither were his discount movers. As he considered his fate, he pulled a large box off the couch in what seemed to be his living room, so there was a place to sit down. Just for grins, he tried to figure out where the contents of that box might go. It was heavy and large, but he had no hint of its contents. It seemed to him that anyone visiting would conclude that he was hopelessly clueless. Why would someone without practical farming experience, and a recent widower without friends in the area to boot, move to the middle of nowhere near the edge of the Blue Ridge Mountains during January?

The moving van had left late on the previous day. Salt was up at sort of a normal (latish) time for him, and he started thinking about Plan A for breakfast. He had no idea where his cereal (or anything else for that matter) was. As he sat down and put his legs up on a box, Pepper pondered what the hell he had thought when he decided to move. He sat there motionless and glum for a bit. And then things got worse: he heard a sound that could only be the doorbell.

Sure enough, it was. A woman carrying a small box of something had appeared uninvited on his porch. He was still thinking through what it meant to have something you might call a porch; he had not lived anywhere with something like that since leaving the farm to go to college in the Midwest. As he looked out the window of the door, he noticed that it had started to rain and observed that a porch protected uninvited visitors from the elements. Which way did that cut?

Panicked, Pepper looked down to remind himself of what he had on. Sweatpants, an old hoodie he had once worn while painting a room in his old apartment, and ancient tennis shoes that showed their age. He had not yet shaved, and his hair was unkempt at best. In contrast, he could tell that his tallish visitor was wearing a dress under her raincoat and had medium-length or a bit longer well-groomed auburn-colored hair and flat black shoes that were not showing signs of age. She was thinnish and seemed to be wearing a smile under her mask.

Pepper broke through his introverted nature, summoned all of his courage, and opened the door. He concluded by her cheerful "Welcome to the neighborhood" look that they were not going to get along.

She introduced herself as Margaret Hatcher. "Not Thatcher," she said. "Call me Margie. Everyone does. I live about half a mile down the road and noticed the moving truck pulling away. I was baking some chocolate chip cookies today and thought you might be able to use a sugary energy booster."

Pepper was standing in the doorway, holding the door half-closed, when it finally dawned on him that he was being impolite and had no choice but to invite her in. And there was the chocolate chip cookie factor—homemade chocolate chip cookies scored big points.

Pepper stumbled a bit but managed to say, "I'm embarrassed by the state of things here, but please come in and allow me to find a place where you might safely sit down at a proper social distance, and let me find one of my new masks. I'm sure I have some somewhere."

"Not to worry," she said. "I'll keep my distance, and there is no such thing as an easy and orderly move. We Welcome Wagon volunteers see all kinds of disasters."

"Welcome Wagon?" queried Pepper. "I didn't know it still existed." "Well, it actually doesn't—at least not here in a formal way," explained Margie. "But a few of us in a book club try to do what we can to help newcomers adjust to Carterville and feel welcome. It's just the right thing to do, and we meet some fascinating people this way. Will your family be joining you today?"

"Sorry to say I don't have a family," explained Pepper. "My wife passed last year, and we didn't have children. So, besides a younger sister, I'm alone."

"I am so sorry. I didn't intend to open wounds," she said sincerely. "Your question was perfectly natural—and no harm done."

"Thanks," said Margie. "If you don't mind another risky question, what brings you here?"

"I shouldn't admit this, but to be honest, I was just sitting here wondering that myself," mused Pepper. "What am I doing here? The obvious answer is that I grew up here on this farm until I went to college. Although I never came back, except for holidays, it ended up being mine when my parents passed. My sister didn't want it, and I was willing to take the farm as my share of the estate. At that time, the Yoder family was actually farming here, and when my parents passed, the Yoders moved into the house. They couldn't afford to buy the farm, and I hated to sell it from under them, though I'm told that 150 acres are not big enough to work financially. They were good, hardworking folks who treated it like it was theirs. I never made much on the deal, but I didn't need much."

"I didn't know the Yoders well," said Margie, "but they seemed like nice folks."

"They are," said Pepper. "They decided to retire from farming toward the end of 2018. Jack Davis, who went to school with my sister and is younger than me, called and said he wanted to rent the land and barn to be part of his farming operations, but he wasn't interested in buying. So, as I was winding down with my law firm in DC in the wake of my wife's death and the dislocation created by the COVID-19 virus, it seemed like coming back home might make for a good, fresh start for the rest of my life." He paused, looking out the window toward the mountains but not really focusing on anything, and then commented as much to himself as to Margie, "Holy cow. I'm sorry to burden you with my life history. I've got to watch that."

"That's okay. I asked the question," she replied.

"Okay, Margie. Turnabout is fair play," said Pepper. "What's your story? Are you from around here?"

"Yes and no," she said. "I attended James Madison University, about forty miles south of here. I was dating my husband-to-be then, and we were both education majors at Madison. He was from Carterville, and I was from a suburb of Philadelphia. We both student-taught here in town and ended up with offers in what was not a great market for teachers. After we graduated, we got married and moved here. He was a teacher and basketball coach. He coached junior high, then freshmen, and eventually the boys' varsity basketball team. I taught high school English and ended up as the assistant principal at the high school."

"Any children?" asked Pepper.

"No," she replied. "I guess we were overexposed to kids at school, so we never had our own. My husband passed in an auto accident several years ago, but I didn't have it in me to move. Besides, for better or worse, we virtually knew everyone around these parts, and my friends and support infrastructure were all here. In that sense, I'm now from here."

"Sorry," said Pepper. "Now I'm the one who's ripping off scabs."

"Don't worry," she said. "I have some scar tissue but no open wounds. Back to you. Do you need some help here? How are you planning to get unpacked and settled in all by yourself? I would gladly come over in jeans tomorrow and help out."

"You just put your finger on the problem," he responded. "I don't have a clue about how I'm going to unpack. My current thinking is that I'm going to find and deal with the minimum I need and then put the rest on hold to see how this move works for me. No offense, but it could be that the whole move here is a massive mistake. I don't know and won't for a while. In any event, thanks, but I think I can handle the bare necessities."

"Okay." She smiled. "I get that. But holler if your new neighbors can help at all. I'm just down the road about half a mile toward town."

"There are a couple of things you could help with," Pepper said. "I could use some recommendations. In no particular order, I need to get a haircut, get some dry cleaning done, and find an informal place to eat that's open for indoor dining and not a fast-food joint."

"Those are easy ones," she laughed. "Dry cleaner is on the edge of town on the left. As for the haircut, do you want a stylist or a barber?"

"A barber."

"Then try Georgie's on the square in town," she said. "You'll either love it or hate it."

"OMG, is this the same Georgie's that was in business when I left home to go to college?"

"The same," Margie smiled. "And there is a good small-town diner called Helen's Place across the street from Georgie's near the county court-house in the middle of town."

"Wow. This will be a serious trip down memory lane."

"Well," responded Margie, "you almost missed them. They are small businesses that were shut down for more than three months last year as a result of the COVID-19 pandemic. Things remained slow even after the lockdown eased up, and I guess they still are. I'm not sure which of the small businesses will make it over the long term. Things have been rough for a long time."

"These have been tough times indeed," remarked Pepper. "Heaven knows when we'll return to normal, whatever that is."

"Well, good luck with deciding what you're going to do," Margie said as she stood up and headed for the door, "and let me know if there's anything I can help with. My number is on this card."

As Margie was nearing the door, Salt yelled: "Hey, I forgot to ask if you know anyone who has a cheap rate for disposal of top secret documents." Margie stopped dead in her tracks, and then realized that Salt was kidding. Both had a good laugh. Salt thought to himself that it's always good to know if your neighbor has a sense of humor.

After Margie left, Pepper returned to his ruminations and box collection. He concluded that the first day in a new place must always be miserable. In the near term, he needed to get to Georgie's to see if he could get a much- needed haircut, not that he was planning to attend the Inauguration or anything like that.

Chapter 4

Back to Georgie's

[January 4, 2021]

After Margie's departure, Pepper felt the need to do anything but unpack. He decided to shave and shower. As he shaved in front of the mirror, he took stock of his 6'1" frame. He had put on weight since his wife's death and had been surviving on too much junk food. He still looked like he was in decent shape. However, he had not been exercising with any regularity. He needed to correct that before things got out of control. His dark hair, sprinkled with more greying as the months marched on, was getting shaggy by his standards. And the longer his hair, the more grey that showed.

Pepper still had coverage on his mobile phone, so he found Georgie's number and called to see if he could get an appointment for a haircut. Georgie himself answered the phone. Georgie must have had caller ID, and Pepper was calling with his mobile, which had a 202 (DC) area code. Before Pepper could get a word in, Georgie hollered into the phone: "Hey, bub, nobody calls me from a 202 area code. I'm not interested in your survey; I ain't buyin' nothing, I don't need a car warranty or health insurance, and I donate nothin' to nobody. Don't call again."

Pepper virtually yelled into his phone as Georgie hung up, "Hey, all I want is a haircut appointment." Pepper had the sense that Georgie heard him, but he must have had too much momentum in slamming the phone down to be able to stop. So Pepper called back.

Georgie was still gruff. "You again, huh? Appointment? We don't make appointments. You come in, you take a number, you wait your turn in the shop, or you do some shopping in the downtown area, and when your number comes up, you climb in the chair."

"Sorry," Pepper said. "I'm new in town and didn't know the rules."

"Ugh, newbies," Georgie grumbled. "Since you're new, I'll give you number twenty-nine if you want a haircut today. I estimate that number will be up in about two hours at the end of the day. How's that work? Don't be late. What's your name?"

"Name is Pepper."

"That your first or last name?" Georgie asked. "Ah hell," he continued, "doesn't matter. The only peppers we have around here are grown in gardens. Are you comin' or not?"

"See you soon. Thanks," responded Pepper.

Pepper puttered around for a bit and then climbed into his somewhat elderly Volvo to drive into town. As he drove, he passed a sign with an arrow pointing straight ahead to the "historical area." Carterville was a small town and county seat with a quaint downtown that included lots of two-story brick buildings dating from before World War II, brick sidewalks, a genuine town square with parking, trees, and the prototypical courthouse, and many storefronts that at one time had windows providing a view into once-bustling shops. Sadly, they weren't so bustling anymore.

It was nearly dark outside when Pepper walked into the barbershop. On the wall were three sets of hooks that held numbers, a different color for each barber chair. Not much had changed in Georgie's barbershop since Pepper had had his going-away-to-college haircut. There was still a red, white, and blue barber pole outside. Indoors, the tin ceiling was still yellowed from the days when patrons smoked at will. The linoleum floor, cast-iron barber chairs, big leather straps used to sharpen razors hanging down the side of the barber chairs, shave cream dispensers, and towel heaters were all without visible change. The shop was much bigger than needed for three barbers, and there were a lot of chairs, but many of them were stacked in a corner to allow for social distancing. Various out-of-date newspapers and magazines were in evidence, and a lot of chitchats were going on. It was almost Inauguration Day, after all.

One new feature was a large smart TV hanging on the wall, tuned to Fox News; another was the barbers' masks. The use of masks by the customers was less uniform, but Pepper put his on.

The biggest difference in the shop was the barbers themselves. Georgie was Georgie, referred to by many customers as the "old white guy." But instead of three caucasians, a second barber was a black male, and the third was a brown-skinned woman. The customers were diverse, though a majority, like Georgie, were old white guys. It seemed like everyone in the shop was treated with equally good-natured disrespect in terms of reactions to their reviews of the election—or anything else for that matter. But it also seemed that the chitchat avoided the most controversial issues. In that sense, it was a little like the Thanksgiving discussion when the uncles, aunts, and cousins visited, and everyone avoided discussing politics.

"You must be number twenty-nine," Georgie said to Pepper. "Have a seat."

A number of the patrons looked like they had already had their haircut, but they hung around, as Georgie later explained, "to shoot the shit." Most of them were acquainted with one another, and most had opinions about the election and what the President's speech would be like. "Blah, blah, blah" got the most votes. Pepper was smart enough not to become an active participant in the banter. That allowed him to escape becoming a target. Besides, the people in the barbershop would figure out soon enough that he was from DC and a lawyer to boot.

After Pepper was seated, Georgie turned the barber chair around, so Pepper could see himself in the large mirror. He wasn't getting any younger. Apart from the grey hair, his face featured lines and a sort of ruddy complexion. Along with everything else going on in his life, Pepper was jolted a bit by his appearance. He just didn't think of himself as old. Maybe it was the lighting in the barbershop. But then there was the math.

Georgie interrupted this train of thought by asking, "What's your name, number twenty-nine?"

"Pepper," he said.

"That your first or last name?" "Last."

"What name do you go by?" "Hmm. Long story."

"That's okay," said Georgie. "We'll just call you Pepper."

"Well—let me try to give you the short version," offered Pepper. "My real first name is Staunton, I guess after a relative or the small town downstate where they hold the Shakespeare Festival. That got shortened to Stan among family members. When I was in high school, people still remembered the Beatles and started calling me Sarge after the song 'Sergeant Pepper's Lonely Hearts Club Band.' That didn't stick for long, and people decided that Salt N. Pepper was a normal progression from Staunton Pepper. Then they started to use the obvious shorthand by calling me Salt. So a lot of people in the family call me Stan and others who know me pretty well call me Salt."

"Got it," said Georgie. "Next time you come in, we'll figure out what to call you. Today, you're number twenty-nine. Are you new in town?"

"Yes and no," Salt responded. "I grew up and lived here till I went off to college. You cut my hair when I was in high school. People around here called our farm the Pepper Place. The Yoders lived there for a long time, and now that I'm retired, I'm thinking about moving back here."

"We heard there was a moving van out there," said Georgie. "People wondered what was going on. Where are you moving in from?

This was getting serious, and Salt said meekly, "Washington, DC."

"Well, son, what are you doing in this barbershop today?" Georgie asked. "Why aren't you getting ready for a demonstration of some kind or an inaugural party? You must have been one of those pointy-headed members of the Deep State. Or part of what we used to call the Trilateral Commission."

"Nope," Salt responded. "The truth is almost worse than that. For the past five years, I have been with a DC law firm; before that, I worked in the Treasury Department and the State Department. But I'm getting over all of that."

"Good for you, and welcome back," said Georgie. "I guess I'll just need to figure out how to give a pointy-headed haircut."

"You know," Salt said, "it's interesting that I haven't heard the words Trilateral Commission since high school. I had an uncle who suspected such a thing existed and that they secretly ran the US government, if not the world. That was the reason he always kept a stash of gold and silver around as a hedge against who knows what. To my surprise, I later found out that there was such a thing as the Trilateral Commission, which included some powerful people. Today, I guess you would call them hedge fund managers, billionaires, business leaders, retired politicians, people who run huge political action committees, and other very bright people. Many show up at the World Economic Forum held in Davos, Switzerland, once a year or in connection with Group of Seven or G-7 meetings; not many were ever elected. Not sure they did any harm in the old days. Still not sure they aren't a positive force."

"Well, there you go," said Georgie. "Seems like your uncle was mostly right."

"Do you really think it exists and does things?" asked Pepper.

"You bet your sweet ass," said Georgie without any response delay. "Let me see," Georgie said, "a bunch of super-rich guys, relatively few of them going to jail because of President Pope, they control businesses like Russia controls them oligarchs or whatever you call them, they can't afford to get involved with drugs, they play with people like they were poker chips, it pays for them to be close with Congressmen and members of the administration, and they don't really ski unless it is really sex. Those guys?"

"Sorry, I guess I touched a nerve."

"Well," said Georgie, "one of those guys had a radio call-in show during the 1950s and told everyone they should buy gold because inflation was coming and they needed protection. He was right about that, and my Dad put a lot of his money in gold and silver. It wasn't much money, but it was all he had. It worked, sure as hell, for about 5 months. Then the radio guy announced that inflation was going down and everyone should get rid of the gold and silver. Of course, my Dad was not a broker, so he had to wait in line to get a trade done. Big F . . . ing surprise. The little guys got screwed just because of when their sell orders got filled. Dad damn near lost it all, we almost lost the house, and he was on the edge of suicide for a month. Yes, I hate those bastards, just like these bitcoin jerks."

"By the way," Georgie continued as he settled down, "Don't worry. I won't shave the back of your hairline until I settle down."

Salt was unsure that was a good warning, so he looked around the shop and decided to try to reduce the outsider bias and introduce himself while Georgie was assembling his scissors and combs. He stood up and started walking around to chat, without shaking hands, of course.

The first person introduced himself as Steve. "I farm here," he explained. "What kind of farming?" Salt asked.

"Good question," responded Steve. "I used to be a grain and soybean farmer. But that was before President Pope double-crossed us and used tariffs to attack China. The return ticket from China hurt badly. Then there was COVID-19 and our current recession. I don't know what I'll plant this spring if anything. The grain markets are a mess. Sorry, but you asked."

"No problem," said Salt. "Sorry about the mess. Despite what President Pope said, I know the tariff disruption has lasted a long time. And the recession has been Godawful."

"You are 100 percent correct," said Steve. "Right after I learned about tariffs, I had to learn about how hard it is to reengineer what they call supply chains, and then all hell broke loose with the pandemic and recession. You know, some people say we are not in a recession; I say bullshit. Nobody would call this normal. Maybe I should do what everyone else around here seems to be doing and plant grapes and get one of those "government giveaway loans," but I'm not sure folks are even buying wine these days. And it's hard to get excited about popping corks for the city folk and sippin' wine with them all day. No offense, of course."

"None taken." Salt next introduced himself to Roy. "What do you do, Roy?"

"I run the men's clothing store down the street—your typical small business trying to survive against Target, Walmart, the Internet, and the recession."

"Good to meet you," Salt said. "After I get unpacked, I may need to come and see you."

"That would be great," offered Roy. "We'll take good care of you."

Next was Warren, one of the black patrons. "I work in the hardware store," Warren explained. "You being in the old Pepper place, you'll need what we have from time to time. Most of our stuff is made in America. If you're looking for service, give us a try. You may need some handyman help, and we can recommend some. You need to know who's who around here. What with business going to hell last year, everyone and his brother is say'n' he's a handyman. Some can't drive a nail straight."

"Thanks," said Salt. "I imagine I'll be a regular customer for a while. And I'm not the handiest guy alive. That's a lawyer disease."

Finally, there was Don. "I don't do much since I retired," offered Don. "Just hoping the government won't crash completely and take away my social security and Medicare."

"We're in the same boat, Don," said Salt. "Having just retired and counting on social security and Medicare, I also hope the government is careful."

"And by the way," volunteered Don, "I'm a hunter, a Second Amendment guy, and a card-carrying member of the National Rifle Association. Just in case you wondered, and I get to DC from time to time for big events."

"Good to know. Thanks," replied Salt. "My dad was a member of the NRA, and I can still remember when I was in school here, and we got the first day of hunting season off from school. Do they still do that?"

"Not officially." Don smiled. "That would not be politically correct, would it? But at least before COVID-19, we had the twenty-four-hour flu around here at certain times of the year, if you get my drift. Not sure what we'll do now. I guess the good news is that you don't have to worry about being six feet apart when walking in the woods with a bright orange jacket on." As Don was leaving, he handed Salt a card with his name and telephone number. "If you ever want an alternative perspective on things around here, call me, and we'll have a cup of coffee."

"'Thanks," said Salt, as he wrote his mobile number (and only number) on a card for Don.

By this time, it was nearing 5:45 p.m., and the other patrons, having had their hair cut and learning about Salt, started to leave. So did the other barbers.

After Don got through the door, he pulled a throwaway cell phone from his jacket pocket and dialed. When the other party answered, Don said, "It appears that a retired federale is moving into the Yoder family place. He seemed to have been a civilian and was with the State Department. He has a law degree but does not seem to be FBI or Justice Department. Thought you might want to know."

The party on the other end of the call said simply, "Thanks. Sounds harmless enough, but let me know if you learn anything interesting. And throw away this phone." Then Don heard nothing but the dial tone.

Salt got back to the barber chair; it was just Salt and Georgie left in the barbershop. In these quiet few moments, Salt asked, "Georgie, this is a good place to get a haircut, but people clearly come in early and hang around before and after getting their cut. Why do you put up with that?"

"It's part of who we are. Most of the folks who hang around here work in town or are retired, semiretired, or unemployed; they have time on their hands, they don't belong to book clubs, there is only so much cable news you can take, and human interaction is a good thing. You didn't see that today, but they like to argue. They also like to get a bit of a shave and a hot towel. A number of these people are just plain lonely. And some are desperate. Talk about desperation; you should have been here last summer when it became apparent that COVID-19 would hold on much longer and stronger than expected. Ugh. This shop was standing room only, and I had to take a few IOUs for haircuts. It was really sad—still is in a lot of cases.

"Anyhow, folks are welcome to hang around as long as I can stand on my aching feet. And they know the rules—the one here the longest leaves when the chairs get filled up and a new customer comes in."

Salt then asked, "How bad has COVID-19 been around here? Did many people get it?"

"I think we had less than one hundred who got it last year and went to the hospital," responded Georgie. "They never did get the testing right, so nobody knows for sure. Something like fifteen died from it. Mostly older folks or people who had some other condition going on. But that damn virus has hung on like a dog with a favorite bone, and it is still in the air here, and folks are still coming down with it. The health risk is really depressing. I thank God for the vaccine. Others have different views.

"You know, the illness was horrible, but the lockdown that people have had to sit through has also been really miserable, and we are still living with limitations on what we're supposed to do. With businesses closing or cutting back, many for good, people woke up to the fact that a lot of jobs were gone forever. You know, we lost a lot of stores here in the downtown area. I was lucky. I lost a lot of business, but at some point, most people decide they need to get a haircut."

Georgie had started to cut Salt's hair, but Salt decided to press his luck. "None of my business, but do you have many women customers?"

"I don't," said Georgie, "but the other barbers do. If you're looking for a good cut and not two hundred dollars worth of color and uppity styling, this is a good place for a woman to come. You didn't see any women here this afternoon because they tend to come in earlier and don't like some of the cursing that goes on later. Now, how do you want your hair cut?"

'Medium, I guess," responded Salt.

"Yeah, you look like a medium type of pointy-headed guy," Georgie said, laughing.

"One more question?" asked Salt.

"Okay, just one more," responded Georgie. "What's with the Hair-i-Care sign behind you?"

Georgie laughed and handed Salt a piece of paper that said at the top, "Hair-i-Care Application." Georgie got up on his soapbox: "All this talk about the green new deal and Medicare for all and forgiveness of college loans, and nothin', and I mean nothin', about controlling or subsidizing the cost of haircuts. So, we set up our own 10 percent discount program. But you have to apply and qualify."

Salt focused on the rest of the house rules then laughed quietly, then asked for the rest of the rules and who decided who qualifies for a discount..

"Well," said Georgie, "I consult with the other barbers, and they get a vote, but I make the decisions if you know what I mean."

"Got it," Salt responded, "this is an aristocracy. But how about question number seven? Is that for real?"

"Hell yes," said Georgie, chuckling. "That's the polygraph question."

"Huh?"

"Well, our customer base is day-by-day becoming a little longer in the tooth and shorter on digestion, if you know what I mean. Anyone who answers that question yes is a liar and does not get the discount."

"Okay." Salt laughed. "But how about number one? Seems to smack of affirmative action."

"Maybe," said Georgie. "We don't have long enough tonight to talk through that one. Just remember that this is one case where someone did what they thought was right in general terms and for their business, without any pushing or shoving from the government."

Since they were getting close to the topic, Salt asked, "How is the Black Lives Matter movement going here?"

Georgie thought for a few moments and responded, "Well, you ask a lot of questions, and now you're getting into touchy stuff. The truth is that the Black Lives Matter movement does not get a lot of play here. There were some mild demonstrations following the George Floyd killing in Minnesota but no violence. Hell, we don't have any statues to pull down, even if a crowd wanted to do that. This is a small enough town that big crowds do not assemble for anything. Nobody buys into violence or riots, but a lot of people—all flavors of them—are beginning to understand that something is seriously wrong with our race relations. Most just don't talk much about it when strangers or people who don't get it are around. Next time you're here, ask Homer about this. That's his Black Lives Matter sign over there in the corner. He went to a couple of demonstrations."

"Hmm," murmured Salt. "That must have been a controversial addition to the barbershop."

"Not really," said Georgie. "Homer is not just a black guy; he's Homer. A person. People know him as a person and like him, even if they disagree with him about things like police brutality. Comfort comes more easily with the known than the unknown. Wasn't it a Secretary of Defense who used to talk about known knowns, known unknowns, and the like? Besides, Homer gives a good haircut."

Salt decided he would shut up and enjoyed the warm towel on his face after Georgie finished his haircut. Wisdom can be found in unusual places. It was good to be reminded of that.

Chapter 5

Climbing Out of Life Among the Moving Boxes
[January 5-6, 2021]

T he next day, January 5, started out better—at least Salt thought so. It felt like it must be warmer outside. The fog lifted, and Salt could see the mountains. Why are they called the Blue Ridge? he wondered. They looked a bit blue when the sunlight hit them the right way—or was he kidding himself? He had read somewhere that the soil's chemistry affected the tree leaves. But most of the leaves were gone. Well, not today's issue. The mountains were tranquil, relaxing, and majestic on their own, and that was welcome. To make things better, the sun had come out. It was not raining. This was not the Rocky Mountains as viewed from Denver or Boulder, but it was pretty damn good.

A few of Margie's chocolate chip cookies were left. The cookies were the only breakfast food he could find (though, truthfully, he didn't look very hard after finding the cookies), so he had several with two cups of coffee. So much for the good news; boxes still remained, and he attacked them.

By the end of the day on January 5, Salt had unpacked and sent late Christmas cards to selected family members. Are people really still sending cards, he wondered, but he sure as hell was not going to send emails (besides, he had no Internet service yet). He had done his mandatory Christmas family visits. He owed a lot of the same people a holiday card and a thank you, so for some it was a two-birds-with-one-stone exercise. He didn't mind that much, but it was more like hard work without Meredith at his side to remind him who was "Uncle Bob". Salt was not good with names; the same was true for small talk. Family meetings were tough. He was a terrible chit-chatterer and was not good at remembering jokes he had heard. He didn't cook at all, so he was sort of one of three designated dishwashers. Even that was not all bad as it placed him near the fridge in the kitchen, where he could reach in and grab a full glass of eggnog from time to time and glance at the football game on TV.

Salt had lived in the District of Columbia, all of his post–law school adult life, but wasn't active in party politics as such. He avoided anything that looked, felt, or tasted like partisanship. He survived by being neutral and good at what he did. He had served under five presidents, and as he finished his government career with the State Department, he had become a jack-of- all-trades, handling tough issues in the background and developing trusted relationships. He had worked with both the more partisan players in the United States and key career diplomats overseas. People sought him out not for favors but for insight and judgment. He wasn't a person who liked to hear himself talk. But when he talked, people listened—at least some of the time.

Salt was by nature a moderate in style and thought—a person comfortable with the ambiguity of being in the middle even if it forced you to think. He was either a moderate Republican or a moderate Democrat; nobody knew. He did vote in the most recent election and for the new president. That was the first time he had voted in a very long time. He remained neutral while with the law firm. But he did not view the most recent election as a close judgment call; it was more of an emergency response.

He had gone through a major adjustment when he left the Government and joined the law firm five years ago. He was again viewed as a seer, but he had to learn to be hyper-responsive to clients—and even to do some "marketing." During his first year out of the Government, he was barred from lobbying directly, and that put a crimp in his style. He was sought out on all things international, was invited to join a company board (he declined, saying that he would rather represent them, and did), and became moderately successful over time. But he was essentially an introvert, never got the hang of selling, and fundamentally remained a policy wonk.

Like many law firms, Salt's firm suffered during 2020 as the post-COVID-19 recession became more serious. There were cutbacks. Strangely, efforts to get back to the expected norm in the fall of 2020 did not precisely head toward a familiar normal.

The virus was not going away, and during the fall of 2021, they were still working on vaccines, with several in process and none fully approved and widely administered.

Salt decided—probably mistakenly—after his wife, Meredith, died that he needed to move on and would gracefully slide out of the law firm toward retirement at the end of the year. He wondered from time to time whether, despite Meredith's death, he would have been asked to retire even if he had not planned to do so. But he never had to find out. Probably just as well.

As Salt flipped among the news channels that evening he was keenly interested in the various and inconsistent takes on what the new President would say in his inaugural address. Knowing that the President's words were important, but that perception sometimes trumps reality, he paid attention across the broad commentator spectrum.

Chapter 6

January 6

[January 6, 2021]

T he next morning, January 6, Salt finished sorting boxes by floor—which meant carrying all manner of loads up an old and creaking staircase with ancient wallpaper on the walls and ceiling.

In fact, in the course of his efforts, Salt noticed that there seemed to be a lot of wallpaper all over the house. It was old and mostly one shade of green or another—in other words, ugly. Salt concluded that removing the wallpaper and fixing the plaster issues that would almost certainly be uncovered if the wallpaper was taken down would be a major investment. Ditto the plumbing. He couldn't bring himself to think about it.

By a little after noon, Salt had had it. Coming around to the realization that the packers had not packed much of his food, Salt drove into town and stopped at the drive-in at the first fast-food joint he came to. He ordered a sumptuous meal of a cheeseburger and fries and turned on the car radio.

Salt's plan had been to go home and spend the afternoon watching an old cowboy movie on a cable channel that he had not known existed. He liked cowboy movies. They didn't force you to think; the good guys wore white hats and always won and got the girl, and the bad guys wore dark hats and always lost. Cowboy movies were not particularly politically correct, especially on gender issues and Native Americans, but that was more than Salt could sort out that afternoon. It was hard to think about cutting cowboy movies out of his life. He had done enough of that over the last year.

As he was headed home with his cheeseburger, Salt turned on the radio. Based on what the radio was reporting, he hustled home, turned on his mini TV, and saw the breaking news.

As Salt focused on the dreadful scene covering the roadways and middle area between Pennsylvania and Constitution Avenues toward the Capitol, the question of how far our citizenry would go in response to a bogus call for action became real. After the kick-off rally at the Ellipse in front of the White House, egged on by President Pope, a group of thousands turned into an angry mob that attacked the Capitol complex in Washington, DC, and police. For some reason, President Pope did not actually get down to the Capitol, but members of the crowd knew what was to happen. It turned into a mean and dangerously ugly crowd, and despite best efforts, the police soon lost control. This group of visitors was not there to look at the memorials, snap a picture and then move on. They had a mission, and whatever it was turned mean and ugly. They weren't there to look at the statues; they were there to weaponize them.

Salt's jaw dropped. Our Democracy lost its modern-day virginity that afternoon and early evening in a closer and more organized assault than anyone--other than the leading participants—expected or understood. As Salt learned over time, through two impeachment proceedings, continued efforts of the press, and the investigation of the very able special house committee formed to investigate the January 6 events, he began to wonder whether the Country's mechanisms for the peaceful transfer of power were sufficient. It was an astonishingly close call. As to whether groups like the Sons of Liberty might succeed, how could January 6 happen?

As he watched the mob scene on a cable station that afternoon, Salt congratulated himself for successfully extracting himself from the Government before these events took place and quickly changed so many things. But it also shook him up. Did that really happen?

Turns out that it did.

Chapter 7

First Client Call

[January 6-7, 2021]

S alt had heard and seen enough of the riots and the related commentary and was about to turn in when his phone rang. He hesitantly picked up the phone with care, but he heard the voice of Don—the guy from the barbershop crowd. He was yelling through his cell phone with lots of background noise. "Salt, Salt, we really need your help. We don't know any lawyers in DC, and about eight of the Sons of Liberty, which we call ourselves, are about to be booked and put in a holding cell in DC. We're in a hallway right now being "processed," but they could hold us overnight. Our people ought to be treated like heroes, and here we are, standing around in piles of shit and pools of piss and vomit (used and half-used alcohol in some minds). All we did was exercise our rights, take a few swings at people, and not use any weapons. You got to get us out of here—or we may be here all night. This is a real shithole. Our true leader, "Alexander Hamilton," will be a great friend if you can get us the f . . . out of here tonight." He gave Salt a case reference number. Salt said, "Don, it is midnight here; I am 60 miles away and not a criminal lawyer. But I know some, and I will make some calls. That's the best I can do. Does your buddy Alexander have money someplace where he can get to it tonight?" And I need an address for everyone and the name and address of a near relative. And, oh yeah, confirm that none of these people have plans to leave the US. So they should not be carrying airline tickets good for use during the next month. The Government wants everyone's passport. If they have tickets, they need to call the airlines, cancel the ticket, and get a refund as soon as possible. It won't be fast unless the Government already has it from the airline—but if the Government has the ticket or a request for it, do not express any more interest in it right how. Wait until you have your first real interview.

"Look Salt, you need to know that Alexander is loaded," said Don, "he's even been invited to the White House. Making bail will not be an issue. Trust me."

Salt was dead tired; it was about 10:30 pm, and he was freezing his butt off in a cold and drafty bathroom with only a wet towel around him. And he understood several other things: this was not his normal gig; there was no way he could find his DC bar card, much less the one issued by Virginia, in the boxes in the farmhouse even if his life depended on it, and it might. He would not accomplish much in DC, where the criminal defense lawyers were churning like a school of sharks; what he needed was a smart "fixer" who knew his way around the courts and creative bail bond providers, and ideally, he could find someone near the jail who was already bailing people out. Someone who understood what it was worth to get Don's crew out of DC. He hit gold on the first call—the guy he wanted to talk to. A former partner of his in the law firm was down at the jail picking up clients like picking ripe apples off a low-hanging branch. The Sons of Liberty were about to be liberated—for now. Better to be lucky than good. And Salt earned his first legal fee—a good one.

Chapter 8

Know Your Clients
(Sons of Liberty) and Their Goals
[January 15, 2021]

L aw firms are pretty particular about who they represent and the implications of—and the potential fallout from—the relationship with the client. They have to be. Salt knew damn well that nobody in his right mind would take on the Sons of Liberty as a client. All he had to do was get on the Internet to understand that there was already a very diverse group of underground and underworks organizations that knew they would have different goals than Alexander - a number of "stopper" differences. His old firm would have laughed in his face. But Salt was interested primarily in "Alexander," who seemed to be what you would find if you followed the money behind the Sons of Liberty. Who are these guys? And what were their real goals? But that was not for today.

But they did meet a few days later. Alexander Hamilton turned out again to be the quiet listener type: low-key, highly educated, and a very successful private investor. He was functionally the head of a very wealthy family office or private investment fund. Maybe a very mini version of Warren Buffet and Berkshire Hathaway, Bill Gates, Battelle, or a sort of non-governmental organization ("NGO"). After it is up and running, it might be able to attract some kind of working relationships with businesses that need to enhance their ESG (energy, social, and governance) profile and credibility. ESG was becoming a very hot topic among both investors and public companies.

Hamilton would not go beyond this point without further guidance. But he was convinced that it might be possible to roll out a fund or funds that focused on identifying or developing funding sources–most likely in private transactions of some kind—that would respond to the pressure on corporate America (and elsewhere) to take ESG seriously.

He would not get into detail without a confidentiality agreement.

Salt stopped him there. "Actually, we should not go forward with this discussion without deciding whether I am representing you. Without a lawyer-client relationship, there will not be a privilege. As President Pope found out, the attorney-client privilege is not an answer to everything, but it is a good start. Neither of us knows whether my representing you makes any sense to either of us. "

Hamilton was quick. "OK, I get that and appreciate your bringing it up. How about if I give you $750 in exchange for an hour of consultation about various legal and related matters, with the agreement that the content of that discussion is privileged and neither of us has any obligation to go any further?" Hamilton called in his assistant and asked him to bring in $750 in cash. While they were waiting for the money, Salt commented that this situation was surreal. Hamilton was quick: "So was our last president, so just get over it. It took a while, but I am getting to the point where I think we might be able to do something positive in this space. Besides, we have already spent 30% of the consulting fee, so let's get going."

What followed was a wide-ranging discussion of various government functions on the fringe of the private sector and examples of permanent staffers who are smart and dedicated, have their heads screwed on right and are effective in dealing with Congress and other levels of the government. Hamilton put it this way: "What I need is the functional equivalent of a Margaret Mead treatise and a 500 level course on how to succeed in government with hair on your head, an operative moral compass and a sense of accomplishment that outweighs your frustration tolerance. It is good to remember that many Members are as frustrated as you are. That is an asset worth thinking about. But we have to overcome centrifugal force.

Another January 6 episode is exactly what is not needed. "What the hell was I thinking?" He asked himself as he hit his forehead with the palm of his hand. "Yes, a major part of the assignment would be to catch me before I get as far as the outskirts of Jerksville."

Several of the group said they needed more meat on the bones.

"OK," Hamilton said. "I can relate to that, but I don't have an organized pitch here. First and foremost, I want to do some lasting good for the country and do it effectively in terms of both cost and quality. I would like it to be replicable. If we are good and put some successful things together, people will knock on our door. That is fine, but the goal here is not to make money. I need to know where capital can be married with need and have the smarts that are hard to find. I know there are some good folks in this zone. We need self-starters—we have grown and know some good folks in the Government who know how to get things done, how the Congress and the multilateral funding sources really work—or don't work—and who are likely to be influential in the new administration. During the course of this discussion, Hamilton made some interesting observations. Some were half-baked, but he was a quick study. And as half-baked as he seemed to be in some senses, he was clearly serious in others.

He would not give Salt any detail without a formal confidentiality agreement, but at a very high level, he wanted to (1) joint venture with the government to provide management and capital at a discount and (2) pool private and public sector talent in challenging but potentially significant efforts. This was all less complicated if Hamilton could, in fact, find others who did not care if the joint venture made a profit. If it did, it would make attracting private money easier. If a profit was not possible, there would need to be a rational tax break of some kind.

Hamilton's generic description was impressive, but it would need to be made as bullet proof and leak-proof as possible, including for the Government. They all needed to listen carefully to the upcoming Inaugural address. What they were thinking about was not a super far reach from what was going on in some corners of the government contracting world, but some T's would need to be crossed. The private sector activity would be primarily with the civilian agencies of the government, without much Department of Defense interface, though that could change over time. "Remember," said Hamilton, "this is not a crazy approach. After all, we are in the process of privatizing space exploration."

Examples of other activities that could be of interest included constructing and managing the smaller, more cost-effective, safe nuclear power plants, large-scale rapid grain movement in response to famine, and critical products and services ranging from baby formula to electronics to general government services.

Hamilton readily admitted that there were many things to be sorted, but he was sick and tired of the country gradually slipping into a downward spiral and becoming an ineffective giant: sort of like the USSR was, say, 65 years ago, before the break-up of the Soviet Union, or risking being chewed up by the Chinese bear. He found politics, particularly in the Senate, to be dead on arrival in terms of getting things done—so he was not a prominent donor. All legislators could do was talk, hurl insults at one another, and engage in self-promotion in their embarrassingly gerrymandered districts.

Hamilton also had some interesting observations about Ukraine, including that winning the impending war was only half the battle. He had studied the US military's recommendations for rebuilding Europe after World War II. He murmured something about General George Marshall and the Marshall Plan. Salt got the drift. Salt's view was that the coming events in Ukraine were, in effect, a potential first module of World War III, a serious war that could expand even further but would not involve the use of the ultimate weapon.

When asked, Hamilton said he assisted with the formation of the Sons of Liberty because he had no vehicle to address his concerns. He thought President Pope might have been different—a fresh breeze from the private sector—different enough to make a difference. He sure was different, but not quite the difference Hamilton was looking for. In retrospect, he said that President Pope was a giant mistake. He was embarrassed about having supported Pope. Live and learn. But his motives here were not political.

Re-making government is too big a goal to be achieved, observed Hamilton. Private capital cannot move without reasonable government infrastructure or too much of it, but you can do more good with sizable and meaningful projects that are not nation-size.

Consider what happened to Vietnam and Eastern Europe after the initial local and cross-border sources of capital had been allowed to come in. It was a minor miracle.

Hamilton was not afraid to learn from his mistakes—like being in the wrong place at the wrong time on the evening of January 6. Salt's analysis of that one: "whopper." Hamilton could and would revise his "do good" portfolio planning accordingly. He would structure and retain long-term solid assets but would invest the balance in the equivalent of private development equity, and he would try to partner with other investors with like minds: businesses that would be used to have to be key players in the renewal and other projects and the affected local governments. It would not be simple, but there were models out there, and Salt's off-the-cuff reaction was that those involved would have ice water in their veins, patience, the ability to earn the trust of local and regional governments as well as national and global governments and investors (including multilateral agencies such as the World Bank and the European Development Bank and non- governmental organizations, or NGOs), and have someone on staff who could provide local presence, local management, and then grow the businesses.

He might also have to move some key people and transition others who did not fit the new business model as it evolved. He did not want a big organization. The dramatic is not often achieved by the meek or groups large enough to develop consensus.

Salt's head was spinning, and he was not able to articulate very much in response to the proposal. "Are you serious about this?" Salt asked. "How much of my time would you want?"

"To be determined, up to 50%."

"Pay hourly, on salary, or against a retainer?" Salt asked. "To be determined. Tell me what you need."

"Can I represent other organizations?"

"Yes, if there are no significant conflicts of interest in your reasonable judgment. It could be a good thing if there were some conflicts—we could collaborate."

Salt then got in a real sentence: "The Government has contacted me about another pretty major short-term project that would probably not involve a conflict, but it is a little unusual. I would need to talk with both parties about it and get clearance to even tell you what is involved. By the way, do you have a clearance?"

Hamilton was not thrown off by the diversion. "I respect that—tell them I recognize that they hired you first and, in conflict situations, have first dibs unless waived. Do what you need to in order to get this cleared. My clearance is above top secret. That's enough for now."

"Who would I report to?"

"Me. Although there are some other like-minded business people who might be interested in joining up, say, as Board members. We would have to deal with them one at a time. But if this works like I think it could, it could be very interesting. I am sort of wanting to create a combination of Common Cause, the Lincoln Project, and a charitable/government investment fund."

Salt then dared to ask: "What is your timeframe?" Hamilton replied, "I would be willing to take 50% of your time starting this afternoon, subject to the conflicts and other administrative crap that would no doubt be triggered. We'll have to get some good administrative support for you.

But this has to stay out of the media until we are ready. No lobbying. I would reserve the right to terminate and deny the existence of the relationship without notice if I learned about us above the fold on page 1 of the Post, Wall Street Journal, or New York Times."

"I need to think about it."

Hamilton: "I would hope so, but please do that with all due speed. I realize this involves a leap of faith."

Salt replied: "We should at least shake hands on the retainer, including conflicts. And I will send you a confirming letter. "

Hamilton's handshake was firm, and he said, "Keep the letter short. Just confirm that we had the privileged conversation. By the way, do you remember we did not return to a number?

Salt smiled: "Yeah. Figured I would wait for you. The reality is that neither of us knows enough to suggest what would be fair. So it is 'To Be Determined.' It should be the least of our issues."

"By the way," Salt asked, "what are you going to call this effort." "Haven't thought much about it," said Hamilton, "for now, let's call it 'Friends of Liberty' or maybe 'Daughters and Sons of Liberty (or DSOL).'

Salt walked out to his car and thought about what had just happened, but his mind was spinning too fast. He needed to get home and have a good dinner and a drink before going to bed. What a day. By the way, he asked himself, type a letter? Assistant? He did not have so much as a business card or a bank account. What would he call himself? He did know that DSOL was dead on arrival.

Chapter 9

Reactions from Afar: January 6 and the Inauguration

[January 6/20, 2021]

I n January 2021, many around the United States and the rest of the world paid more attention to Evans's inaugural address than Pepper did. The new president could not ignore January 6 or the many troublesome issues, but he needed to pull together disparate groups, and the world needed to help the country "get over it." So he could not dwell on the problems. The speech was brief and well delivered but short on details. Salt particularly liked the concluding lines of the speech:

"Fellow citizens of the United States and the world, we are burdened with an inheritance of crises and dysfunction that does not respect political or national boundaries. But we are blessed with the means and ability to respond. We will succeed if, instead of being distracted by trying to assess blame, we recognize that we are indeed in this together.

Our mandate is to overcome the tyranny of our inheritance and chart a better course for all. We can and we will. That starts today."

Overall, Salt was pleased with the new President's words, as were most but not all of the commentators. But Salt knew that talk was cheap.

Salt was very aware, for example, that the senior career staff of the State Department had been decimated by the passage of time for baby boomers and by partisanship for others. The Pope administration had had three secretaries of state in four years and three sets of sycophant staffers to go with each. They would soon all be gone. There wasn't much wisdom to be passed along to their successors. The new President didn't have an overwhelming army of trusted professionals to deal with the results of the weaponization of foreign relations. And then there were the pandemic and approaching recession that flashed signs of hope from time to time but were still significant problems.

Good luck, President Evans, Salt thought as he finished his coffee, had one last cookie, and forced himself to go back to the boxes.

In the late evening of Inauguration Day in Europe, at both Number 10 Downing Street and the home of the Foreign and Commonwealth Office on King Charles Street in London, British officials were huddled around television sets to take in the address and then—after taking off their masks and with inspiration provided by some scotch (rather than the weaker and more common gin and tonic)—assess what January 6 and the speech meant.

At 10 Downing Street, Prime Minister Osborne hosted several of his ministers and other friends for modest drinks and appetizers. The Prime Minister's verdict was short and to the point: "Well, I guess it is better to learn nothing than to be scared to death by something like what President Pope said in his inauguration address. Jesus!"

Little did the Prime Minister know that he was headed for the political dumpster and that he would soon be joining President Pope on the outside looking in. There were some similarities. They were showmen who prided themselves in reckless personal behavior ("party animals"); decisive action; some forms of economic isolation (e.g., Brexit on the one hand and tariffs levied on China on the other); and had followers who were fervent true believers, but could be shrinking a bit.

The foreign secretary's team at the Foreign and Commonwealth Office had a more vigorous discussion about the admittedly hidden meaning of the new president's scant reference to foreign policy and returning the United States to a role of collaboration, leadership, and consensus building. They were more positive in their assessment. After thirty minutes of debate and two scotches on the rocks, Foreign Secretary John Watson asked, "Just what the hell is Stuart Bacon up to these days?"

Bacon had worked with the Evans presidential campaign, had bona fide qualifications and experience in the US foreign service, and was a favorite to land some outward-looking role in the new administration, but nobody knew what. Many speculated that he would gain the secretary of state's seat at the table; others thought something in the US intelligence community was more likely. The new president had not hinted at anything yet but would have to nominate someone to do something soon.

The transition to the new Evans administration had been anything but smooth. Even before Inaugural Day, the Evans administration's plate was full. First, there was the election itself, then January 6 (which the new administration wisely did not take on as an administration issue and left that mess to an effective Congressional Special Committee), and, of course, the stubborn and morphing COVID-19 pandemic, including the need for spending on COVID and other matters that made the economy aggressively move toward inflation and its typical cure—higher interest rates. And these were just the high-value domestic issues that existed on Inauguration Day.

Following January 6, election law and processes were challenged rather than celebrated. Some of the truly shocking events during the 2022 mid-term elections involved the successful search for top secret documents at the president's resort home and forced a focus on the safety of intelligence materials that our allies deemed urgent and essential. And, of course, there were concerns about the security of the election results from foreign interference, which President Pope had invited in, and the risk of voting fraud. The term "rigged" seemed to be on everyone's tongue before and after the inauguration and in court papers and the media. There was litigation challenging the election results that had made it to the Supreme Court, which finally declared a stop to the circus to begin to get in gear. But a precious six weeks had been lost, and the Pope administration had not been exactly magnanimous in terms of cooperation. These diversions had prevented the normal focus on things diplomatic, which worried (and puzzled) the UK and other allies.

To make matters worse, President Evans was a newcomer to the international scene at the beginning of his term, having focused on the myriad of serious domestic US issues during the campaign.

So the experts outside of the United States were largely guessing when spouting opinions of what the new US administration would mean for the somewhat tattered state of US foreign relations.

The British foreign service team watching the inauguration from London had its own issues. They were dealing with: an unsteady Prime Minister, who was about to resign; chaos as to who would replace him and when and how; dealing with the negative impact of Brexit, which had pretty clearly been oversold; and the unfortunate and rushed trade talks with the European Union and others, exacerbated by the severe and never-ending spread of COVID-19 and its variants, inflation and the absence of a truly dominant UK political party.

And as if these were not enough, in the next wave, Russia invaded Ukraine in late February 2022 (though they had been at war since 2014 in reality). With Ukraine in the picture, just about everything else got worse: inflation, frightening layers of spending, a currency crash against the dollar and the Euro, other market crashes, and a historic heat wave during the summer. Where was Churchill when you needed him?

The Brits had been hoping for discernable direction from the new president. But rather than articulating a detailed and cogent definition of the United States' foreign policy, the inaugural address presented the equivalent of a thousand-piece jigsaw puzzle with no detailed picture to go by.

A very similar discussion was taking place in Berlin, where it was an hour later. In that capital, the new chancellor, foreign minister, and their closest advisers watched the address together while maintaining a safe level of social distancing. Like the Brits, the Germans were intensely interested in how the new US administration saw its role in the world. Given the stakes in Ukraine, the emergence of the post-Brexit European Union, and developments in Asia, principally surrounding China, including the risk that China might use Russia/Ukraine as a model for China/Taiwan, the United States might not ever be able to return to the role it played prior to the Pope administration, much less prior to the Iraq War.

There was some very welcome and significant progress in the form of the enlargement of and collaboration among members of NATO in relation to Ukraine. And the AUKUS treaty between the US, UK, and Australia, announced in September 2021, which is focused on the US and the UK helping Australia to acquire nuclear-powered submarines, was a welcome development, particularly in light of the Pope administration's walk away from a huge multi-party Asian trade treaty.

The United States was still needed as a counter to other lesser but dangerous powers and as an example of how democracy and capitalism coexist and flourish together. And then there were the lingering effects of COVID-19 on health, the effects of climate change on living and working conditions, and the softness of the business climate throughout continental Europe.

Similar inconclusive assessments were taking place in places like Moscow, Beijing, Tokyo, New Delhi, Tehran, Jerusalem, Ankara, Paris, Brussels, Canberra, Ottawa, Brasilia, and Mexico City. There were lots of calls. Moscow called Ankara, who called Saudi Arabia, who called Pakistan, who broke with tradition and called India, and this went on through four layers of government in each case. And then there were the pundits. All were in the same boat: individuals, officers of rank, leaders of those governments, as well as pundits around the globe, were hopeful in some cases, worried in others, but in either case, not at all sure why.

And just when you thought things could not get worse, too many US citizens became familiar with supply chain issues through the lens of a baby formula shortage. And the global climate was going to hell almost as fast as inflation.

Chapter 10

Cutting Ties to the Past
[January 20-24, 2021]

The next few days involved trying to absorb the meaning of January 6 and the Inauguration, moving boxes, and taking stuff out of them. This was harder than he thought it would be. He was not only throwing into a box things that Salt would no longer need because of his limited range of activity; he also found some of Meredith's things. That forced him to stop, go downstairs to sit on the couch, and think about his wife's death, how much he missed her, and what to do with her things. She was not only a spouse but also a best friend and confidante. He hadn't fully appreciated what a jewel she was until she was gone. He felt terrible that, because of the pandemic, it had not been possible to even have a proper memorial service for her. And, of course, the grief process was exacerbated by the fact that he was quarantined and isolated for several weeks after her death, and that was followed by weeks and weeks of working from home where he lived alone. He was miserable and lonely and wanted to get out of the apartment.

Several counselors had urged him to deal with his wife's things long before this. That was good advice but a road not taken. Now, tears that had not previously been shed flowed freely down his cheeks. After an hour of quiet sobs and introspection, he concluded that, for better or worse, he needed to move on, and keeping his wife's wardrobe in a closet of an old farmhouse would be like inviting ghosts in to play. She would disapprove.

What do to with her clothes? Donate them, obviously—but where? The Wi-Fi wasn't yet hooked up in the farmhouse, so his internet access was limited to his phone. Rather than relying on his mobile, he looked for and somehow found the scrap of paper with Margie Hatcher's phone number on it and called her for advice. It was an awkward call, but she was accommodating.

With Margie's advice and encouragement, he loaded the boxes full of his wife's clothes in his Volvo (it took two loads) and delivered them to the thrift shop run by several local churches.

This made him feel both worse and better. But that seemed to be the way the week was going.

Salt had not taken a good hot shower since the move, and he felt grimy as well as whipped. The movers had packed some soap and shampoo, and much to his delight, he found that the water in the bathtub worked. And it was hot. There was no shower—only an old cast-iron tub with a hose he could use to wash his hair. It felt good enough, and Salt thought maybe he was getting close to rejoining the human race- about time.

Rejoining the human race involved eating something other than cookies and cheeseburgers. Salt put on some clean clothes and decided to try Helen's Place, the diner recommended by Margie.

Salt drove into town and walked into Helen's after reading the sign on the front door, now required by law, saying that all of Helen's employees had been tested for COVID-19 within the past two weeks, had their temperatures taken when they came to work for the day and were required to wear masks. Patrons were also warned not to move the furniture, which was set up in compliance with the current and ever-changing social distancing requirements for indoor food service.

Helen's was clean and orderly but not fancy. It was a sort of Silver Diner- looking kind of place, but the booths, napkin holders, jukeboxes, and utensils were genuine rather than faux old. Salt thought to himself that the same could be said of the diner's staff.

Salt got a booth and asked if he could order a drink. The diner had no hard liquor and only local Virginia wines—some of which were actually pretty good. He ordered the red Helen sold by the glass, a side salad (Meredith would have approved), and the meat loaf. He learned that he was being served by Helen herself, so Salt introduced himself. The diner wasn't busy, allowing Salt to chat with Helen, who turned out to be a character. It was lucky that Salt was a good listener.

She detailed for Salt the effects of the COVID-19 virus and the recession, the painful layoffs Helen had to do, how close Helen got to closing up, and the time she threw the keys on the table in front of the landlord, explaining that he could take over the damn diner if he wanted, but she was not paying any more rent until she could open up. She was still hurting financially and very tired of wearing a mask.

Margie Hatcher walked in as he sat there thinking about Helen's comments. She saw him and walked over. "How are you doing?" she asked. "I know from our call you had a tough day."

"I did, but I think I've worked my way through it," said Salt. "Thanks again for your help." Salt realized she was still standing; he asked if she would care to join him.

"I would be glad to, but I don't want to intrude," Margie responded.

Salt smiled. "The only thing you would be interrupting is the sound of silence." Margie sat down a safe distance away and ordered a glass of white, and they exchanged small talk, including some about politics. Salt followed his policy of talking politely about politics in general while actually saying very little about his. He got the impression that, like himself, Margie did not advertise it but was somewhere in the middle of the political spectrum.

They shared a bit more about their backgrounds. "What kinds of things did you do when you were with the Treasury Department?" she asked.

"Well, most of it was pretty boring now that I look back on it. I spent a couple of years in the Treasury Department's Office of Foreign Asset Control, better known as OFAC," explained Salt. "One of its functions is to define and administer US sanctions programs. Those programs take advantage of the relative strength of the US economy and the broad reach of our financial institutions and markets. Essentially, the government, through OFAC, can prohibit so-called US persons—a very broadly defined term— from engaging in transactions or trade with a country, a business, or a person. Over the years, that has included countries like Cuba, Iran, Russia, Syria, North Korea, and the like. The events in Ukraine led to the largest and most aggressive economic war in our history.

The folks in the areas where I used to work in the State Department are on fire. There are risks down any path you take.

"That sounds pretty complicated," said Margie. "Isn't there a risk that countrywide sanctions could have unintended consequences for the innocent—like starting what may be the opening of World War III?"

"Fair question," said Salt. "In more recent years, OFAC has become more targeted and, rather than going after countries all of the time, has sometimes focused on particular entities and individuals that US persons will not be permitted to deal with. This is becoming a critical feature of the Ukraine situation. For some of the targeted Specially Designated Individuals, as we called them, this produced a world of hurt. They ran the risk of having tied up in knots big sums of money that touched banks doing business in the

United States. They would retain advisers to try to get them out of the target zone, and some US persons would try to get licenses that would allow them to do particular types of business with a sanctioned party. That's also the sort of thing I worked on when I was with the law firm."

Salt finished, "Well, that concludes a short course on the part of my career. I warned you. Pretty boring."

"I would say it's complicated and interesting but not boring," responded Margie. "Did the sanctions work?"

"What I'm about to say is a personal view only," cautioned Salt. "The answer is yes and no. Did it change Iran's foreign policy? Some but not so much. Did it punish people trying to do business with Iran and, therefore, indirectly penalize Iran? Yes. Is Iran trying to manipulate around the sanctions?" Yes. Will it ultimately change Iran's overall posture? Not in and of itself."

The conversation then drifted in Margie's direction. Salt was a better listener than a talker and learned quite a bit about Margie. He wondered why, after five years, she had not remarried. Maybe, like him, she was still in love with her spouse and just could not get over it.

It was good to have some casual human interaction. Salt could not remember the last time that had happened with anyone, male or female. For the first time, during dinner, Salt noticed things that went below Margie's surface attractiveness. She was smart, informed, well-read, fun, a volunteer for good causes, and pretty in her own way, with medium-length auburn hair, brown eyes, and a strong chin line. She clearly took good care of herself. She also made great chocolate chip cookies.

And she was just plain nice. At the end of dinner, Margie offered to have him over to her place for some home cooking if he was interested. "Sound's great," he replied, surprising himself with his swift response.

"I'm having some friends over for dinner next week. I think you could tolerate them, and they're sure to be interested in the newcomer who is actually a native of the area." She wrote down the address, date, and time and handed it to him.

At home and after going to bed, Salt remembered the last time he had had a meaningful discussion with a woman. His mind was blank on that subject, but he knew he had not been to bed with a woman other than Meredith while married or since she died. None of this helped him sleep. He added to his to- do list, next to his bed, buying some sleeping pills and going to the liquor store.

Chapter 11

Beltway Beckons

The next week started uneventfully. More boxes, more donations to the church thrift store, more memories, and a better understanding of what an old farmhouse would require in the way of modernizing. It was daunting but nothing compared to the call he got on his mobile around ten thirty in the morning.

The call was from Stuart Bacon, who the news reports had named as a likely pick for secretary of state or a comparable position, in terms of influence, in the West Wing of the White House. Maybe the director of national intelligence, another cabinet-level position that oversaw the US intelligence community, including the Central Intelligence Agency, the National Security Agency, and others. Salt knew and respected Stuart as a thoughtful guy who had survived being in several cages full of politicos. His sustained diplomatic service under several presidents in an era of extreme political turbulence was even more impressive. Stuart was a survivor without the level of baggage that normally accompanies that tag.

"To what do I owe the honor of this call, Stuart?" asked Salt. "And before you go any further, congrats on being wherever and whatever you are. I wasn't sure that people of your quality could survive these days. It's one of the few recent developments that I find comforting."

"Thanks, Salt. That means a lot coming from you," responded Stuart. "This is a busy time, so I'll get to the point. We would like to pick your brain, and to that end we'd like you to come to DC for a meeting on Monday afternoon at the White House. The meeting would be with me and one or two others. Probably not the President, though the President knows I'm making this call and why. We have a lot of bridge-building to do with lots of people, including alienated allies, if there is such a thing, and we need your thoughts about how to go about that."

Salt was shocked and took several seconds to settle himself. He had no clue that he would get a call of this nature. "Thanks, Stuart," said Salt, "but I've been out of the game for five years. I'm a dinosaur when it comes to this sort of thing. And if the President or the President's supporters thought much about my views, they would have asked during the campaign." Salt didn't add that he probably would not have answered a call from a political campaign.

"Salt, the fact that you have been out of the game, as you put it, is one of several reasons we're calling," explained Stuart. "Not much good happened while you were gone. You don't have recent baggage. And you have perspective, which is important. You're also well respected, both here and abroad. You may not be a unicorn, but you're in that family. All we're asking is that you make a trip to DC and sit down with us. You owe the country that much."

Salt hesitated momentarily, knowing there was likely more going on here than met the eye. But he could hardly refuse. He said, "Okay, but all I'm agreeing to is one meeting that will almost certainly disappoint you."

"Great," Stuart replied. "The guards will expect you around 1:30 p.m., and bring some ID. You know the drill. And thanks. By the way, will this mobile number I called work for the next few days in case we need to move things?"

"Yep," said Salt, "at least until the Russians bring down our telecommunications systems."

"How about email?" asked Stuart.

"You can text me on my phone, but I don't have Internet here yet. Don't send anything very long. I'm getting used to no email attachments. See you Monday."

Later in the day, Salt got a voice mail message from Stuart suggesting that since the meeting was not until Monday afternoon, it would be helpful for Salt to stop by the CIA on his way down the George Washington Parkway into DC and meet with Louise Roseaux to start the process of getting his security clearance updated. Salt had no intention of doing anything that required a clearance update.

The move to the farm had not been an overwhelming success so far, but it had not been a complete disaster either, and it was early. Salt ignored the message from Stuart and the one that came in later in the day from Ms. Roseaux.

Salt drove back into the dreaded DC traffic on Monday morning, allowing plenty of time for delays. He hated traffic—even the slightly lower volume that the COVID-19 lockdown and recession had brought about—but at least today, it beat unpacking moving boxes. Fortunately, the weather cooperated. Although overcast, there was no precipitation. Out of spite, Salt did not drive down the George Washington Parkway past the CIA, instead taking Interstate 66 all the way onto the Roosevelt Bridge and Constitution Avenue. He was late enough that he avoided the rush hour toll. The drive gave Salt time to think in the quiet—and without the distraction of what still seemed like hundreds of remaining boxes—about what this meeting could really be about. He had no idea.

As he pulled into the White House, he momentarily panicked, thinking he had forgotten his briefcase. Then he recalled that he didn't bring one. It was hard to imagine walking into a meeting in the West Wing without a briefcase or an empty one. The outdoor guards asked whether he was carrying. "Nothing other than my keys, wallet, and mobile," Salt responded. Their eyebrows went up quizzically and screamed doubt and uncertainty.

"How about a briefcase?" one of the guards asked. They looked at Salt with questions in their eyes and eyebrows raised when he pointed to his head and said, "keep it all up here. Too easy to forget your briefcase." That in itself almost made the trip worthwhile.

As he checked in with security inside the White House, one of the officers told him that Mr. Bacon had left a message that the meeting would need to start about an hour late, but the guard had been instructed to call Ms. Roseaux, who would greet Salt and meet with him during the delay. The inside security guards asked if he wanted a mask but didn't force him to wear one since he had a certificate confirming that he had recently been tested for COVID-19. Still, they took his temperature with a fancy electronic gun.

Sensing that the new administration had a different view of masks than the Pope administration, Salt took the mask. They asked again about his briefcase, and Salt was delighted to say again that he didn't have one. Then they forced him to deposit his mobile phone with them. It was five years old and a bit of an embarrassment. But life went on. And he still missed his Blackberry.

Having no choice, Salt went with Ms. Roseaux into a small, barren room in the West Wing. She was tall, trending toward skinny but muscular, dressed in a severe black pantsuit, with mid-length black hair worn straight. Her skin was dark enough that she might be the product of some mixing and matching. Whatever, it worked, even with the mask on. And she was very proper and polite. "We're sorry about the delay, but we can put the time to good use if you're willing to give me an update on matters relating to your security clearance, which has expired under the terms of President Pope's 2019 revocation of the security clearances of former senior intelligence personnel."

"But I have no intention of needing a security clearance," said Salt.

"I'm sorry, Mr. Pepper, but the nature of the meeting you are here for is such that you cannot attend very much of it unless I believe you are eligible for the highest level of security clearance. This won't be a wasted effort, even if nothing comes of the meeting."

"Are you attending the meeting, Ms. Roseaux?" asked Salt. "Yes," she responded.

"Can you tell me what it's about?" asked Salt. "No."

"Do you know what it's about?"

"Only on a superficial basis," she responded.

Salt continued a bit more harshly: "Would you kindly tell me what you know about the meeting?"

"I understand your frustration, but you'll soon learn," she calmly explained. "In the meantime, let's not further delay the meeting. As I said, I need to preliminarily clear you before you can be told about the meeting or allowed to participate in it. Surely you're curious."

"Okay, but this is nuts. Kindly note my objection." Salt was huffing and puffing through his mask.

Salt spent the next hour responding to Louise's endless checklist of questions and describing his activities since leaving the government five years ago, his personal and law firm business dealings, his finances, those who he regarded as friends (a short list), his drinking habits, his gender preference, details as to his travel outside of the United States, and his contacts outside of the United States. For once, it was good to be boring.

Toward the end of the session, he asked Ms. Roseaux, "So, who are you? What's your background? Why are you going to be in this meeting?" "That's classified at a very high level." She smiled, not warmly. Then they finally got the call to come into the meeting.

Chapter 12

Selling Salt at the White House
[January11, 2021]

They moved the discussions into a larger and more formal but still nondescript and cold conference room in the West Wing and were soon joined by Stuart Bacon and his assistant, Norman. After abbreviated small talk and introductions, Stuart began the discussion by emphasizing that what was said in the room needed to stay there, with the exception of briefing the President.

Stuart opened. "Salt, as you can imagine, we have spent a massive amount of time and effort assessing our diplomatic relations since the election. Those efforts have been hindered by litigation over the election results, a boorish lack of cooperation from the Pope team, and issues such as the FBI's subpoena issued to President Pope. Nevertheless, we have been identifying candidates to assume positions of significant responsibility in the intelligence agencies, internationally-oriented slots at the Treasury, ambassadorships, and of course, positions with the State Department and USAID. I will be either the secretary of state or here in the White House as director of national intelligence.

"We have been consulting with friends and foes about what the issues are and what our staffing should look like. Frankly, things are worse than we imagined. Our foreign relations are very troubled. They were bad before the COVID-19 pandemic, worse as the pandemic and recession took hold, and now look like a very troubled enterprise. We still have some very talented people in the diplomatic corps, but we have also lost a host of good people to firings, retirement, and disgust with the last administration. The good people still here will need to stretch and grow in their responsibilities. Many of them can. But we need reinforcements."

"Let me stop you there, Stuart," said Salt. "For a host of reasons, I'm not the right person to be serving as a reinforcement. If that's what you have in mind, we can call time-out now."

"That's not exactly what we have in mind," responded Stuart. "Let me finish. As you know, the United States suffered significantly diminished credibility over the past five years—even before January 6."

"Yeah," said Salt, "how in God's name do you explain that one? Whew!"

"Well," responded Stuart, "you've got to deal with it, whether addressing friend or foe. Some of these governments actually wonder whether we are headed toward a civil war. We are variously viewed as volatile, xenophobic, racist, withdrawn, self-absorbed, unreliable, and untrustworthy. The lack of trust is a profound and severe problem. We have reluctantly concluded that people viewed as political appointees or otherwise closely allied with the new administration will not be as effective as in the past. At least in the near term, what they say to others in the world will often be treated as just more blah, blah, blah—and only effective for as long as that person is around, at best.

"How do we fight this? With a new and very closely held approach. We need investigation and guidance from someone who is not viewed as political poison and, more importantly, has a reputation among career diplomats in other countries for being trustworthy and maintaining confidentiality. Someone who views Twitter, Facebook, and Instagram as the enemy and never to be used. In other words, we need a friendly dinosaur from those days of yesteryear when looking someone in the eye meant something. We need this dinosaur to consult with the trusted core of the diplomatic structure of other major countries and organizations—outside of the pressures created by publicly announced positions and the media—and then report back, on a very high and sensitive level, his or her findings and recommendations."

Stuart continued, "Apart from the obvious—Ukraine—to which we have to give special attention, what are the issues of most importance? What do they need to see from us? What treaties can or need to be patched back together? What makes sense in that regard for the United States as well as others? Can we salvage existing alliances and create new ones?

"Apart from attacking even more aggressively the continuation of the coronavirus pandemic and fighting the recession, what should the priorities be? We've now had more than a year to offer the transition plan. Everyone knows where the issues have been, but we need to step up. We need you to be part of that.

"We would give you a short list of priority targets. We think the consultations need to start with the UK, but to a large extent, you would control your own agenda and priorities, with periodic reports back as needed and per a schedule.

"You would essentially be your own boss and report directly to the President and me. There would be no Senate confirmation. We would brief the leaders of key congressional committees as to what you're up to, but you would not be scheduled for public appearances. We think our members of congress can deliver that much.

"You would be a troubleshooter and a diplomatic relations turnaround specialist. Should be a great challenge and an incredibly important service to the country." Stuart paused.

"You've got to be kidding," responded Salt. "What you're describing here is not mission impossible; it's mission suicide. It won't work. And I'm the wrong guy to try. I am virtually anonymous. This is nuts. Did you find this in a bad book or a worse movie? What did I do to you to deserve this kind of thing? Come on, man!"

"Well, tell me what you really think." Stuart sighed. "And by the way, thanks for not saying no in the middle of that blast. At least you understand the degree of difficulty here. But what a great capstone for a career this could be. I would be tempted to do this myself, but I'm too politicized. On the other hand, you have a low profile and could pull it off. You would be surprised how often we've reacted positively to mentioning your name in discussions with allies about this initiative. I'll be honest, people do not come to your name by themselves, but if you ask them about Salt Pepper, there is a positive reaction, wondering out loud about it."

Salt growled. "You mean you cleared this with others before even mentioning it to me? What the hell, Stuart?"

"Well, Salt," Stuart said calmly, "we could hardly sell it to you and then be told by key allies that you're a nonstarter. Admittedly, some allies were more enthusiastic than others. And we ran a few other names through in addition to yours. Some people may have thought you were a placebo of sorts, but the reactions were neutral at worst, and a number were enthusiastic. There is a hunger worldwide for the United States that is rational, trustworthy, and willing to lead. You won't have trouble lining up meetings, even with those who were ambivalent."

"And how would the nutcase who takes this job get things done in terms of support?" Salt asked. "Most people like me have no infrastructure. I have no entourage and don't want one."

"We will, of course, provide support," Stuart explained. "We don't see this as being a big team. You have met Ms. Roseaux, whose real name will remain secret for the time being. She has been with the CIA in several roles, speaks French, Arabic, and Russian, knows who's who at the Agency and State, and believes in this cause. Her parents were French and American."

Stuart continued, "I think you need to think about this a bit more before we go any further. Admittedly, this is not an obvious next career step for someone in your situation. Why don't we call it a day and allow you two to get together over the next few days to discuss the next steps? But time is not on our side."

As if on cue, the door opened, and the President's head partially popped through, giving the room a thumbs-up and his patented smile. "Thanks, Salt, for thinking about this. We need your help." And then the President disappeared before anyone could stand up or say anything.

Salt knew he had to nip this in the bud. "Look, Stuart, this may seem ungrateful, but there's nothing to think about; I just moved out to the edge of the Blue Ridge, for God's sake."

Stuart wasn't taking no for an answer. "All we ask is that you and Ms. Roseaux get together and discuss it. I'm sure she would be glad to come out to see you. If we can't get you, at least tell us how you would do this or something like it. Thanks, Salt."

Stuart left abruptly and flashed a thumbs-up on his way out. As Salt left the White House, Louise gave him an encrypted phone for use in connection with this project and her phone number for "temporary use." She said she could come out to see him any day that week. Salt said she should aim for Thursday and warned that his farmhouse looked like it had been hit by a tornado.

"I'll be there at one o'clock." She smiled. "No lunch needed.".

Chapter 13

Enter Louise, Stage Left

[January 14, 2021]

The next day was Thursday, January 14, and the doorbell rang at precisely 1:01 p.m. It was Louise, dressed again in a black pantsuit, smiling, and clearly ready to get going. She wasn't wearing a mask but took a socially distant seat at the kitchen table and declined his offer of a mask. Salt also offered coffee; she preferred water. Salt asked again if well water would do.

She responded, by shaking her head. No.

Salt responded truthfully, "Sorry, but I have never bought a bottle of water." She took a glass of the well water, not asking if it had been run though a filter. Salt concluded this was going to be a long afternoon. No sense injecting more irritation than necessary.

Louise started out with her remaining litany of questions. That took the first hour and a half. Salt wasn't good with names and had to agree to come up with information for a long list of non-US citizens he had come into contact with over the years as well as US citizens who could attest to his straight arrowness. Salt must have passed that part of the test because she did not up and leave in the middle. In reality, Salt was a pretty plain vanilla guy.

After producing another glass of well water, Salt decided it was time to set the stage for more serious talk. "Now that we've gone through all that, what is this really about? You're not dumb, but you're playing dumb. You're not that good at acting. You've been around—in the Agency and other related organizations—for a long time, so you're a survivor in tough environments. You're not likely to want to babysit a retiree. Tell me who you are and what Stuart wants from me."

"Fair questions," she responded. "I'll go against the grain of all of my training and trust you and your discretion. You seem to have some, and that's more than you can say about many men. I've done many things, including being a CIA field agent. I have been loaned to Stuart for this project. I grew up in the United States and France, did undergraduate work at the Sorbonne in Paris, and was recruited after that by the CIA in part because of my language skills. My real name is not Louise but Marie Louise, but the Agency thinks that sounds too French, so I'm Louise. I have gone through the full range of training with the Agency, including martial arts and firearms. I'm a perfect shot. I've served in Asia but more in Europe, especially Eastern Europe. I have used firearms in the field. There have been fatalities but no innocent victims. Those who have passed got what they deserved. I'm not a female Jason Bourne, but I'm good at what I do. But I want to do more, something more subtle than my prior assignments. I would like to be attached to the diplomatic corps in a significant role, but most of those roles seem to go to white males. I am not a male, and I have mixed racial origins. I need a mentor and some experience that counts. Nobody in their right mind would think that attaching myself to you and this role that Stuart is making up as he goes makes sense. But I think you may have more to you than meets the eye. I'm willing to experiment and invest some time and effort around this."

"Okay," said Salt, taking a deep breath and trying to take all that in. "You win the contest for candor, but several more questions. First, what do you mean by being attached to me? I don't need either a helper or a bodyguard."

"Wrong," she said. "That's what I thought at first, but if Stuart's hairbrained scheme works at all, you'll be subject to some level of risk. We'll get back to what Stuart wants. Still, suppose you're successful in calming some of the global diplomatic disarrays. In that case, you will be viewed as an inconvenient and dangerous person by those who benefit from disarray— and there are plenty of those, both in the United States and outside. Perhaps it's the worst, but you need someone to watch your back."

Salt came to life. "Whoa," he said. "I would never create or buy into that much danger. You can't make this stuff up."

"I'm not making this up," she responded. "If you're even modestly successful, you'll be upsetting the efforts of people like the Russians, the Iranians, and the North Koreans. Russia has arranged for former spies to be poisoned in the UK. You must know the stories of the 2006 poisoning murder of Litvinenko and then the attempts a decade or so later on two others, Sergei Skripal and his daughter. God only knows what the Iranians have done through ISIS and otherwise, and North Korea's supreme leader hired women to knock off family members in the Singapore airport. The good news is that you don't think you're good enough to pull this off, and if you're right, you have nothing to worry about."

Salt thought for a moment, rubbing his chin to get rid of nervous energy. "Even if you're right, you don't seem like the type who would want to follow me around as a bag carrier."

"Now, you hold on," she nearly yelled. "I'm no damned bag carrier. I'm a woman, making me seem less dangerous to some, which is a tactical advantage. But I'm fully capable of being equally vigilant eyes and ears in sensitive meetings, and you will need that. So get over it, and be glad I'm willing to humor you and play-act as a second fiddle. You may be the conductor, but I'll be the concertmaster—and a good one."

Scrambling to get out of this mess, Salt countered, "You've seen my file. I need to see yours."

"No objection here," she said.

"I'm not suggesting for a minute that any of this makes sense," said Salt. "But assuming it did, this would involve a lot of travel, presumably together. In this me-too era, how does an old white guy like me feel safe from being accused of harassment or something like that?"

She laughed. "You really are a dinosaur. The chances of you being able to force me to do anything I didn't want to do is zero. Less than zero. You might end up in a bed, but it would be in a hospital. Relax."

Salt felt the blushing take over his face.

"Feels like that's a good place to stop for today," Salt suggested.

"Not yet," she said. "I'm under orders not to come back without understanding where your head is on all of this, even if it is up your ass. That's a direct quote from Stuart."

"Very diplomatic," Salt commented. "First, you tell me you can whup my ass, and now you say my head may be up my ass. I feel like I have a nuclear hemorrhoid attack. Are you always this gentle? Are you sure you want to be a diplomat when you grow up?"

"Sorry," she said. "I thought you could handle someone being direct." "I'll get over it," Salt countered. "You leveled with me earlier, so—also against my better judgment—I'll level with you. I'm very confused about what I want to do with my life post-retirement, post-marriage, post–everything I cared about. I doubt anyone can pull off what Stuart has in mind— whatever that is. But I've been surprised by recent discussions about how much our diplomatic yo-yo game has messed things up for a lot of ordinary people in ordinary places. Trying might be worthwhile if there's a 2 percent shot at helping."

"If you want to do this, you need to decide fast; there are other candidates, though you're the preferred party at this point. Moreover, you're the only candidate I'm attached to, so I'm in your corner. What else do you need?"

"The next step," Salt responded, "is for you to get me permission to fly to Canada on my nickel to meet with Rene Marchand, known as Ray in the United States and Toronto, and talk to him about this. Ray is a lawyer with a big Canadian law firm, has a lot of diplomatic experience, and is a good friend from the days when he was involved in the Canadian foreign ministry and UN delegation, and I was with State. I trust him and respect his judgment. I want to see what he thinks about the world in general, US-Canadian relations, Europe, and this nutty idea of Stuart's. The mission-impossible element is getting permission to spill the beans to Ray. To be clear, I'm not saying I'll do anything, but I am thinking about it. If Stuart says no, that's fine and understandable, and then my answer will be no thanks. By the way, I want to use that encrypted shoe phone you gave me to get hold of Ray. And no, you're not invited to this meeting. Again, to be clear, I'm paying my own way up there if we can get the meeting cleared for me. No strings attached."

"Fair enough, I guess," she hissed. "I'll be back to you tomorrow or Saturday." Noticing that the afternoon was gone, she said, "I need to head back to DC but would like something to eat first. Have any suggestions?"

"I could also use a bite to eat," said Salt, "but there's still nothing in this house. Follow me into town, and we'll have a quick bite downtown at the local diner."

As Salt and Louise were waiting for their meal at Helen's, Margie walked in with a female friend. Salt thought about the line from Casablanca in which Bogart says, "Of all of the gin joints in the world, she had to pick this one." He introduced Louise as a colleague and was surprised he was blushing again. Louise noticed.

Chapter 14

What Keeps Local Leaders Awake at Night

[January 22, 2021]

F riday, January 22, was the date of Margie's dinner party. Prior to taking a shower and finding in his collection of boxes a sport coat to wear, Salt spent the day thinking about his meeting with "Alexander Hamilton," what he said he wanted, what he probably really wanted, what he probably really needed, and how deep Salt was willing to go. Then Salt's thoughts turned to the meeting with Stuart. There wasn't that much to think about. No matter what Stuart wanted, Salt needed to get into the details and make sure they were on the same page about whatever "it" was. Stuart outlined the real challenges and opportunities, but Salt didn't see himself as being what the doctor ordered. And he was tired, both mentally and physically. This was not what he had signed up for. Come to think of it; he didn't sign up for anything.

How did this happen?

He arrived at Margie's smallish single-family home a polite ten minutes after 6:00 p.m. Salt wasn't the first to arrive, but he was not the last either. Margie answered the doorbell, opening the door and greeting him. "Glad you could make it, Salt. I am pleased to be able to introduce you to some good and interesting friends." She then took his temperature with one of the new- fangled electronic thermometers and confirmed that Salt was okay. She also commented that they would not violate the maximum ten-person rule and would do their best on social distancing. Margie also delicately asked if Salt needed or wanted a mask. He saw that others were not wearing masks and didn't want to look like the Lone Ranger, especially since his temperature was normal, so he declined.

Margie first introduced Salt to Mary and George Anderson. Mary was president of the largest local bank, Carterville Community Bank. It seemed that George, who was less outgoing, was an entrepreneur of sorts who also did some teaching on the side. Both George and Mary were obviously brilliant. They had two teenagers getting close to college age.

Also interesting was Alan Greene, the president of Carterville University, and his partner, Angelo. They did not mention any kids. Despite its name, the university was fundamentally a well-regarded liberal arts college. The university designation came from the school offering graduate degrees in teaching. Both Alan and Angelo were very outgoing. Salt missed what Angelo did for a living. Alan was black, and his scholarship was in history, focusing on the post–Civil War reconstruction era. He had fascinating perspectives on the Black Lives Matter movement and related topics, including progress, made (and not made) since reconstruction.

Bob and Betty Reardon were a bit more reserved than the others. Bob owned the local GM dealership ("Come and see me if you need a good deal on a pickup for use on the farm"), and Betty stayed very busy with four kids and activities at the local Catholic church.

One other couple associated with Margie's book club or the Methodist church she attended was also there. Never good with names, Salt did not pick up theirs, but they were not handing out business cards either.

Given the inauguration on January 6 and the continuing impact of the recession and the Black Lives Matter movement, the discussion over a tasty and healthy salmon dinner inevitably turned to politics and related topics. The dialogue was naturally awkward as the other guests tried to figure out where on the political spectrum Salt stood and how he voted, all without asking directly. Nobody wanted to ignite the equivalent of a family fight over the Thanksgiving table. Salt finally acknowledged, "I know everyone is wondering, given my background in what President Pope used to call the swamp, what my politics are. It's pretty unexciting. When I worked at the Treasury and State Departments, I didn't vote.

I just thought it was better to be apolitical. I'm sure that hurt me in some senses, but it also saved me in others. This most recent election was the first presidential election in many years that I have voted in—since I was then out of government—and I voted for President Evans. I'm basically a boring middle-of-the-roader."

"There! I told you, you would not get anything out of him," Margie exclaimed as she passed the salad. "You really have to squeeze things out of him." Everyone chuckled politely.

"Well," said Mary Anderson, who was clearly ready to unload on someone, "as a banker, I'm curious about your views on the recession, the massive business loan programs initiated two years ago, and the direction of interest rates. Bank stocks were up for a time and are now bouncing everywhere. We bankers go crazy with rate volatility, which can cut either way at the bottom line. That couldn't last without inflation going sky high; now they have done a U-turn and raised rates starting late last year like there is no tomorrow. And is it the Fed or the President who is making these changes, really? My God. All of this means, first, that we can't be comfortable with the independence of the Fed; second, there is very little dry powder left if we need to do more from a monetary standpoint; and third, that it is tough for banks to make money these days. We went from an inverted, or nearly inverted, yield curve to the point where the yield curve became almost irrelevant and is now trending higher. Ugh. And, of course, the federal deficit has exploded thanks to President Pope's first tax cut and the massive COVID and recession relief packages. Now I ask you, and I am sorry to be so blunt— as I always am--can anyone top that smelly collection of crap?" she asked rhetorically.

"I'm glad to share my thoughts on those subjects," said Salt, "but these are only my views, and they're not worth much. And I'm no economist. Of course, neither was President Pope. I have no idea whether pushing up interest rates and the other significant steps with being implemented by the Fed and the Treasury are right. Something had to be done to pull the economy up out of the correction, that's for sure.

It's still too early to tell, though. The stock market sometimes seems to hint that things are once again headed in the right direction. I do know that creating doubt as to the independence of the Fed is a terrible thing. It diminishes the reputation of the Fed and makes it much harder for people here and abroad to give the Fed the benefit of the doubt. I'm concerned that we may no longer be in a position to lead interdependent international efforts to stabilize the global economy. Instead of leading, we're just part of the pack."

"I can assure you that, despite what all the government has done, people will buy cars if the price is reasonable and they can get the vehicle they want," commented Bob, the GM dealer. "But this is a two-fur. Despite the inflation, because of the computer chip supply chain situation out of Asia, our industry cannot get cars to the dealer's floor fast enough to respond to pent-up demand."

During the pause, Margie picked up the salad plates and served the salmon, wild rice, and green beans as the chatter was subdued.

Responding to Bob, Salt said, "I guess the only good news is that you have been able to borrow at very low rates from Mary's bank, partially under the special small business loan programs that were rolled out in 2020." Nobody referred to the excesses of those programs.

"Well," said Mary, "we still have the huge-and yes, I mean huge-- you heard it here first--problem that inflation is high, high, high, interest rates are wandering everywhere, a real recession is coming--mark my words, and don't tell me that I didn't warn you about all of this. OK—I'm done, and please pass the wine in my direction. Oh—wait a minute, and how about that damn war in Ukraine? By gum, we have our issues there—wherever it is-- and now we are sending treasure –big treasure— and all of our best equipment there. It is hard to imagine the audacity of those folks. Our people cannot get a new car, and the Ukrainians won't accept our used guns."

"I'll say it's a mess," piped in Bob. "Our farmers around here—even little old Carterville—depend on being in a cross-border market that works.

Pope and his tariffs on China, the backlash against our farm products, and the recession and now Ukraine are not helping me sell new pickups to farmers with grain to haul but nowhere to take it. That's for sure. All of us feel this strain at a time when we see the big R—recession—comin' through our front door."

That led to a discussion of the challenges of getting things both into and out of Ukraine and other places in central and eastern Europe. Warren, the hardware guy, spoke up. "We all know China is a challenge for us. OK. Spilled milk. But now we are having trouble getting wheat and other food products and hardware out of Ukraine, given what amounts to a naval blockade on the Black Sea. Who the hell has ever heard of Ukraine? And now we're going to give them a free ride into NATO. And then let's assume that Ukraine wins the war after another five years and someone knocks off that SOB Putin."

That got Angelo's attention. "Capital S Shit," said Angelo, "I had not even thought of that. Oh my. Get used to $35 hammers. We really are treating them better than if they were part of the United States. What gives?" Do you really think good ole' Uncle Sam would rebuild our houses if we were bombed? Nope. Welcome to the real world. Pick between this house trailer or one of the one-bedroom cinderblock apartments that we're pretty sure will get started before the end of the year."

"Right," said Mary. "Without getting into names, I can tell you that more than a few farmers around here are losing sleep over how to get through another year. It's sad, and their bankers are also stressed." With that, the guests finally focused on the main course.

"So, you're saying that things international directly affect both the business and mood of relatively remote financial ecosystems like the Carterville area?" asked Salt as Margie and others cleared the main course dinner plates.

"Absolutely," said Alan Greene, the college president. "I'll give you more examples. At a time when clear demographic trends reduce the number of prospective college students in the United States, the recession and the following second dip exacerbate affordability issues, and many in the middle and lower classes are questioning the cost and value of a college education.

We are offending non-US governments and families who have sent their students to us. Many of those students can't get visas. And we're struggling to provide needed greater levels of financial aid to domestic students.

All of this mush about free college and forgiveness of student loans that became standard progressive fare during the last presidential campaign and is now revving up again will never happen, but the chatter has an effect. Sometimes perception is reality—at least for a while. This is all on top of the government passing a tax bill in 2017 that doesn't help the needy very much but does hurt the level of charitable contributions because they're not deductible by those who standardize. I could go on, but you can understand why we see things as being very interdependent. You don't need to be an economist to figure this out, but we have them at the college, and they have."

"How is your enrollment holding up?" Salt asked.

"Oh my," Dr. Greene replied. "The reality is we don't know from semester to semester. Parents remain concerned about things like adequate COVID- 19 testing, kids living in dorms and eating in large dining halls, and whether we will ever have to go back to being virtual with these new strains of COVID, and now we're seeing the Monkey Pox. We're holding our breath to see how many students actually show up for the second semester, which we have delayed a few weeks to give more time for the disease to be more fully eradicated. I do concede that the vaccines have been miracles."

Margie saved the day with a cold chocolate dessert of some kind. "Maybe," Salt commented, "we need to hit pause in this discussion, so we don't allow this great dessert to melt entirely! We haven't even gotten to sanctions and the new breeds of the coronavirus and the Monkey Pox."

All agreed and turned to lighter dinner chatter, mellowed a bit by the consumption of dessert and more wine.

At the end of the evening, Salt was one of the last to leave. "I hope you weren't offended by being in the target zone all evening," said Margie.

"No, I actually enjoyed myself," Salt said. "Everyone was both polite and interesting, and I learned some things. Besides, the food was great, and seeing what an organized home looks like was nice. I owe you dinner, but we'll have to go out. I don't cook; you know I don't unpack or clean."

"I would enjoy that." Margie smiled. "There are some nice country inns in the area where you can have a good dinner. And I won't pepper you with questions."

"Good," responded Salt. "It won't happen right away, as I may have some travel in my near future, but you have a rain check—one that works without the need to have rain."

Chapter 15

Farming in the New Normal

[January 25, 2021]

A few days later, Salt woke up in a good but thoughtful mood and started the day with two cups of coffee and no cable news blaring. He had been surprised by the level of sophistication among the dinner party participants on Friday evening and a bit by the strength of their continuing unease. The views of real people outside the Beltway were refreshing and enlightening. It was clear, from those at dinner and among Georgie's barbershop patrons, that people were not at ease with their government, regardless of where they were on the political spectrum. They had become less interested in fireworks than trustworthiness. Maybe the Democrats were wise in not allowing the party to drift too far to the left. Salt's take was that most of the Carterville folks he had met were slightly to the right of the center. They had not wanted to vote again for President Pope, but they damn sure had not been looking for revolutionaries either.

Salt's thoughts were interrupted by a knock on the back door. He thanked goodness he had gotten dressed when he woke up.

Jack Davis, Salt's new tenant farmer, was at the door. Jack asked Salt if he had a few minutes, and Salt was glad to oblige and poured coffee for each, bringing Salt up to three cups.

"Sorry to bother you, Salt," said Jack, "but I'm in a bind and need to be honest with you, especially with you moving out here and all."

"Sorry to hear that, Jack. How can I help?" responded Salt. "Terminate our lease on the farm."

Salt sat quietly for a few moments, trying not to look as stunned as he was. "Wow, Jack. Our lease is less than a year old, and I tried to be very fair with you. What's the problem?"

Jack sighed. "It's complicated, but the short version is that farming doesn't work anymore as a way for the little guy to make a living. When you're losing money on every bushel of grain you grow, you can't make it up in volume. When we entered into our lease in late 2019, I thought I could make it by, in effect, spreading my fixed costs over a larger number of acres. That should have worked, but the market just plain sucks. Things were bad before COVID-19, and now even worse because of layers of shutdowns, the recession, and a trade war I don't understand, and on top of that, Ukraine. Beats me how the hell Ukraine can hurt this much. Never heard of the God- forsaken place until about a year ago. What I do understand is that I can't continue as I have. I need to farm the acres I own, do my best, and find another job to cover the shortfall. I won't have time to farm your 150 acres, and even if I did, that would only make things worse unless, of course, you want to pay me to farm your land."

After some fast thinking, including around the fact that he needed someone to look after whatever was in the barn, Salt asked, "Assume for the sake of discussion that the grain market improves. Would you want to lease the farm again?"

"Depending on the lease terms and the market, yes," said Jack. "But those are big ifs."

Salt toughened up a bit. "You know, Jack, I don't have to let you out of the lease. But I was to get a share of the profit, and it's not such a big deal if there is no profit. But if I let you off the hook, I'd be doing you at least a little favor."

"I get that," said Jack, "and believe me, I don't like to come asking for favors. I was awake all night thinking about this discussion. I'm a man of my word. But at the same time, marching into bankruptcy is sort of a crazy strategy. And you know that's likely a lose-lose proposition."

"And I get that as well," replied Salt. "Here's my proposition. We'll suspend the lease of my farm to you for one growing season—say until October 31, 2023. At that time, we will reassess and either put the lease into effect for 2023-24, terminate it, or change the deal somehow. You will maintain the barn and equipment in exchange for my agreeing to do that. If you want to plant my farm or part of it, and if you need to go out of pocket to do that, we'll discuss what it costs on an item-by-item basis, and I'll cover the agreed-upon cost. Finally, we will keep this discussion confidential."

"That's more than fair and okay by me." Jack smiled. "Do we need something in writing on this?"

"I'm fine if we shake hands on it—or these days touch elbows or bow to each other," said Salt. "If you want to get a lawyer, that's fine by me, and maybe you should since I'm a lawyer, but I would rather work this out between neighbors. And even though you're here walking out on our deal, I'm prepared to trust you."

"Works for me," confirmed Jack, who continued: "Salt, you're from Washington and a lawyer. Can you help me understand how these tariffs on stuff to and from other countries are supposed to work? Even forgetting the effects of the recession, the tariff battle with the Chinese is killing a lot of farmers in this country, and once those markets get screwed up, trying to get them back in working order is nigh unto impossible."

"I'm happy to try, but they can work in lots of variations and are not entirely simple, and then there's the theory and the reality," said Salt.

Salt then explained, "Let's assume that Country A has a state-controlled economy and a surplus of certain metal products and decides to get rid of them in the United States by lowering the price to below the manufacturing cost. One approach by those in the United States hurt by this type of conduct would be to accuse Country A of what is called dumping— that is, dumping cheap metal products on the market, which hurts US metal product producers but helps US buyers of metal products. Assuming Country A is a party to a trade treaty with the United States or is one of the 164 members of the World Trade Organization, the United States might file a dumping complaint with the World Trade Organization.

Or the United States might decide that would take too long and might or might not result in relief from the dumping. Instead, the United States might assert a 'national security' exception to trade treaty dispute processes, take things into its own hands, and impose a tariff on the metal products sold in the United States by Country A.

"The tariff, in effect, increases the price of Country A metal products sold in the United States and, in theory, levels the playing field in an effort to persuade Country A to stop trying to dump the metal products in the United States at artificially low prices. But it operates like a tax on US buyers of the metal products."

"Where does the grain come in?" asked Jack.

Salt continued, "In response to the US tariff on metal products, Country A might reciprocate by imposing a tariff on other goods, like grain, sold by US producers to buyers in Country A. The tariff sort of levels the playing field by offsetting Country A's reduced volume of sales of low-price metal products with a reduction in the volume of grain bought by purchasers in Country A. Country A understands the linkage.

"So the tariffs, in effect, hurt US grain farmers and Country A buyers of grain, and hurt Country A sellers of metal products and some US buyers of metal products, and help some US producers of metal products, and can result in multiple rounds of reciprocal tariffs or other countermeasures."

"Ugh," commented Jack. "Feels like a lot of unintended consequences here at home in the good old USA."

"You're getting the picture," commented Salt. "There are several problems with all of this. First, as a practical matter, the metal products tariff may or may not dissuade Country A from dumping the metal products. Second, US buyers of the metal products in our example will, in effect, pay the tariff imposed by the United States through increased prices, so it feels like a tax. Third, Country A may decide to impose counter-tariffs on other goods from the United States—like farm products—resulting in what is loosely called a trade war.

Finally, Country A might decide to offset the tariffs by manipulating its currency pricing against the US dollar, so the price of metal products in US dollars, in effect, goes down and offsets the tariff."

"Okay," said Jack. "I get that in general terms, I think, but it's complicated, and I'm not sure what's going on here."

"Fair enough," said Salt. "So, let's get closer to home. Assume, for example, that Country A buys a lot of wheat from the United States, in effect, from farmers like you. Country A engages in activities, such as stealing US intellectual property, that the United States wants to discourage. The United States then decides to try to change Country A's behavior by imposing tariffs, roughly equal to a reasonable licensing fee, on selected Country A goods, such as consumer electronics that are imported into the United States from Country A, Company B reciprocates by either cutting back on its purchases of US wheat or imposing a combination of tariffs and quotas on US wheat, in either case hurting the United States but more directly the farmers who have benefitted from the sales to Country A. The targeted behavior by Country A may or may not change. But it's pretty certain that US wheat prices will crash, and you know the rest of that story better than I do."

"Man, oh man, seems like there should be a better way," commented Jack.

"You just said a mouthful," responded Salt, "but keep in mind that in early 2020, the United States and China signed a trade deal that, in theory, was supposed to fix some of this as between the United States and China. But then along came the COVID-19 pandemic, which the United States blamed on China. That complicated an already very messy state of affairs. Frankly, assessing whether the trade deal with China was on or off was hard. Only time will tell what, if anything, comes of that in whatever is the new normal." As he was speaking, Salt was thinking to himself how right Jack was and about the provocative discussions at Margie's dinner party. Maybe there was no escaping this stuff.

At the end of the discussion, Jack clearly had one more topic he wanted to discuss. "Anything else on your mind," asked Salt.

"Well, I was just thinking," Jack responded. "If you really want to get a take on how middle America feels about things, talk to a good, down to earth minister, not one of the television evangelists. Nothing wrong with them, but you want to have a different kind of discussion about the con-gregation. And then get yourself to a big county or state fair. Just go and listen to America—the real America—talk. Find out how others feel. But no matter what, don't tell them you are a lawyer from Washington, and you're here to help." They both laughed.

Chapter 16

Feedback from the Fair

[January 27, 2021]

Based on Jack's other recommendation, Salt decided to go to the "fair" to learn more. It was too early in the year for most places to hold fairs, but there was a fair-like event in one of the Midwestern cities within driving range through the mountains in Virginia, Pennsylvania, and West Virginia. A lovely drive but not so relaxing when you have to battle trucks and a mixture of rain and fog.

After getting into Ohio, the landscape gradually transformed from mountains to rolling hills to flat farming land. The glaciers must have been pretty darn powerful to mold the landscape so dramatically. Overall it was a pleasant drive, but gasoline did not get any cheaper as he drove west.

On the drive, Salt worked on his pitch line to get other folks to talk. He got it down to: "The thinking right now seems to be that farmers and others in the sector could act carefully from a COVID standpoint, get out of the house and barn and breathe some fresh air, and maybe just get by on the hair of their chinny chin chins. (Carrying a gun, especially an assault rifle, was less likely top of mind.) What do you think, brother?" The more he thought about it, the less Salt liked it. So, as on most occasions, he decided to wing it.

The plan/non-plan worked well with some. The event was far smaller than a major fair, of course, but it was interesting from the standpoint of what was going on in the farming business, and Salt was not looking for cotton candy and ferris wheels. It did not look like the jumbo disc/harrows that had an impressive wingspan of about 35 feet were selling fast. Ditto, the huge and also impressive combines. But hell, these machines were so big that you would need to have a massive farm just to have room for them to turn around.

Developing reasonably priced self-driving combines would take a while, but that time was coming.

In another booth, the "super seeds" (Salt's name for them) were on display, with salespeople explaining what their seeds could do in a COVID-shortened growing season. These seeds were hardy and produced plants with consistent characteristics. And you never know; you might get two plantings in and out in one year. The seeds required an add-on piece to tractors, but as the lead sales guy, Marty, said, "Don't worry about that—no payment due until three months after harvest." Naturally, the seeds were expensive. When asked, they acknowledged that they were not selling this quality very hard, and they said they had some product lines that had not yet been proven but seemed to be more productive and resilient in the hotter and drier climates. Most of the seed products had several varieties, like variations of wine, based on different varieties or types of grapes. Using the different breeds of seeds in different growing conditions also gave you different characteristics. The timing was great in the sense that you could buy now, plant very soon and pay later after selling the crops. And at the exhibit, the farmer could also learn about new grades of equipment, seeds, fertilizer, etc., without sitting around and waiting for the start of the next planting season.

"Are these seeds considered to be 'genetically modified?'" Salt asked. "Yes, but that's a technical answer."

"Doesn't that mean you cannot sell them in the EU? "

"Yeah, but that's for right now. It can't last for long. Hell, you don't even know if it has any health effects. And haven't you read about the war in Ukraine? A hell of a big chunk of Europe's cropland is in the war zone, and crops were being blocked from getting into and out of places like Odessa, where Putin's boys can shoot 'em up. The timing is great for us for all kinds of reasons. To make money, you have to take some risks."

Returning to the seeds, another visitor asked, "do you have to rotate crops more aggressively?"

"Well, that is recommended because they say the extra vigorous growth saps more out of the soil. You know what they say, 'no pain, no gain.'"

They started talking with another farmer, "Max." He and his spouse ("Mimi") were there to see a presentation on some high-end machinery. Max was the real deal: straw cowboy hat, overalls, boots he called shit kickers, and a mustache. Salt bought coffee all around and got started. Salt introduced himself and asked: "I've been wondering, Max, how big does a family farm need to be to be viable nowadays?"

Mimi interrupted: "Hold on! You just used the word 'viable.' If you're trying to sneak into a discussion of abortion, forget it. Touchy."

"Oh no, not at all, ma'am," Salt assured them. Salt explained that he was a part-time free-lance reporter and was trying to learn more about the business of farming with all that was happening in the world. He started with the size of the farm. "How big does a family farm need to be in order to survive financially? I have heard 500 acres."

Max had another sip of coffee while he thought about Salt's question. Then he started talking. Before he answered questions, he outlined his "rules of the road." That meant no quotes, taping, names, or pictures. Salt said he agreed with the rules, they shook hands, and then Max started with another set of rules. "Rule number 1, don't ruin your soil. Period. One great harvest is not worth having to rest your soil for a year before you use another non- natural planting. Number 2, the EU is a stickler on genetic modification. And why not? We can't be growing and selling stuff that hurts people. Number 3, our margins are really, really razor thin right now. We can't afford this fancy stuff. And finally, this magic seed crap is pure horseshit. I experimented with some of this stuff in a small plot on my farm—the only real difference: it costs more. May do well in a greenhouse. In the real world, not so much."

Salt tried to get back on track with his number of acres needed question. "Nah," said Max. "Maybe 30 years ago, but not today. I assume you're asking about a beef cattle farm, not milkers, and you want to grow a lot of your feed. In that case, it's 1,500 today and creeping up from there due to inflation. Milk cows? They need less room. So the number of acres depends a lot on the size of the herd. For a decent-sized herd, maybe 350 acres, but it depends on many things. How level is the land? Is it open, or does it have a lot of wooded areas?

The bigger the farm, the more cows you have, the more feed and acreage you need, you get the point. It's a circle. There are no doubt some efficiencies of scale, but less than you think. You know, 95% of the farms in the US are family farms. But the 5% probably have more total acreage than the 95%. That's what is going on here. And people wonder why farmers are on edge. They should be, and that's why some of them get involved with some of these right-wing groups that showed up in DC on January 6.

Another visitor in the crowd followed up: "What do people see in these right-wing groups?"

Max rubbed his chin and thought for a moment. "These folks are the same as 95% of us. All they want is fairness—a level playing field with the rich, the ability to make a fair wage for a fair day's work, financial and physical security, and a government that listens once in a while."

Salt found Max to be direct but credible. So he asked the wide-open question and got another cup of coffee for everyone. "How's farming doing these days in general?"

"It's great if you like to work harder and harder for less and less," said Max without hesitation. "Everyone knows about the climate change problems. That's why swindlers are trying to sell seeds that don't need water. Hell, we are even affected by international stuff. Take the tariffs on grain being sold to China. It's just like a sales tax that we have to pay for. Hell, none of us wanted to be Secretary of State; that's a tough job. But don't F . . . up our markets. Interest rates are way up, and I am not sure where the Fed is going. Sure wish Pope was still in there to keep them straight; we're all going to have more debt. You know, people liked Pope because he seemed to hear us, was not in other people's pockets, said what he thought, stepped on other people's toes, and was crazy enough to make people think he might do drastic shit. He has baggage, but who doesn't?"

Salt commented, "You just said a mouthful, Max."

Max just grinned. "Sorry, what was your other question? Oh yeah, climate—crazy shit going on out there. Never seen anything like this.

"Seeds, equipment, fertilizer, and petroleum products are much more expensive nowadays. Especially fertilizer. Big time--unbelievable. So we're having trouble planting, growing, and selling enough and transporting enough wheat, even though a third of the world is hungry. We have more other crops than we know what to do with, and we can't sell them to people who need them. Why? China tariffs. Russia sanctions--whatever that is, and Ukraine. A lot of others. Hello world, wake the f . . . up. Max stood up and said, "thanks for the coffee and for listening. Now go do something, and don't buy any of those damn nuclear seeds."

Salt ran into another gentleman who sold all kinds of new and used farm and industrial equipment machinery and did the financing. He happened to be black. Salt asked the big broad question again, "How do you feel about government these days?

"I am not smart enough to answer that," he said. "I know I am not proud. Even though I know some folks who went to DC on January 6 and were involved in some horrible stuff at the end, I don't blame them. Remember that movie where the TV anchor goes nuts, sticks his head out the window, and yells, 'I've had enough, and I'm not going to take it anymore.' That's how I feel, but I don't know what to do about it. One thing needs to happen: we need to feel like this country does better when we work together. Right now, seems like there is too much of what we used to call centrifugal force, but for our democracy to work; we need to think and act together. I need to think I am better off with all of the elements of this country--including white cops--than I would without them. But it's hard for me to believe my family is better off living in a country that sells assault rifles to kids with racist content on the Internet. The black/white thing, guns, domestic terrorists—it's all a product of friction and who is making it and who is not. Black men are sick and tired of having to have "the talk" with their teenage sons. We don't know what is going on in DC—other than dirty politics, but we feel forgotten. I am sure it feels that way in the big city also. People talk about improving our democracy; I don't know what that really means. But I do know how a partnership works. That's what we need in this country. Are we living in different states, or more like different countries? Seems like different universes most days."

Chapter 17

Reverend Doctor Sherman

[January 31, 2021]

S alt had not been to Church recently, and it was embarrassing to have to ask too many questions about the churches –or generate too many suggestions. Ultimately, he took Georgie's advice regarding where to learn more about the community. It seemed to Salt that his rules for these discussions had to be honest, but don't volunteer too much and maintain control at all times. He figured that he might not get into a discussion at all if he started with the fact that he had worked for the government for a long time.

He decided that his story line—partially true—was that he had been raised as an ultra-conservative Methodist but was turned off by things like discouraging kids from playing cards, being negative overall about [insert religion or denomination you don't like, but not your own] playing cards even with no or fake money (never did understand how Monopoly got an exemption), dancing other than square dancing at the church, and the hell and damnation that were certain to come his way almost no matter what. Felt like the book of Revelation was the beginning and end of the Bible. So Salt had ultra-conservative Methodist baggage from long ago. It may not have been fair, but there it was.

He showed up at what turned out to be Margie's church on the following Sunday, January 31, after the Inauguration. Notwithstanding having to listen to comments about January 6, evenhanded and at the end of the service, which seemed rational—and not too long—he hung around and introduced himself to the Reverend Doctor Timothy Jefferson Sherman (known as "General Sherman", the fellow who marched an army through Georgia, not a popular guy in the south after the Civil War). The middle name of Jefferson helped.

At least until Confederate names like Jefferson Davis went out of style, with some Union Generals also getting the boot. Dr. Sherman clearly knew the area backwards and forwards based on the sermon.

In the post-service receiving line, Salt introduced himself as new to the area and wondered if the General (as Dr. Sherman was called) could find some time to give Salt an overview of the Church and the area. The General, who up close bore a remarkable likeness to Morgan Freeman in terms of physical appearance and booming voice, said yes and that Tuesdays were generally open in the afternoon. Done deal. Doctor Sherman then asked Salt, "By the way, are you the newcomer to the area who Margie Hatcher mentioned to me?

Salt responded shyly, "Who knows for sure, as she has not mentioned it to me. But she is a very nice person, has made some introductions, and makes great cookies."

"That's her," said Doctor Sherman, "see you late Tuesday afternoon." Salt started for his car and, of course, saw Margie across the parking lot.

They waved but did not talk.

Salt thought a lot about the Tuesday meeting and whether he should just cancel. Dr. Sherman would surely think he was an ogre of some kind, a nutcase, or both. It took about as much courage to cancel as to go, so he took the path of less immediate resistance and did not cancel.

Salt arrived at 2:00 pm sharp, and Dr. Sherman had him wait in the office for just a few minutes he finished with another congregation member. After very few pleasantries, Salt became increasingly uncomfortable with the whole set-up. He blurted out, "I'm deeply sorry, Dr. Sherman, but I got this meeting under false pretenses, and I assure you I will not bother you again." He stood up and started for the door.

Dr. Sherman hollered in a deep voice that sounded like it could come out of a burning bush on a mountain, "Hold on, brother. I am glad you came, as Margie told me a few days ago that she wanted me to sneak you into a meeting somehow. She does not want to meddle but thinks you are wrapped as tight as a snare drum head and may explode.

"The recent loss of a dear wife, moving too quickly after the death, coming to an area that you sort of know but where you don't really know anybody, bad time of year to move, can't use your new grill, looking at some kind of weird job, and so on. She's right. It won't be your fault if you don't just explode from pure stress. So, we'll call this Margie's meeting, which is not tainted by your deceit. Relax, have some of my special tea, talk freely, and no more bullshit. How's that?"

"Do I have a choice?"

"Not really, but I rarely take hostages. And by the way, remember that I don't have the ability to clothe this discussion with an attorney-client privilege, but the priest-penitent privilege is still alive and used, in one form or another, in most places. Our entire conversation should be subject to that privilege except as we agree to the contrary."

"Regardless, talk. Tell me who you are and why."

To his surprise, Salt started to talk and continued for about 45 minutes. Dr. Sherman interrupted on very few occasions to direct the conversation, but he had a light touch.

When Salt had finished his story, which was candid, Salt looked at his watch and blurted out, "Jesus, I started talking and never shut up. I am deeply sorry. I talked for an hour and wasted your whole afternoon. I am surprised; this has been a bit like a security clearance interview. I don't think we got into sensitive stuff, but I guess I should ask, do you have a clearance, Dr. Sherman?

"Yes, but that is all I can say about it." Salt was surprised, and visibly so.

They looked at each other silently, and then, after a long silent minute, Dr. Sherman said, "My story is pretty simple. Grew up in the inner city, was recognized as being intelligent and a smart ass, and good on the basketball court when I paid attention, maybe because I was tall and maybe because some thought I looked a little like Bill Russell (of course, you white guys think us blacks all look the same," he chuckled), "but Bill Russell was OK by me).

I was fortunate to have a couple of ministers as serious mentors who, for some reason, were willing to try to make me make something of myself.

I got a scholarship from the Army when I went to college and joined the rangers at the same time, spent six years in the dual program and then another four full-time with the rangers, and then went to seminary because my head was about to burst—like yours right now—if I did not settle down somehow. After seminary, I served as an assistant pastor in several churches and landed here—not exactly the best fit. But we have a hell of a choir, and that brings people back."

"OK," Dr. Sherman concluded, "that's enough for today. Think about this, and we'll get together again in a couple of weeks."

"One more piece of advice—Margie is very popular around here. Do not hurt her. Period."

"Got it," I responded, heading for a drink and a burger plate at Helen's Place. In honor of Margie, I started with a salad.

Chapter 18

Evening Church Meets DSOL

[February 4, 2021]

S alt felt he had to show up at the next church service held in the evening, and he did so on February 4, a Thursday. He did not attend with anyone, though he waved at Margie as she walked in.

The congregation was modestly diverse from a racial standpoint, and the services were consistently moderately full. It was an old church building, constructed 75 years ago with the typical red church brick used by the more well-to-do congregations, lots of heirloom items placed around to show off the church's history, a few stained glass windows, beautiful wooden pews that were hard enough (no pew pads) to make it difficult to doze off, and a grand old pipe organ. From the back of the church, which is where Salt sat, as always, he saw mostly white and grey hair.

The opening procession had the choir and Dr. Sherman walking from the back of the sanctuary to the front, and when they reached the front and turned around, they were surprised to see at the back of the sanctuary about 15 men wearing blue head coverings, a la the Ku Klux Klan, but clearly differentiated from the KKK, standing in a line across the back of pews. A few were carrying side arms, but no long guns were visible.

Dr. Sherman had sensed that trouble might be brewing, so before the procession started, he had asked the church softball team manager to bring up to the foyer in the middle of the church a couple of canvas bags they used to carry their softball bats. When the kid came up, he had mostly whiffle ball bats. Dr. Sherman asked the kid if he knew who Teddy Roosevelt was. "Yeah, I guess. He was President or something like that."

"Right," said Dr. Sherman, "and do you know what he said about getting into fights?"

"Nope."

"Well," Dr. Sherman said, "Roosevelt said that in situations like this, you should speak softly and carry a big stick. So go back downstairs and bring me that wooden baseball bat with Hank Aaron's name on the end of it." The kid got the message and the bat.

Dr. Sherman confronted the visitors and said that Church always welcomed visitors and invited the group to take a seat.

Their leader responded, "We aren't here to worship; we're here to talk." "Well," said Dr. Sherman, "that's OK too, but since a lot of people are here to worship, kindly step aside for those who want to leave."

"Good idea," said the leader, and he said to the leader of the other group, and he and others stepped aside to allow about two-thirds of the other group to leave. Margie and Salt stayed where they were, but with Salt inching his way toward the bat bags. While that was happening, Dr. Sherman took off and laid aside his robe, mantle, and other evidence of his minister's role. Stripped to his shirt and pants and holding the bat he had picked up, Dr. Sherman said, "OK, now what can we do for you? You are still welcome to have a seat and worship with us. Please." None of the visitors moved, but the leader stepped forward.

"Thank you," said Dr. Sherman, "I hereby declare this service concluded, with whatever happens next not to be construed as happening during a church service or at the instance of the church." While speaking, getting rid of his minster gear, and picking up a bat, Dr. Sherman made clear two things: the church service was over, and Dr. Sherman was in pretty good shape. Then Dr. Sherman said, "Look, if you really want to talk, you have to lose the guns."

"Well," said the leader, it's pretty damn clear to us that you don't really want to talk. You want to bash us. Now listen, the Sons of Liberty, we don't go around bashing people. We don't like oppression ("Damn right", the group said nearly in unison). And our reputation would go to hell if we have our way with a bunch of churchies who average 20 years older than we are. ("Damn right"). So here's what we're going to do.

We're going to free you because we don't think we are in danger anymore, and we'll send you a list of demands. ("damn good idea, right on").

"OK," said Dr. Sherman, "but what will it be a list of?"

The group leader thought about that for a minute and said, "There you go again messing things up. We demand that you receive our list." ("Damn straight")

"OK," said Dr. Sherman. "We'll receive it if we receive it. And one other thing. The local papers are going to call us about this meeting. We're going to say that we had a peaceful meeting and agreed to receive some papers from you before another meeting if we think one would be useful." Dr. Sherman then yelled, "did everyone hear that? If the press calls, that is all we're going to say."

The church members mumbled, "OK," and the group leader said to his followers, "Refer the press to me, and I will just tell them we had a meeting and we got all we asked for." Then the group left quietly.

Salt walked over to Margie and was smiling. "After an incident like that, I could use a drink and a piece of chocolate cake."

"Sounds good to me," said Margie. "I hitched a ride out here and need a ride home."

"Deal," said Salt.

They got to Helen's for a drink of Virginia wine and some cake, and Salt then dropped Margie off at home. There was no serious talk other than about the Sons of Liberty. And it was hard to know what to say about them. Salt could only put two words together on their way to Helen's: "Holy Shit."

Chapter 19

Canadian Reality Check

[February 8, 2021]

Louise passed her first test with flying colors by getting the Canadian junket approved, so Salt called to arrange to meet with Ray Marchand in Canada. Ray split his time between his law firm's offices in Montreal and Toronto. Salt asked him for two to three hours in either city for a highly confidential matter that would not result in any revenue for his law firm.

True to form, Ray said he could clear Monday afternoon in Toronto.

Early Monday morning, Salt drove into Dulles airport, boarded a small regional jet that was operating despite the coronavirus and recession, landed in Toronto, went through customs, grabbed a cab and noticed that the driver was wearing a mask, put on his own, and then experienced the traffic hell that was the Gardiner Expressway from the airport to downtown Toronto. He was glad he had scheduled plenty of time for transit. After grabbing a cold- cut sandwich at a shop in Ray's building and putting on his mask again, he took an elevator up to the forty-third floor and waited. Suddenly, this seemed like a nutty idea again. How was he going to explain this in a rational way? And who would believe the idea had a prayer of success? Thank goodness he had picked an old friend to try this out on.

Ray walked into the office reception area and greeted him with a booming voice; even through his mask, his gladness to see Salt was evident. "I have wanted to see you and share stories about US politics. What's up?"

"Nothing we can discuss in your reception area," cautioned Salt. They headed for a small conference room.

After they were ensconced in a small but comfortable conference room with a great view and each had a cup of coffee, Salt and Ray exchanged pleasantries and generally caught up.

Salt asked about Canadians' view of their young prime minister following Canada's recent failure to gain a seat on the UN Security Council (losing to Norway and Ireland), whether he would prevail in the next election, what that meant for US-Canada relations, and how Canadians were reacting to the early days of the USMCA treaty that replaced NAFTA.

As they were completing their catch-up, Ray said, "Salt, before we get into the details of whatever is on your agenda, I need to ask you about a couple of things. First up is something that is just slightly more than a year in the past, but given everything else going on, it seems like a long time ago. I am talking about the Black Lives Matter movement and what is going on in your country in terms of racial issues and gun violence. The use of the military to clear Lafayette Park during the George Floyd disturbances last summer was scary—it looked more like Russia than across the street from the White House. And then, in the sharpest contrast possible, there is January 6. My God. After pausing, Ray continued. Many of us can't understand how the US got here. We in Canada feel a little like the younger sibling of an older brother who has been convicted of a serious crime. We don't understand, and we're lost without that older brother."

"Well," said Salt, "as an old white guy who likely has a few racist bones in his body, I am not the most qualified to speak to that topic, but it needs to be recognized and dealt with as the shameful situation it is. We have to do better in all kinds of ways. Dealing with police profiling and brutality is just a starting point—and a relatively easy one. We haven't yet gone far enough there. These issues and our urgent infrastructure deficiencies may mean we need what amounts to a Marshall Plan for America.

Salt continued, "As to January 6, it is truly not understandable on its face. I don't know any more than you, as I have not seen anything that has not been on TV. I think the special congressional committee has done an excellent job at a high level. I don't see how the Department of Justice can duck, but time will tell. It is hard to read the Attorney General. But he is principled; in fact, I am still sorry that he is not on the Supreme Court, yet another tough topic we could discuss for hours at another time.

Going back to the race issue, I've not tried to explain it like this before, but consider two museums in Washington, the Holocaust Museum and the National Museum of African American History and Culture. Both are evidence of shameful racial treatment with major impacts on the world. These things make you wonder, how in the world did that happen? Going to the African American museum takes you through the experience of blacks over four hundred years in what is now the US. History and teaches us that, to a significant extent, the United States was built on the backs of blacks. But because of our history, sharing of the opportunities that represent the fruits of that labor has not been fair.

"You know, there have been many outstanding and recognized accomplishments by blacks in the US, but the thing is, they have to overcome not only competition but a terrible history of bias that creates barriers of all kinds. There is systematic racial bias in the US. Period. We all need to understand that. This will likely never be fully remedied, but with its rainbow of supporters, the Black Lives Matter movement may force more fairness. The movement needs to be broad, determined, and successful. This is important. Its time has come, and in the long run, those protestors are actually doing the United States a great service."

"It is interesting that you raised two sorts of reciprocal issues: Black Lives Matter and January 6, which could be called White Lives Matter, or maybe some White Lives Matter. I really can't get into January 6, but it ain't over 'till it's over."

After a few moments of silence, Ray responded. "Thanks. Maybe that is a useful way to start thinking about it. Let's switch gears and move on to a third matter. How in God's name did the US flub so badly the response to COVID- 19? We are sitting here in early 2021, essentially fifteen months after the pandemic began, and the US is still fighting what amounts to a third or fourth wave of the disease without ever really getting your arms around it, while second and third-tier countries have done as well or better. You guys have the best epidemiologists in the world and have thrown billions at it without getting it under control. And you have a massive recession and job loss to boot. How did that happen? We all hope that one or more of these vaccines will do the trick, but only time will tell, I gather."

Salt responded quickly. "One word: leadership. Maybe a few others, like divisive politics and lack of popular will to make sacrifices for the greater good for longer than a couple of months without good leadership." And maybe something harder to understand—a deep desire to tell someone that they can shove it, and I am not taking any damn vaccine to prove to the world that I don't need it and can make my own decisions.

"OK," said Ray, "now for the biggie, January 6." Salt sat back and smiled. "I guess I should have had a briefing paper on this one. As I said earlier, the truth is, you know about as much as I do. I don't have anything other than political briefing papers. The major newspapers in the US are doing a really good job on this, and we'll see the special committee report eventually. The only thing I can tell you is that it looks like some people in the Pope administration played some kind of role, it will take a long, long time to figure this out, and it will be a big story. The fact that the Vice President finished the Electoral College process that had to be done on January 6 is a big deal. Beyond that, stay tuned."

"Well," said Ray, "January 6 was unbelievable for those who have seen it on TV up here, which is nearly everyone, and the media is full of it. I gather you are not here to talk about any of those topics directly, but as a friend and in the interest of candor, I need to say that the racist and right-wing anarchist political views and also the crazy things that come out of the mouths of some of your ultra-progressives are frightening. The editorial writers up here wonder what is in store for American democracy over the next few years. Are we to add an American impeachment to our annual medical checkup and colonoscopy? These things detract significantly from the ability of the US to regain its leadership role in the world. The United States is diminished by this history you describe and the related current events. People just shake their heads."

"Well," responded Salt, "you would know these things are not easily controlled. We have our President Pope, who is gone but not really, and you have your young PM to contend with. Then, the USMTC seems to be off to a good start. See, we've already agreed on something.

Now we need to turn to other aspects of US politics, which is what I'm here to talk about, but with important ground rules. Ray, I hate to do this, but I need to say up front that if you cannot agree to the ground rules, I'll fully understand, and we can cut this way short."

"Okay, friend, lay them on me," Ray responded.

Salt began, talking slowly. "The ground rules are first that this meeting never happened and you won't write it up; second, you never discussed the subject matter of this meeting before it became public if it ever does; and third, you can't share the content of the meeting with the Canadian government, where I know you have lots of good and reliable friends, unless I clear it. You and Canada would get a head start but not an exclusive. In return, I will follow the same rules, except that I can share the content of this meeting on a confidential basis with Stuart Bacon, who knows I'm here, a colleague from the CIA I would be working with, and President Evans."

"Hmm," murmured Ray. "Well, you have certainly piqued my curiosity. Since you're saying it's your way or the highway, I guess I have no choice, but this better be good. In order to have some balance here, I need to be able to discuss the general subject of whatever this is on a confidential basis with our foreign minister. No detail and nothing in writing."

"Thanks, Ray," responded Salt, who, without thinking, held out his hand to shake and then quickly pulled it back. Both smiled at the gesture. Salt then started talking through the barebones outline that Stuart Bacon had shared with him. After getting through that, Salt said, "So there are two basic questions for you, Ray. What is your assessment of the diplomatic status, influence, and credibility of the United States, and does this hair-brained scheme have a chance to improve things?"

"Well," said Ray slowly, "there are a lot of layers to this. So I'm going to do what you Americans only sometimes do when you say you are going to tell it like it is. I'll actually do that."

"First, America is viewed as somewhat racist and xenophobic. We've already talked about race, and the xenophobic nature of your immigration policies has the Statue of Liberty weeping under her mask. Enough said.

"Second, there is genuine concern about the stability of the government. Even today, former President Pope is giving his seal of approval to certain candidates. Why, in God's name, does anyone care about what his twisted mind thinks about candidates? This is an element of the trust factor. One would think that Pope's loss would have offset much of the concern, but then you have Pope, who is not in prison and making political speeches. How can there be a trust factor when some people and some of your media think Pope should be in prison and others would make him president tomorrow, and all of this when you have a current president who is a good guy but may not be renominated by his own party when there is no obvious successor: Incredible.

"Third, the trust factor. If this were a business deal, you would say, 'we just cannot deal with these people.' Even though there is trust in President Evans, these other factors mean that nobody, and I mean nobody, trusts the United States on a long–term basis anymore. We don't trust your word, your actions, your motives, your politics, your people, or your follow-through. Assume President Evans is sort of like what we think he is: a decent, if naïve, middle-of-the-roader. One proper administration is not enough to undo the doubt. Trust dissolves a lot faster than it forms. If the president is trustworthy, can the president be reelected? Who and what follows? Because your politics are so screwed up and divided, nobody knows. The divided politics give rise to a divided government in both the administration and Congress. And there are lots of showboating and promises that could not be kept even if the promise maker wanted to.

"Think for a moment if you were a German or a Hungarian. If you are German, you are going to lose your Russian natural gas in the winter and have cold kids because of the Ukrainian war. That may or may not be so if you are Hungarian. So, in either case, you keep an extra blanket and call it President Evans to make the kid feel more secure? And what of the immigrants from Ukraine they are hosting?

"Finally, we have the results of the Pope administration causing the shrinkage of the diplomatic corps. Nobody knows who is left and stable. The US diplomatic corps seems a shadow of its former self. Clearly, there remain some very good and loyal people—and they are very good—but not enough.

In some areas, the diplomatic infrastructure needs to be rebuilt almost from scratch. No offense, but it speaks volumes that Stuart has decided to bring you, who amounts to an outsider, in from the cold to start fixing some things. And then there is the fact that nobody is comfortable with their current read of the situation—or how stable it is. The last administration seemed to clean the house every so often in order to eliminate dissent. What will things look like in a year?

Ray took a breath and continued: "Think about all the things the United States has backed out of, threatened, or criticized: the Paris Climate Accord; the Trans-Pacific Partnership; NATO; the Iranian nuclear treaty; the World Health Organization and the World Trade Organization negotiations with Russia on the New START nuclear arms reduction treaty; even UNESCO for heaven's sake. Nothing is safe. Real countries don't do this sort of thing. It is one thing to say some things are out of whack and need to be fixed. It is another to tweet insults on a regular basis and abandon treaties by tweeting.

"Unbelievable.

"Those of us outside the United States will be in a show-me mode—prove that leadership is different, that there is followership in the electorate and Congress, new blood in the diplomatic corps, stability, and credibility—and a succession plan. Thus far, the support for the Ukrainian war is a positive sign. Let's hope Europe does not tire of that war too soon.

Ray continued along the same lines for an hour or more, including details on issues in which Canada had a particular interest. Salt occasionally interrupted with a question or carefully worded objection. Salt had been taught by his father not to try to argue with an angry person, and Ray was using the occasion to unload on Salt.

"Well, I asked for it," acknowledged Salt. "And you gave it to me, though I noticed that you did not complain about the lack of follow-through by the United States on buying Greenland. Recognizing the depth of the problem is only step one. How do we start to fix it?"

Ray thought for a few minutes. "As I said earlier, there is no shortcut available here. You can get started, but there will be no miracles. Start by undoing as much unnecessary damage as you can. It is helpful that NAFTA was redone as the US-Mexico-Canada trade agreement, or USMCA, with some beneficial changes. Beg your way back into the Trans-Pacific Partnership treaty and the Paris climate accord. Make your devotion to NATO clear. And by the way, that does not mean you need to buy your way into a better place; other countries should pay their fair share. Think creatively about Iran, though that one may not be recoverable. Stop making things worse in Jerusalem. And, yes, leaving Greenland alone is okay.

"Then show the world you're serious about rebuilding your team and your image by starting to fill key ambassadorships, solid members of the diplomatic corps, or other serious people. Break the habit of trying to make big donors into ambassadors. You can't afford to do that right now, even though big donors were no longer safe from removal under President Pope.

"Jettison all Twitter accounts. Period.

"Get your act together on US immigration. I know this is very hard, but in recent years, this has created a huge stain on the US image, which it can ill afford.

"Get used to the idea that on the economy, climate change, terrorism, cybersecurity, and so many other things, the United States is no longer independent but rather interdependent. A first among nearer and nearer equals, if you will. The United States is no longer a private island. You can't accomplish very much unilaterally anymore.

"Before you get on a plane to be the roving secret diplomatic fixer, make sure you know how far President Evans will go along these lines. The worst thing for you would be to overpromise and underdeliver to the countries you'll be meeting with. The only thing you have going for you is that not many remember you, and those who do still think of you as a straight shooter. Don't lose that. Get the President to give you comfort on these issues.

"And by the way, my friend, you may as well make it clear that you're not willing to do this forever because that's how long it will take.

"So, will it work? Not in the short term. It might help over the long term if you're not double-crossed. It will not undo the last four years—that will take a long time. It would be a start, might help, and can't hurt."

At the end of an intense discussion that eventually became more two-sided, Salt thanked Ray and said, "This is why I needed to talk to you. I appreciate it."

"What else can I do for you?" asked Ray.

Salt hesitated for a moment and then said, "There is one other thing I want to ask about. What is Canada's view of the World Health Organization these days?"

"My God," said Ray. "Why do you ask about that? It is important, but you already have a long list of highly visible diplomatic issues to think about. Even with COVID-19 still hanging over us, I would not get tangled up with the WHO controversies as a priority."

"I appreciate that," responded Salt quietly. "It's a personal matter. My wife, Meredith, was a nurse and contracted the virus during the pandemic. If I take on this other stuff, I owe it to her to see if the world's health threat response systems can be improved."

Ray responded carefully. "I don't know enough to comment, but I'll make some quiet calls. The WHO didn't cover itself with glory on COVID-19, but I don't know whether that was China, the WHO, the Pope administration, or all of them screwing things up."

"Thanks, Ray," said Salt quietly. They finished with a much more normal conversation and best wishes.

Salt had a lot to think about on his way home. The last thing he needed was more aggravation, but the Gardiner Expressway to the airport during rush hour reminded him of Washington traffic.

And to make things worse, he forgot that he would be going through US customs in the Toronto airport, not at his destination, and he had to run to avoid missing the flight. He sat quietly during the short flight, trying to digest what he had heard from Ray and thinking about the next steps. Shortly after landing in the early evening, he decided to stay overnight in Tysons, Virginia, near Langley. He would call Louise and try to get together that evening somewhere quiet where he could debrief her and get her reaction. He needed to talk to someone, and right now, she was the only person on the face of the earth he could talk to about this.

Chapter 20

Back of the Envelope Principles

[February 8, 2021]

They got together in a quiet corner of a restaurant in McLean. The greying evening crowd was thinning out quickly, and they could sit at a social distance and avoid using masks after they were seated. Salt was dead tired but needed something to eat and relax and have someone to talk with. Louise arrived a few minutes after he did and asked for the debrief. Salt started talking, aided by a masked waiter bringing a Manhattan, which Salt sipped, and a large glass of water, which he guzzled.

Salt opened by asking Louise if she had ever seen the movie Get Smart and if she understood the meaning of the phrase "cone of silence." She answered in the affirmative. "Good," said Salt, "because we're now in a very secure cone of silence. This does not even go as far as Stuart unless we agree it should. Agreed?" She did.

Salt opened the discussion by summarizing his chat with Ray. He then said, "Louise, I have to be honest. I don't see how this project is going to work. There are serious issues here that cannot be resolved even during a four-year presidential term. I initially thought this might involve a four-month commitment. It involves way more than that. And I would need high-level support for meetings outside the United States and commitments for changes that could be reliably delivered upon. I'm not sure President Evans and Stuart can deliver. I could end up looking like more of an idiot than I actually am."

Louise was quiet for a few moments. She looked at Salt and realized he was stressed out, and this gig was on life support. She tried to be comforting. "Okay—let's start with what we can control. We can't control the fact that this is going to take a longer and more sustained effort than you thought. That is what it is.

To kick off the effort, you need more detail about the Evans doctrine— or whatever you want to call the President's foreign policy—than you now know and, if there is enough coincidence of thought, extract some promises. Let's think about what you need."

Louise pulled an envelope out of her purse, found a pen, and wrote "Necessary Principles" across the top. The waiter came by, and they ordered another round of drinks and some appetizers. They then got to work on the envelope.

They started broadly with Salt pontificating what was needed and Louise understanding that he needed to vent. As the discussion continued, she pushed back more often and with more force. Ultimately, they decided to limit Salt's Necessary Principles to ten, then eleven, and then twelve. It was not easy.

This is what the first iteration of the list looked like:

Necessary Principles

1. Stuart Bacon is the secretary of state or director of national intelligence.
2. Pepper is not on organizational charts but reports directly to Bacon and President Evans, including reasonable direct access to Evans.
3. Professional diplomats will be put in place as ambassadors in places like Canada, the UK, France, Germany, Russia, China, Australia, India, Turkey, Japan, Israel, and Mexico as existing assignments expire.
4. Good faith attempts to rejoin Paris Climate Accord.
5. Good faith attempts to rejoin Trans-Pacific Partnership (TPP) treaty.
6. Much more limited use of tariffs.
7. Ukraine—not sure if there is a role for Salt—it has plenty of attention
8. Unconditional support of NATO.
9. Arms control discussions with Russia (after Ukraine),
10. New and different approach to North Korea, coordinated with South Korea and Japan.
11. Reopen good faith discussions with Iran and parties to the nuclear treaty (Joint Comprehensive Plan of Action).
12. Commitment to restore senior professional staffing at State Department.

"Well," said Louise, "that is for sure a full back of the envelope. And the assessment of the President being able to deliver on all the items is no f...g way. But some of this is easy. Take the State Department staffing, for example. Not an issue. But the ambassadorships, on the other hand, are a different story. You know that many of these—not all—have already been promised to big donors. Hard to imagine President Evans picking up the phone to call a big donor—call him Jack—who has been promised London and saying, 'Jack, I've got good news and bad news. We have a guy you've never heard of who is about to waste two years of his life on a diplomatic mission impossible. We need to humor him, and he says he won't take on the mission unless we put a professional staffer in charge of the embassy in London. As a result, you don't have to move to London and meet the queen and all of that. But we have some pretty exciting opportunities that you can pick from. And if you help us reduce the campaign debt, there is always Norway or the Caribbean.' The President is going to say, 'Salt, you don't know my donor Jack, and you don't know jack shit about the realities of this stuff." And that will be the end of this exercise. I think Ukraine is out of bounds—nothing to be done there quietly, and maybe we can pick up some dropped balls elsewhere.

"Sounds like a good result to me," Salt nodded.

Louise responded, "Just for the hell of it, let's call the back of the envelope we have been using, Envelope A. We will start a new summary on this cocktail napkin and call it Napkin B. Let's see where the give might be." They started through the list and discussed each point, item by item.

Somewhat to Salt's surprise, Louise took the lead this time through.

Maybe it was the alcohol.

"Stuart needs to be secretary of state," she stated. "Director of national intelligence is just too limiting. You need Stuart to help move the State Department bureaucracy or what's left of it when need be. And you need to be able to get into the Oval Office when need be, so number two is okay as is. As we discussed, item three, the ambassador thing, is a nonstarter."

"But that could be a strong early signal to the key countries, and it's easy to do from a logistics standpoint," protested Salt. "It would likely find bipartisan support on the Hill."

"Get over it," Louise shot back. "Think of something else."

Salt took another sip of his Manhattan and thought for a few minutes. "Let's require that, in the G-7 and selected other countries, there be a senior person acceptable to me that is read into the project and reports directly to Stuart, not the ambassador. This project will be out of bounds for political appointees."

"Worth a try," Louise responded. "Items four, five, six, and eleven should be acceptable as they are. Items four, five, and six were part of Evans's platform, and Stuart will insist on item eleven. How about item seven and NATO?"

"Well," said Salt, "unconditional is a strong word. How about if we say, 'strong support of NATO that does not assume we stop pushing them to pay for committed defense costs,' or something along those lines?" Louise gave a thumbs' up as this was already in process. No reason not to have a gimme on the list. But Salt and Alexander were aware of several important projects that were not going anywhere. Could any of them be rescued? Pepper and the team needed the courage and discipline to walk away from things that looked attractive initially but did not progress fast enough. They would need early wins.

"Okay," responded Louise. "And arms control negotiations with Russia and fixing Ukraine?"

"Important but outside the scope of this and way over our heads," acknowledged Salt.

"Done," she said. "Now, for the easy ones, North Korea and Iran."

"I don't know," said Salt. "I'm too tired and have had too much to drink to take those on. There are no answers. Just say the approach to those countries is to be closely coordinated with allies. That's all that can be said, but those issues will be front and center in discussions with many countries, especially those who have supported aggressive sanctions. But we need to put on the list, when appropriate, the New START talks with Russia."

"Okay, let's look at Napkin B now," Louise suggested. And they did;

Necessary Principles—Napkin B

- Stuart Bacon is secretary of state.
- Pepper is not on an org chart but reports directly to Bacon and President Evans, including reasonable direct access to Evans.
- In G-7 and other selected countries, a direct contact in the embassy, acceptable to Pepper, will be established with such contacts reporting to Pepper and the secretary of state with respect to this project; the project is not to be shared with political appointees.
- Pepper stays out of Ukraine unless invited in for narrow assignments
- Good faith attempts to rejoin Paris Climate Accord.

- Good faith attempts to rejoin TPP.
- Much more limited and targeted use of tariffs (Ukraine excepted).
- Strong support of NATO not to foreclose pressure on member state defense spending. Expansion of NATO favored.
- The approach to North Korea is to be closely coordinated with allies, especially South Korea and Japan.
- Approach to Iran to be closely coordinated with allies and parties to the Iran nuclear treaty (Joint Comprehensive Plan of Action) that the US withdrew from, and stay out of wars in the Middle East.
- Commitment to strengthen senior professional staffing at State Department.
- Meaningful and rational comprehensive immigration reform.
- The rapid movement toward renewed New START talks without requiring China to participate.

"Okay, for now," said Salt, "but I need to sleep on this. I'll call you in the morning. Sorry to ask you to do this, but I don't have a computer with me. Can you get this typed and cleaned up a bit? I doubt the president will be impressed with a napkin. The real question now is, assuming I'm still willing to try to do something, what is my next step? Meet with Stuart?"

"No," Louise blurted out. "We—not just you—need to meet with the President and Stuart ASAP and in person. You need to unload on them with the input from Ray in Toronto, show them the Napkin B list, and watch how they react. And if this is going to get launched at all, that needs to happen sooner rather than later, that's for sure. Now, get some rest and call me in the morning."

As they were walking out of the restaurant, Salt asked to be reminded where the nearest Marriott was, and as they said good night, Salt added, "By the way, do me a favor and don't throw those napkins away. I may want to frame them someday—or shred them."

Chapter 21

Napkin Negotiations

[February 9, 2021]

T he following day, Salt called Louise on what he now called the "shoe phone" and said he was willing to meet with the President and Stuart and gauge their response to his report on Canada and Napkin B. He asked if Louise could arrange for the meeting. Her answer was a bit frosty. "No, this is a meeting that you need to set up. Let me know what you arrange."

"Sorry," said Salt. "I thought you were insisting on being there."

Louise was doing a slow burn. "I am, but you need to make that happen without me looking like your calendar keeper. This is a test. Don't screw it up."

Salt called Stuart and left a message asking for a prompt meeting with Stuart and the President that Louise would also attend. Stuart called back several hours later in a huff about how the President had a day job that did not involve fitting Salt in when it suited Salt. Salt responded, "Sorry, but I thought this was a priority. Call me when some slots become available. In the meantime, I'll go back to the farm and unpack a few boxes."

"Don't do that until I get back to you," Stuart demanded. "You know, it's going to be hard to make this work if you live two and a half hours away."

"Yep, life's a bitch, but it's my life. And most of these countries you want me to talk with are not in our time zone anyhow, and the flights will fly out of Dulles, which is closer to the farm than Reagan National." After the call, Salt decided to take a walk around the nearby Tysons mall, which he had not been to for years while waiting for Stuart to call back. He was surprised at how empty the mall was—of both people and stores. The COVID-19 pandemic and the recession had clearly taken a toll. There were lots of For Lease signs.

Salt wasn't sure, but based on the few store windows he looked at, it seemed remotely possible that his wardrobe was out of date. But he had several suits that had been made in Hong Kong, and he decided he'd be damned if he would get rid of those.

Stuart called back in a few hours. They were on with the President at nine o'clock the following day. Stuart advised him to stay put in the hotel in McLean, and as long as he was around, Stuart said they should get together at a private club in DC that evening so they could prepare. "I'll have to bring Louise," said Salt.

"Damn right," responded Stuart. It seemed like she was in.

Louise drove, and they met Stuart at 7:30 p.m. in the corner of a sparsely populated dining room. They each ordered lightly and started on a bottle of pinot noir. Salt opened with a recounting of his meeting in Toronto with Ray. Stuart did not seem to be surprised, acknowledging that he had been given similar, if less pointed, lectures by diplomats from other countries. But Salt's version from Canada was another wake-up call. Stuart was in sales mode.

"Hell, if we thought it was easy, we wouldn't have asked you," commented Stuart.

"And if I thought it was easy, I wouldn't be laying these take-it-leave-it demands on you," said Salt quietly.

Stuart came to life. "Whoa. What demands?"

"Look, Stuart," said Salt, "before you get in a huff, look at this from my standpoint and that of other countries. I just can't get myself in a situation where I represent the US position on issue X to be solution A when solution A is a nonstarter in the United States. I'm a dead duck if that happens. And beyond that, I need to know the US position on key issues before I decide whether to even try doing some good here. I need to cover my ass in advance. And the same concerns apply to Louise."

"Just show me the damn list," growled Stuart.

Louise handed him the typed version of Napkin B. Stuart started to read and began to twitch.

Stuart looked at Louise. "Louise, do you buy into this list, or is this Salt pouring salt into open wounds—no pun intended?"

"I'm in," she said.

"I was afraid of that. Look, I could bitch and moan about this, but that would not be productive. You guys have got to look at this at two levels. Frankly, the President probably agrees with most of this. And so, the President and I can have your backs at one level. But there is a second level that's a reality. The President can't act—or appear to act—unilaterally on a number of these issues. There is the State Department buy-in—thanks for your vote for me as secretary, by the way—but I'm pretty sure you don't get a vote. And then there is the dysfunctional Congress. We can talk to the President about his core policies, and I will tell you what I think, but we can't have you blabbing about the President's position on this stuff before he takes a public position. His ass also needs to be covered, for Christ's sake."

They then walked through the list item by item and discussed the issues, nuances, and practical problems. It became clear that important factors for all at the table and the President would include (1) who Salt and Louise would be relating to, (2) whether those persons had loose lips, and (3) how strongly Salt and Louise would articulate the President's position on various issues. And there were also factors X, Y, and Z: how would this play in the mid-term elections, more than a year out, could this operation possibly surface during the mid-terms (yes), and if so, how would Congress, our allies and our voters react, and do we need to get someone on the team to be set up to one for the team and, if so who? Probably a TBD item. Who is willing to take one for the team if there needs to be a sacrifice?

"Yuk," said Louise, "I think you need to work on your recruiting pitch Stuart."

All at the table knew Salt, as the semi-retired outsider not known by many among the diplomatic intelligentsia, would be the candidate. Brutal.

"This is very "yuk," Louise said to the group. Salt just meekly held up his hand. "Beats a firing squad, I guess."

As they were wrapping up, Stuart simply said, "Thanks. I'll meet with the president at nine, and we'll see you at 9:15. The most we will have will be until 9:45."

Louise dropped Salt off at the Tysons Marriott. There wasn't much to be said. Besides, Salt was not in the mood to give her an opportunity to comment on his wardrobe. Down deep, he already knew what she thought.

Chapter 22

West Wing Input

[February 10, 2021]

Salt picked up Louise in the morning, and they arrived at the White House at nine o'clock. After having their temperatures taken, waiting for fifteen minutes, and pulling up their masks, they were shown into the Oval Office. That office, in and of itself, was intimidating. It was apparent that President Evans was not done moving in, but that did not detract from the awe factor. The Oval Office was the Oval Office, after all, and it looked pretty much like it did on TV. Salt wondered to himself how the hell he had gotten there. Stuart was there, and the President was jovial and welcoming. Maybe the President was a morning person. They exchanged pleasantries, but the President was not into much small talk today.

"Let's cut to the chase, folks. I appreciate your talking to your buddy in Canada, Salt, and the thoughts outlined in your Plan B paper. And I understand why you need me to cover your backsides—otherwise, we will blow your credibility, which is what you bring to the party, Salt. So, look, three things. First, I would be crazy to do something that would destroy the mission. Second, I have looked at your paper and agree with what is outlined. I think we need to drop the immigration bullet for now because nobody knows yet what comprehensive immigration reform is— so it's meaningless. Third, I can't go public with positions on these other issues now. That's just a political reality. You folks are rightly focused on things international. I get it. But only US citizens vote in our elections, and we have a ton of domestic issues that just landed in our laps, including COVID-19, the recession, the deficit, and Black Lives Matter. Reminds me of the old Johnny Cash song, 'fifteen tons and what do you get, another day older and deeper in debt.' We don't any longer say, 'America first,' but the reality is that domestic issues, like health care, finishing the recession recovery, and the Black Lives Matter movement, need to come first.

Look, you can honestly represent my position to be consistent with your outline, but if someone leaks it, I may have to deny it. Plausible deniability. "Yep," the President said, staring at Salt and sighing, we don't have to like it, but we're here for the greater good. That means we really have to be very careful about who you talk with and what you say to whom.

"Finally," the President concluded, "I agree entirely with trying to keep this team out of Ukraine. It is already swallowing people."

"That's it," he concluded. "I need to know by noon tomorrow whether you're willing to undertake this mission. If not, no harm is done. If yes, we need to get a move on. By the way, I got the line about direct access to me. That's okay, but the reality is that Stuart and I are of the same mind on this. Your first port of call should be Stuart, but if you need to talk to me, we'll get you in as we did today. Besides, I'll want regular updates. Have a good one."

It was apparent that they were being dismissed. But Salt wasn't done. "There is one other thing, President Evans," Salt injected.

"What's that?" the President asked.

Salt looked out the window so his face was not visible to the others and said, "I need to add one more item to the Plan B agenda."

Stuart and Louise gulped. The President looked quizzical.

With damp eyes, Salt turned to the President. "My wife, Meredith, died last year of the coronavirus while working as a nurse in a major hospital in Northern Virginia. She had been a nurse for many years but managed several years ago to get into a doctor's office to have more regular hours. When the pandemic arrived with force in this area, she volunteered to work in the emergency room of a major hospital, she contracted the virus, and it killed her. If I'm going to take on this assignment, I owe it to her to look into how we address global health threats, including whether the World Health Organization needs attention. I'm sorry, but that needs to be part of the package. Please be assured that I have no interest in being part of a blame game on this."

The room fell silent. After a few moments, the President responded. "Two things. I'm very sorry about your wife. But words like that are meaningless, really. I get that. If you want to explore the world health morass, okay, and we will provide some staff and other support. But it cannot get in the way of the rest of the agenda. We are not going to let the WHO fall apart any time soon."

The President stood up and saluted. Shaking hands was out. There was nothing more to say, and Salt and Louise left. Stuart followed in a few seconds.

"That went as well as it could have gone until the end," Stuart remarked. "I wish you would have given me a heads-up about that, Salt."

"Sorry, Stuart," Salt responded. "It came as a bit of a surprise to me, to tell you the truth. You have a right to be pissed."

Stuart paused for a moment, taking in Salt's response, and then said, "It would be great if you could decide today what you're going to do. If that happens, we will try to schedule briefings for you starting tomorrow afternoon. We would like to have this kicked off with meetings—probably in the UK—next week. And Salt, I really am very sorry. I didn't know how Meredith died."

Salt and Louise left, climbed into Salt's dirty ten-year-old Volvo, and crossed the bridge into Virginia. What they needed was a quiet coffee shop with glazed doughnuts and chocolate croissants. They found one, got what they needed for their caffeine and sugar fixes, and sat in a socially distanced area.

Louise broke the silence. "Well, we got most of what we asked for."

"Sorry for the surprise, Louise, but my new ask was actually pretty spontaneous," explained Salt. "After it came to me, it became important." Salt paused and then changed the topic. "I'll say one thing, neither of us has ever been or ever again will be, in a meeting anything like that. Holy shit!"

"So, what do we do?" she asked.

"I guess I don't have the courage to say no," Salt admitted. "If I say no, I see myself getting up in the morning every day, looking in the mirror, and thinking what a chicken shit I was for saying no. But that doesn't mean you need to have the same hang-ups. Where's your head?"

Louise paused for a few moments. "You're right. And even though I don't care for playing second fiddle in this ensemble, I'm in. And playing second fiddle means I have plausible deniability like the President."

Salt grinned a bit. "This reminds me of when I played basketball in high school. I sat on the end of the bench unless they needed someone to go in and take a beating in a game we were losing by a mile. It was hopeless."

Louise said, "But despite the odds, you went into the game and didn't quit."

"Right," acknowledged Salt.

"So," said Louise, "tell me more about this world health element of the program."

Salt looked puzzled. "Well, to be honest, I don't know. I haven't really thought it out. We need to get a lot more homework done on this, and you can take a pass on that element of the program. You didn't sign up for this on either of the napkins."

With some wonderment, Louise leaned forward and asked, "Are you thinking of taking on the World Health Organization and the United Nations? Maybe your real name is Don Quixote."

Salt responded, "The World Health Organization is essentially the United Nations. If a country belongs to the United Nations, it can be a member of the WHO. There are nearly two hundred members. At the risk of oversimplifying things, the WHO is supposed to stop or at least arrest things like the coronavirus. That didn't happen in connection with COVID-19. I have a feeling that, like our government, the WHO could have done better, but my guess is that the WHO is essential, and most of the fault lies elsewhere. But I have no interest in a backward-looking investigation and trying to assign blame. That wouldn't make Meredith rest easier.

The history is of interest to me only to the extent it illuminates what needs to be done to fix things. I'm interested in speed and effectiveness. It no doubt makes sense to have something like the WHO, but maybe we need to have something more. Perhaps a combination of the Epidemic Intelligence Service of the Centers for Disease Control and Prevention and small dream teams of experts can act as pandemic special forces units, go into consenting countries, do the necessary, and ask later for forgiveness rather than waiting for permission. Maybe this already exists, but I need to know. This needs much more thought than I have given it, and multiple investigations are already ongoing. Two things we know for sure now are that pandemics are not mere historical anomalies but serious stuff."

Louise thought for a few minutes and then said, "Well, it's admirable and probably needed, but I have to get my head around it. In the meantime, we need to jump on phase one if we're going to agree to proceed. I think you need to call Stuart."

Salt called Stuart and gave him the news.

"Great," Stuart said. "Show up at the State Department at noon tomorrow for the beginning of a day and a half of briefings. Bring five passport photos and think about buying a decent suit. They still wear suits overseas. You'll be a consultant to the State Department, and we will negotiate a fair per diem compensation and expense deal over the next few days. You won't become wealthy doing this, but you knew that. Let me talk to Louise."

Salt handed the shoe phone to Louise, who mostly listened and, from time to time, said, "Uh huh." When the call was over, she handed the phone back and said, "I need to go home and pack and also pick up a bunch of stuff at the Agency, so please take me back to my apartment. You need to go shopping. I'll pick you up at the Marriott at 11:00 a.m. sharp tomorrow."

"Okay, boss," deadpanned Salt, "but I will do my shopping by buying American in Carterville."

Louise shook her head and rolled her eyes.

Chapter 23

Small Town, Small Business Ills

[February 12, 2021]

I t was late enough when they got back to the Marriott that Salt decided to have a drink and dinner there and stay overnight.

The next morning, he remembered that he owed Margie Hatcher dinner. He screwed up his courage and called her after breakfast before getting on the road. "I apologize in advance for this short notice, but I owe you dinner in return for your inviting me to your dinner party. I know this is very short notice, but I wondered if you had time this evening. I'm headed out of the country on business, and if I don't pay up now, it could be a while."

"That would be fine if you have time," Margie said. "Despite my crowded social calendar, I just happen to be free."

"Great," said Salt. "Where would you like to go? This only place I know is Helen's Place, which is fine, but there must be somewhere else."

"I can probably get us in for dinner at a nice country inn about eight miles out of town if that would be okay. The food is good, and it's quiet," she said.

"That works for me," said Salt. "And thanks for being willing to make the reservations. Let me know what time to pick you up."

"Unless you hear from me, pick me up at five thirty for a six o'clock reservation."

"Will do," Salt responded. He was surprised at how pleased he was about this.

As Salt drove back to the farm on Thursday morning, he started thinking about what he needed to do to get ready for the trip.

He needed a new suit and a hair trim, and he might need a new country casual shirt for the evening's dinner. Rather than going to the farmhouse, he drove into Carterville and parked near the men's store owned by Roy, who he had met at the barbershop. He walked in and saw Roy, apparently the only human in the store, though it was a weekday morning.

Salt greeted him, saying, "Hi, Roy. You may not remember me, but we met at the barbershop a while back. I need a suit, and I hope you can help me out. But I need it today. Can I get that done today if it needs altering, so it fits?"

"I'm the owner, the salesperson, and the tailor," said Roy, "so that won't be an issue. And this time of year, I compete with college basketball for customers. I can fit it in if we have something you like. What size do you wear, and what are you looking for?"

Salt responded, "Something very boring, like a blue suit with a new white shirt and a tie that's any color but red and is not too long. I'm probably something like a 38-tall or a 40-regular, but it's been a long time since I bought a suit off the rack. Back in the day, when I traveled to Hong Kong, I got some suits made there. But for a variety of reasons, I won't be going back there any time soon."

"Well, let's see, a 40 regular should be about right," said Roy. "You know people are wearing suits less and less, so we don't carry very many, and the ones we do have are mostly plain vanilla, like what you're looking for."

As Roy looked through the racks, Salt asked, "How's business these days? Does the trend toward business casual hurt you?"

"Well," responded Roy, "honestly, we're hanging on by our fingernails. There are lots of factors. Most recently, the COVID-19 lockdown was a killer—in many ways—and we had to let everyone but me and one other fellow go. The recovery has been slow. Millennials don't shop in stores like this in small towns and want all casual stuff. For that matter, they don't shop in stores. They shop online and sometimes rent their clothes rather than pay for them. Beats the hell out of me.

When they do go to a store, they go first to Target or Walmart, and after that, to see what's left of Macy's or something similar in a mall where there are other things to do. Guys your age come in here, but they're mostly retired and not spending much on new clothes or are still working and are afraid they will lose their factory job to a cheap immigrant or as a result of the recession. Or they're farmers who don't have money for clothes but would trade me several bushels of grain for a new shirt. Anyhow, all they buy is overalls. And then there's pricing. I sell mostly stuff that's made in the good old USA. These other places get their stuff from China, Bangladesh, southeast Asia, Mexico; you name it. The price competition is fierce, and you sure as hell can't make it up in volume.

"But enough about that—you have three choices: a plain navy blue suit or a couple of pinstripes. Want to try one on?"

"Let's start with the blue one," said Salt. It would work with tricky alterations to shorten the sleeves and take in the chest. Roy helped him find a white shirt and a conservative, not-red, not-too-long tie. Roy asked Salt to put on the new suit in the back room. Then Roy put his mask back on and started marking up the suit for the alterations.

"By the way," Salt asked, "what's the dress code for dinner at a country inn around here?"

"These days, there are no dress codes," said Roy. "People wear the darndest things. But a city slicker your age, you need a sport coat." Roy added a tweed sport coat, a shirt, and trousers to boot. Fortunately, the sport coat and trousers did not need altering, and Salt walked out with those. "Come back for the suit at four thirty," hollered Roy as Salt walked out of the store.

Chapter 24

State Department Global Briefing 101

[February 12, 2021]

They arrived on time at noon the next day, Friday, at the State Department, had their temperatures taken as they entered, were issued masks, and were hustled into a rather lavish conference room with a light lunch and five people waiting for them. None of these folks were household names, and it seemed unlikely they were political. They were bright and clearly wondered what the hell was going on, but they were also smart enough not to ask. There was the inevitable PowerPoint projector but no briefing books. Stuart joined five minutes later after the standard introductions had been completed and folks had started on their sandwiches.

Stuart grabbed a sandwich and then convened the meeting, speaking through his mask. "Louise and Salt, we have been joined by a group of senior geographical and subject matter experts to give you a general update on an extensive range of topics today and tomorrow. This briefing team has been told that I will likely be nominated to become secretary of state and that the President and I have asked you to engage in some highly confidential meetings overseas that will require you to have a solid level of general knowledge but not be on the cutting edge of policies, which in any event are in the process of being formulated. Your efforts will be in the nature of information collection rather than negotiation or policy promotion. These backgrounder sessions have been scheduled for today and tomorrow based on an assumed departure for the UK on Monday morning. You will note that there are no briefing books here. We intend that you walk out of here without any paper other than your notes, which we trust will be very limited.

Before you leave tomorrow, you'll have special diplomatic passports that, despite the bans prohibiting Americans from traveling into the UK and EU due to COVID-19, will get you into those regions, so please give your photos to Eric here."

Salt meekly cleared his throat and said, "Oops. Bad start. But I don't have any passport photos with me."

Stuart sighed. "We expected as much; Eric will fix that problem and get your COVID-19 testing done during one of your breaks. Any other questions? "How about Ukraine?" asked Salt. "Better question," responded Stuart. "There is a sense in which Ukraine changes everything. The stakes are much higher, and the breadth and depth of impact on international trade are not comparable to these other engagements. The impending Ukrainian invasion by Russia, expected any day now (was actually February 24), affects not only Ukraine and Russia but as well other former Soviet Bloc countries in the area, Ukrainian grain and gas sales, the effect of sanctions and counter- sanctions, and many others. The situation may impact others, such as China's thinking about Taiwan, migration into the countries' economies, steel supply, critical food supplies in the area, famine-struck areas of Africa, and so on. We are intentionally aiming to wall you off from Ukraine. We have our best people on that, which may be an early version of World War III, but we also need to keep a focus on this important but lightly staffed assignment. With that, Stuart took his leave.

The briefings started with the current state of play in various regions and countries and provided some helpful commentary on people and issues. The afternoon sessions covered Europe in general and the larger countries: the UK, its uncertain politics, and the recently concluded and last-minute post- Brexit trade treaty with the EU; the risk of a post-Brexit breakup of the UK; the European Union, including the declining stability of the EU, the euro, the pound, and European banks; the issues associated with the rise of state aid to enterprises such as airlines; the continuing relevance of the G-7 and G-20; and then Russia, Ukraine, Turkey, Iran, Syria, Saudi Arabia, Yemen, Iraq, and Israel; and the AUKUS treaty providing for Australian access to US submarine technology.

During these discussions, they also touched on the trend toward fragmentation of the global economy and its uncertain implications, including the risk that the Chinese would try to attack the US dollar's status as the global reserve currency. There was also a wake-up on COVID and its variations, drought, including in the US, monkeypox, and the like, all potentially very serious. They broke off at 8:00 p.m. and then started again at 9:00 a.m. the next morning. The geographical focus continued with the rest of the Middle East, Africa, China, North and South Korea, Japan, India, Australia, the ASEAN countries, South America, Mexico, and Canada.

The subject matter discussions focused on the effects of sanctions and tariffs imposed by and against the United States (ongoing issues included the departure of the US from the Trans-Pacific Partnership and the effects of US withdrawal; the early demise of the US-China trade treaty (since reversed by President Evans), developments in Hong Kong; the early days of the USMCA; the Paris Climate Accord and the effects of US withdrawal and its anticipated re-joinder, the impact of other issues on climate control; NATO and the effects of perceived US indifference, including the surprise reduction, now reversed, of US (made stronger since the beginning of the Ukrainian war); recent G-7 and G-20 meetings and the ongoing impact of US insults; the emergence of autocratic governments in places like Hungary, Poland, Turkey, and Cambodia (not to mention Russia and China); supply chain issues; and finally the effects of direct access by the leaders of hostile nations to President Pope and the lack of records of what was said and agreed to.

Again, each of the briefings included a who's who discussion of the key players from the countries involved in the subject. Those individual backgrounders were as lively as they were important.

Salt and Louise asked a number of questions, and Salt learned early on in the discussions that Louise was at least as up-to-date on things as he was, probably more. Earlier in the week, he had thought of her as being in the way; now, he was moving in the direction of being grateful for her involvement.

The briefings took the promised day and a half into late Saturday afternoon. After the sessions broke up on Friday evening, Eric appeared with envelopes for Salt and Louise.

The envelopes included diplomatic passports—several of them with different names and fake ID materials as well. They each received certificates of successful completion of very recent COVID-19 testing that would be as necessary as a passport. Louise's envelope included papers designed to allow her to carry a concealed pistol in several countries. Salt did not say anything but wondered what that was about. There was a note from Stuart saying that Peter Banks of the British Foreign and Commonwealth Office, who Salt knew from the old days and respected, had blocked his day for meetings with Salt and Louise the following Tuesday. Finally, there were commercial airline tickets in coach for the 9:00 a.m. Monday flight from Dulles to Heathrow Airport, with a separate note that Stuart would try to get them on government status in the future. The good news was that they were not in the middle seats in light of the then-continuing low travel volumes associated with the coronavirus. But then nobody was. The package had them staying at a Marriott near the old US embassy in London.

Louise dropped Salt at the Marriott in Virginia so he could pick up his car and his minimal baggage. "How long do you think we will be out of the country?" Louise asked.

"Beats me," responded Salt. "No return ticket is in the envelope, so I guess I'll pack for a week. By the way, do you really plan to pack a pistol?"

"Yes, I always do when in the field," she said. "But don't worry. I'll spend some time on the practice range at the Agency this weekend. See you on Monday morning." Salt's eyebrows went up, but she took off before he could say anything.

Chapter 25

Salt and Margie Temporize

[February 13, 2021]

S alt had to hustle to get out to Margie's in time for dinner. He was wearing his new sport coat and trousers when he picked up Margie for dinner. Under her winter coat, Margie was in an attractive dress and sweater, probably a little dressier than Salt's new outfit, but he was no judge of that stuff.

Margie guided Salt through about eight miles of back roads in the winter- evening darkness to a bed-and-breakfast that also had a restaurant. On the drive there, Margie had to focus on giving driving instructions, so there was no need to worry about awkward conversation pauses. When they arrived, the dining area reminded Salt of the Inn at Little Washington but less fancy. It had a log cabin feel and look, but like everyone else, they had to spread out the tables to comply with social distancing guidelines. The restaurant was not full, and masks were few and far between.

Margie broke the ice after they were seated on opposite ends of the table and had settled on a bottle of white. "Well, this isn't a first date, but it feels a little like one. Thanks for the payback on dinner; I hope you like this place. This is neither DC nor the Inn at Little Washington."

"You're welcome," replied Salt. "It's been a long time since I had dinner with someone who wasn't a client, colleague, or someone with an agenda. Plus, I'm on the introverted end of the scale unless I'm delivering messages. And I'm sure the food here will be fine. I'm just glad it's quiet."

"Well," said Margie, "introverted is okay, as I share that trait and am able to endure silence. I just hope you're not delivering messages tonight."

"No messages, but I do have some questions."

"Okay, you go first, but then I get my turn. But before we get into Q and A, maybe we should look at the menu. The seafood here is usually pretty good."

Salt started the Q and A before they could order. "So, you've been here, and I've been gone, in each case for nearby a lifetime. I'm the functional equivalent of a newcomer. What makes this town tick? Is it surviving? And what kinds of people are here now? Why do they stay?"

"Wow," said Margie. "That is a half dozen questions, and they're hard. Let's start with something easy—the population is about thirty thousand and holding pretty steady. There are good and not-so-good parts of town, but none of it is ugly. There needs to be some investment in the downtown, and you worry about more and more empty stores and houses that are in danger of falling into disrepair. I don't know if we'll ever really recover from COVID-19 and this recession. There is no discernable movement from the DC area into Carterville. People were still moving out to the outer edges of town when they could, and then the places where they spent money day-to-day changed. But very few people are moving these days.

"This town is pretty diverse in lots of ways, including racially," Margie explained. "The people are farmers, small-town merchants, workers in some light manufacturing businesses, most of which are somewhere in the automobile-manufacturing supply chain and worried about that, and some giant distribution facilities out off of Interstate 81, folks who work at Target and Walmart on the edge of town, and people who work in a wide range of positions at the college and the hospital. The college and the hospital are by far the largest employers. You heard from Dr. Greene at dinner at my place that the college is worried about enrollment in the near term, not because the college is not good, but based on demographic trends. But the hospital seems to be solid. Maybe it's because we're all getting older. We're lucky to have a good community hospital and a college. They provide a good base and attract sound citizens."

Margie paused for a sip of wine and then continued. "This is not the most sophisticated place in the world, but a lot of the people here care about the community and have values that are important.

They watch out for one another. The schools are not superb, but they're solid. Church membership is slumping as the baby boomers thin out, but likely better than at most places, and the churches are active. Bottom line— this is a good place to live. Many people value diversity, and others put up with it, and most could not do much better if they moved. This is an ecosystem that works—at least for now.

"By the way," Margie inserted carefully, "speaking of churches, you would be more than welcome at our church. It's none of my business, but to quote President George W. Bush in a conversation with reporter David Gregory, 'How's your faith?'"

"Hmm," responded Salt, "that's a far-out question. The truth is, I haven't figured that out. It's something I need to think about and sort out for myself. If there is a God—he or she wasn't there for my wife when she was dying, and my wife was a really good person. She was a Christian in every sense of the word. I haven't gotten over that yet, and I'm not sure I will."

"Well," Margie said, "sorry I brought that up, but if you ever want to talk about it, there are people here who would be glad to do that. But enough on that topic."

Salt thought for a few moments and decided to change the subject. "Going back to the local hospital, I was interested to learn at your dinner party that the local hospital seems to be thriving. That's a good sign as well as a good thing. Have opioid overdoses hammered it, or has this community been able to avoid that crisis? And how has it held up under the coronavirus stress?"

"I honestly don't know the answer to the opioid question, and my guess is that the hospital doesn't talk much about that kind of thing. I would be glad to introduce you to the president of the hospital, but he's pretty tight-lipped.

"Or you could talk to the editor of the local newspaper, which now comes out only three days per week. The editor is very smart and inquisitive; you would almost certainly end up telling her more about you than you would get out of her."

"Never mind. I'll take a long-term rain check on meeting the editor," said Salt, "though I don't have much about me that would be interesting to the media. How did the hospital do during the coronavirus challenge?"

"We were pretty lucky," said Margie. "Last year, we had about seventy-five hospitalized cases and eighteen or so deaths. The hospital was able to handle the load, though I hear they're still waiting for the promised federal money for the no-pay stays they had. Our health care team was great.

"The diversity of this area extends to political views, as you may have picked up during your barbershop visits," added Margie. "There was likely a strong contingent of people who held their noses and voted for President Pope in the last election. Down deep, a majority are politically moderates for the most part, and they were offended by candidates who seemed to question the importance of normal folks. It would be hard to characterize this as a flyover country, but we don't think of ourselves as members of either the East Coast elite or what some referred to in 2016 as the deplorables. We think nobody is deplorable—except for former President Pope for some of us."

Salt asked, "How do people feel about the new president?"

"Most of us think the jury is still out on Evans," responded Margie. "On domestic issues, the President looks, feels, and acts a bit like a socialist in moderate's clothing. You know the line: if it looks like a duck, walks like a duck, and quacks like a duck, it's a duck. Evans said what was necessary to get elected. But the inflation rate has been a killer, the war in Ukraine looks like it could last forever, and an inability to get things through the US supply chain has turned toward the absence of need for a supply chain since people had stopped buying. Foreign policy is not something I've thought a lot about. But most of us want to bring our troops home and repair bridges here rather than in the Middle East."

Margie added, "Sorry if I offended you anywhere in there, but you asked. I don't normally go on like this. Time for me to have some wine and shut up. But we need to order first."

The masked waiter appeared, and they each ordered the crab dip appetizer, a small Caesar salad, and the venison house special for the evening. Salt thought for a few seconds about how this meal would compare to what he would be having in London in a few days, but he didn't go there in the discussion.

"I agree with you on the local political climate," Salt said. He went on to describe his unscientific political football game experiment at Georgie's barbershop. He wondered out loud how fairly the game was being described, as it was definitely a game in which the rules determined the outcome.

"I give you credit for even thinking about trying that," said Margie. "You had to be ready for verbal abuse; that took guts."

"Time will tell about that, but striving for moderation and collaboration is a cause for me. Now, tell me about the farmers here. It seems like things are tight."

Margie responded between bites of the appetizer. "Yes, things have been tight ever since President Pope created havoc in the grain markets with the tariffs on China, and the recession only made things worse. As you know, I'm not a farmer, but I know many of those folks, and based on what I hear, many of the local farmers were stretched when the tariffs were imposed, and things got worse when China, in particular, imposed its own grain tariff and quota system and stopped buying as much US grain, and then the coronavirus hit. The government provides some subsidies, but nobody wants a handout. And nobody thinks the new normal will be as good as the pre-COVID-19 normal. Once you change buying patterns, they're changed."

Salt pressed on. "How about manufacturing? Any impact there from things international? Domestic US manufacturing has been in a mild recession since sometime in 2019."

Margie responded, "I don't really know. My impression is that the uncertainty created by the China trade issues and, for a while, the process of replacing NAFTA with the US-Mexico-Canada trade agreement threw a wrench into things, so to speak, and of course, things got a lot worse in 2020.

Yes, uncertainty, no doubt, has a cost. But the strikes that took place with several auto worker unions a year and a half ago also had an impact here in the form of lost income. It seems that our trade policy should focus on increasing what we sell overseas and job creation and security. Wasn't that what Pope was preaching when he was elected? I sometimes wonder how he defined a good deal. But maybe that's just me.

"Now," she said. "I've already told you that I know nothing about foreign policy and am not really that interested in it. Yet, here we are, and it's your turn to talk and stop asking questions. What is it that you do again? At the party at my house, several people came away thinking you had answered that question, but then they thought about it and realized you had said nothing."

"Guilty." Salt laughed. "The reality is that I don't know what I do. As I think I've told you, I spent the past five years practicing law, primarily in the trade area. Nothing unusual or exciting, but we tried to get rid of wasteful blockages where we could or open doors to new trade in other cases. Before that, I was in the State Department and Treasury and worked on the same issues as when I practiced law—just from a different perspective. When I moved out here, I had assumed I would retire, certainly from the practice of law and probably from everything else. An old friend of mine in the government called me last week and asked me to take on a short-term consulting gig, and I think I will do that, though the parameters are not yet defined—except that I can't say much more about it. It will involve some travel, and I had to go to Roy's men's shop this afternoon to upgrade my wardrobe a bit. I expect to be gone for a week or so. I have Jack Davis looking after things on the farm while I'm gone."

"I'm glad you and Jack are getting along," Margie said. "It's none of my business, but from what I hear, he'll need some help to get back on his financial feet. He's a good guy, so thanks. But now, back to you. You just created as many questions as you answered, but I won't badger you with more questions about what you'll be doing. Sounds like it would be a waste of time. But what do you think? You are now what amounts to the local guru on things political. How do you feel about the new President and how all of that is going to work?"

Salt responded, "Oh, I'm no guru. And I'm not sure how the new President will work out. I'm more moderate than the President seems—at least based on the election campaign debate rhetoric and what the President has said. I'm squarely in the middle on most issues. I'm concerned about the new administration on a number of fronts. But the President also has to get things through Congress, which until recent times has involved a lot of compromises. I guess I'm as interested in what is doable with the new administration and Congress as I am about where the President stands on theoretical issues. So I guess, paint me hopeful but guarded. I'm virtually certain that I'll see pretty much eye-to-eye with the new administration on foreign relations. My bigger concern is what's happening on the domestic front."

At this point, the server signaled that the main course was almost ready, so they finished the appetizer and switched to red wine to drink with the venison.

"Foreign relations sounds pretty exotic to those of us out here in the sticks," said Margie. "And complicated."

"Yes and no," said Salt. "It's less complicated than you think. In the final analysis, people all over the world want what's best for their families and their countries, and in most cases, they would trade positions with an American in a second.

"We need to remember how fortunate we are and that—with some exceptions—human nature tends to favor the same basic goals all around the world. Many complicating factors get in the way, like greed and hunger for power, but in my experience, those diseases do not infect everyone."

"On that hopeful note," Margie said, "let's order dessert early so you can get home at a decent hour and unpack a few more boxes tomorrow before you start packing your bag."

"Good idea," said Salt, grateful to be left off the hook in terms of answering more questions.

On the way back to Margie's, things were quiet in the car until Margie spoke up. "This is rather awkward," she said, "but for now, I think we should remain friends and not think about taking it further. We seem to get along well enough, but we come from different universes, and I am not sure which universe you are headed for."

Salt was taken back by what she said but knew she was probably right. He sure was not clear about how to organize his future planning, so he haltingly responded, "Well, I have not thought about this in the depth you have, but you are probably right. But I hope this does not mean we cannot be friends and see what develops over time. Let's face it, there are not that many compatible people of our ages around, and I am not going to go on a dating game show."

"Oh, absolutely," said Margie. "In fact, when we get back to my place, why don't you come in for a nightcap? We can toast friendship, lack of commitment, and the absence of awkwardness."

Salt sighed and began to breathe again. "Sounds great, and thanks, Margie."

When they returned to Margie's, she poured drinks and said, "excuse me, I'll be back in a moment." Salt wandered around the living room and looked at what Margie had on the walls. That can tell you a lot sometimes. Then he saw Margie's reflection in a mirror on the wall. He was not sure he believed it. As he turned around, he confirmed that she had let her hair down and was wearing a black nightgown.

Margie said one word, "Friends?" They fell into each other's arms and had a serious nightcap. Friendship is a good thing.

Chapter 26

Briefing at the Barbershop

[February 21, 2021]

S alt didn't need a haircut, but he could be a shaggy mess by the time he got back from a week in London if he didn't get a trim. He dropped in at Georgie's to see what the wait was like. Then he remembered it was Sunday. There were no college football games or good basketball games this afternoon, so Georgie opened for a few hours. All of the barbers were busy, and it would take an hour or so for his number to come up, so he said Salt should take a number and come back later after lunch. He noticed that "College Basketball Today" was on the TV on the wall, with commentators focused on yesterday's games and the coming week and drawing a lot of attention. The extra chairs were still stacked in the corner, so there was room for social distancing. Indeed, the barbershop seemed to have almost as many full seats as the arena where the game was being played. "What time do you suggest I show up?" Salt asked.

"Best to show up when this program is over, so aim for one thirty," said Georgie.

When Salt returned after lunch, Max was the first barber to be available, so he climbed into his chair and asked for a trim. The shop was full of patrons who had gotten their hair cut (or not) and were there to watch the commentary as if the barbershop were a spin-off of Buffalo Wild Wings that required masks to be worn. There wasn't much interest in the following week's games, so the chitchat focused on yesterday's game and how bad it was; which was more corrupt, Duke or North Carolina; why the high school basketball coach had not been fired ("haven't had a decent coach since Matt Hatcher"); the nutty impact of social distancing on college athletics; and then, of course, politics.

The consensus on the new President was "wait and see." The crowd grudgingly recognized that the President had been positioned as a middle-of-the-roader. Still, folks were perceptive and recognized that presidents seemed to go through at least four policy stages: (1) what it took to survive the primaries and get the nomination; (2) what it took to win the general election; (3) what emerged during the first hundred days as reality set in; and (4) what it took to get reelected. Homer was of the view that the country needed to give Evans a chance, but Homer was a bit further to the left than the consensus view. Georgie agreed with him. Don, the retired NRA member who Salt had met during his last visit to Georgie's and was pretty clearly there to watch the big-screen TV, was not a fan of the new president.

"I just don't trust President Evans," Don explained. "This new crew will want to take away our guns. At least you could trust Pope and his crew."

Georgie laughed. "Don, give me the name of a single politician you have ever trusted."

Don smiled. "Well, Georgie, you got the point there."

"So, Mr. Deep State," Georgie said, turning to Salt, "where do you come out on the new president? Did you vote for Evans?"

"Don't let him trick you into talkin' too much," piped up Ellen, the third barber. "It's none of his business. He'll trap you if you're not careful. He preys on newcomers."

"For the first time in years, I voted for the President," said Salt. "Like a number of government employees, I purposely did not vote for government positions when on the government payroll. I followed that practice with the law firm until this most recent election. In my mind, there was really no choice in the last presidential election, but I got there partly because I think the President is more moderate than most think, and I bet most of your customers are more moderate than they think of themselves as being. You have to look at that question holistically."

"What does that mean?" asked Don, the hunter.

Salt responded with some trepidation. "Well, for example, I bet that most people in here believe that the government spends too much and are worried about the national debt, especially after the humongous amounts we have spent and are continuing to spend in connection with COVID-19 and Ukraine."

"Right," said Don.

"Exactly," said Salt. "It is conservative thinking that many moderates share. Now, let's go to your concern about the President taking your guns. Do you think the Second Amendment gives you the right to own a tank?"

"Nope," said Don, without having to think for very long.

"How about a shoulder-mounted heat-seeking missile launcher?" "Hmm," said Don, "closer call, but probably not."

"Okay," said Salt. "How about a bazooka?" "Nope."

"Colt .45 pistol?"

"Absolutely protected," said Don.

"I agree with you, Don," Salt announced, "and I would put your Remington hunting rifle and your shotgun in the same category. Where we probably run into disagreements is on assault rifles."

"Correct," commented Don.

Salt decided to push a bit. "But you see, we agree on as much or more as we disagree on. And I would bet that your concern is really not so much assault rifles as it is your lack of trust. You think if they can get a ban on assault rifles, they won't stop there and will go after your shotgun."

"Not saying," stated Don firmly.

"My point is that most of us agree more than disagree on big issues. Those who you can't say that about are extremists," Salt commented. Then he asked, "Georgie, can I take those flyers off your bulletin board?"

"Okay, I guess, Mr. Deep State. Half of them are about events that happened weeks ago anyhow."

"Thanks," said Salt. He interrupted his haircut, got out of the chair, and walked over to a cork bulletin board that was about thirty-six inches wide and twenty inches high. After removing the flyers from the bulletin board, he pulled out a pushpin and stuck it in the middle of the bulletin board. He explained, "Imagine that this bulletin board is a football field where we place players based on how far left or right they are, politically speaking. In the aggregate—that is, taking into account a whole range of issues—I place myself right on the fifty-yard line. Well, let's make it the forty-five-yard line or five yards to the left. I'm in the middle on most issues. I bet if you ask your customers to place themselves on this field with a pushpin when nobody is watching, most will be between the thirty-five-yard lines. Not all, but most. Why not try it for a month and see? Call it a new form of political football." He headed back to the barber chair.

"I'll think about it," said Georgie. "But you have to tell us who you are. The more I listen to your smooth talk, I think you must be an agent of the Trilateral Commission or maybe something worse."

"There have been lots of conspiracy theories about the Trilateral Commission over the years." Salt smiled. "If you want to worry about organizations with dangerous influence, focus on the incredibly well-funded political action groups—on both the right and left politically—funded by the very wealthy and hoarding millions today after the Citizens United Supreme Court decision."

"I think you avoided my question," said Georgie.

"Sorry," said Salt. "The truth just is not very exciting. I'm a lawyer who just retired from a law firm in Washington and previously spent some time in the government. You can Google me, but you won't find much more than that."

Homer finished with Salt, and Salt got out of the chair. "Sorry I have to run, but I enjoyed the conversation. Try the bulletin board thing. I think it would be interesting. But be fair on how you explain it."

Ellen said, "We'll make sure he's fair about the political football game."

As he was leaving, Salt added, looking at Homer, "By the way, Homer, that's a good sign you have there in the corner. Good for you." Homer did not say anything but smiled and nodded toward Salt.

Salt then asked Georgie, "By the way, how is Hair-i-Care doing?"

"There could be a new Hair-i-Care application the next time you come in, but you still won't qualify." Georgie smiled as Salt hustled out to pick up his new suit from Roy, who had agreed to finish the suits today and meet Salt at the men's store. He also needed to clean up his car.

Don left Georgie's right after Salt and called the same number he had called after his first encounter with Salt at the barbershop. The other party asked, "What's up?"

Don responded, "The new ex-fed was back at Georgie's today, spouting off on gun control, left-wing zealots, and all manner of things. He tries to make himself seem harmless, but he doesn't fool me. I think this guy could be trouble down the road. I still doubt that he's undercover FBI, but it's hard to tell for sure."

"Okay, thanks," said the other party. "I'll have some homework done on him and get back to you. But stay away from him and don't create any trouble until we decide who and what this guy really is. Maybe this is a false alarm. What's his name again?"

Don thought for a moment. "He goes by Salt Pepper, but I guess his real first name is Staunton or Stan or something like that. Remember, he was a lawyer in the swamp in DC."

"Okay—thanks," said the other party, "but tell me more about the discussion." After listening to Don, the other party said, "Sounds to me like this guy is just a Goddamned liberal who escaped from DC. He won't get in the way of us demonstrating against more COVID-19 lockdowns or other things we've heard about. Stay cool until you hear back from me."

Chapter 27

London Transit Thoughts

[February 22, 2021]

S alt spent Sunday unpacking more boxes, adding to his giveaway pile, and thinking about what he needed to pack for London. There had been a time when he traveled enough that even international travel had become routine.

But that was years ago. And a few things had changed.

Salt got a good start on Monday morning—while it was still dark—so he could easily make the morning flight from Dulles International to London Heathrow airport. The grief he would take if he missed the flight would be unimaginable, starting (but not ending) with Louise. It was a good thing he started early because Interstate 66 was a mess with what they called in the Washington area a "wintery mix"—which in the real world meant nothing. Still, in the DC area, it meant big traffic issues, and of course, Louise beat him to the lounge on concourse C, even with his good start.

She wisecracked about his being later than her, but fortunately, neither Louise nor Salt was a morning person, so they were both mostly content to read the paper and the latest Economist while waiting to board. And, of course, there wasn't much they could talk about on the flight the way over. The seats in economy (not business class, of course) were in a two-three-two configuration with seven seats per row and two aisles. Salt and Louise were in one of the two-seat pairs near the window, but even in an empty plane with no middle seats occupied, there was not nearly enough privacy to allow for a substantive discussion, especially since one had to basically yell through one's mask to be heard. Flight attendants and passengers alike were provided with and required to wear masks while on board the plane.

Salt spent a good portion of the seven-hour flight trying to get his head around the fact that he was on the flight at all and how the discussions with Peter Banks of the British Foreign and Commonwealth Office should open up. Salt tentatively settled on using some of the concepts from the Napkin B discussion with Stuart for openers.

Louise was also focused on the Peter Banks meeting but, to some extent, occupied herself by trying again to figure out Salt. He seemed simple at some levels but was also complicated. As to the meeting with the Brits, she was willing to go with a variation of the Napkin B outline.

After landing in London and gathering their baggage—at about 10:00 p.m. London time—Salt asked through his mask if Louise wanted to take an Uber to the hotel.

Louise responded crisply, "Never leave an unnecessary trail when traveling. Cabs are the most anonymous, the Heathrow Express train is next, and Uber leaves too much of an electronic trail. And keep in mind that there are cameras everywhere, especially in London."

They made their way down to the Heathrow Express train in the terminal's lower level and were fortunate not to have to wait too long before boarding. Salt had a genuine fondness for London, but the relatively short train trip to London's Paddington Station in the dark was anything but scenic. When they arrived at Paddington in the late evening, the station was nearly empty—a good thing since that meant the queue for a cab wasn't very long. They queued up in the line for a black London cab, noticed the near uniform use of masks in the station, and, after getting to the front of the line, made it through the mostly empty streets of London without incident. They eventually (a little after 11:00 p.m.) arrived at the Marriott at Grosvenor Square, near the former US embassy. Thankfully, Louise took care of checking them in since she knew what names and credit cards they were using for the two rooms.

Fortunately, the bar at the hotel was still open—not always the case in London—and they were able to chat for a few minutes in the quiet, though Louise reminded Salt that the walls of a bar this close to the former US embassy could still have ears, and they needed to be careful.

She commented that she was surprised that Stuart would spend so much on a hotel for them, especially one that could leak. Salt could not decide whether he thought Louise was nuts or cautious. It didn't matter, as they would be playing by her rules. The rationale for Stuart's hotel choice became clearer when a fellow by the name of Ed Jordan, who held a nondescript title with the US embassy, joined their table at a social distance and suggested another round.

Louise knew Jordan from a prior encounter, but Salt knew nothing of him. Jordan explained, "I know damn little about who you are, Salt. I don't know what you're doing here, how long you'll be doing it, how Louise is involved, or whether any of whatever you're up to makes sense. My orders are to serve as a liaison for you, help when asked if it's a reasonable request, not mention you to anyone in London, and stay the hell out of the way and out of trouble."

"Glad to make your acquaintance, Ed," said Salt, "and we'll get along just fine since I know just a smidgen more than you do about what we're doing here." Jordan knew that comment meant that Salt and Louise would not be talking, so the chatter turned social and was rather short-lived. They exchanged contact information and broke up. Louise and Salt were getting ready to deal with the jet lag when trying to get some sleep. At least BBC news was on the telly.

Chapter 28

London Day – Openers

[February 23, 2021]

Neither slept well, and they ran into each other in the restaurant at eight o'clock the next morning. It wasn't crowded—a good thing since the seating was spread out. Each had a traditional English breakfast with lots of coffee rather than tea. Salt asked Louise what she knew about Ed Jordan. The answer was virtually nothing. They decided to minimize contact with him.

They then exchanged views on how the meeting with the Brits should go and then left for the meeting via an anonymous black cab.

It was rush hour in London, but even in the UK, which had developed more control over COVID-19 than the United States, the lingering effects of the pandemic were still apparent. This was visible in the auto and foot traffic and the many face masks and social distance between pedestrians. Salt didn't mind the slow traffic very much. He enjoyed London's look, feel, and history and was disappointed that skyscrapers were beginning to dominate the skyline of the areas called the City and Canary Wharf in particular. Salt, being a traditionalist, preferred lower buildings with less glass. He particularly enjoyed the Whitehall and Westminster areas. But he knew that his traditionalism would have to give way to the cost benefits of taller buildings; he would just have to get over it. He commented to Louise that he was thankful for the height restrictions that still existed in the District of Columbia.

Even with the reduced traffic, the pace was slow as the cab crept from the hotel to the British Foreign and Commonwealth Office on King Charles Street, near St. James Park and Churchill's War Rooms. They arrived on time (which is to say ten minutes early), had their temperatures taken, were issued fresh masks, and were shown into a lovely, very formal conference room that no doubt had a remarkable history.

If only those silk-covered walls could talk. Peter Banks and three of his colleagues joined them in a few minutes—a diverse group of millennials.

Peter was nothing if not polite in a perfectly British manner. He was also exactly how one would picture an experienced UK diplomat—straight out of central casting. He was probably 5'10", on the thin side, with black hair, and was wearing an impeccable dark blue suit and traditional tie. He had no doubt attended the right schools. After the necessary introductions, which were a bit more condensed than normal, Peter opened up and got to the point: "I hope you don't mind that a few of my colleagues have joined us. Stuart did not give us a perfectly clear picture of your mission, so it was hard to know who ought to be in our meeting. I can assure you, however, that none of the lips in this room are loose, and these are some of our most thoughtful folks."

"Thanks, Peter," responded Salt. "That's perfect, for we're not entirely clear on how to describe our mission. Saving the world order would sound a bit grandiose, but it's not too far off."

Salt continued. "With the understanding that we're all colleagues in the art of foreign relations and operating under the proverbial cone of silence, let me be direct. Some in the new US administration, including the President, are painfully aware that the world order has deteriorated largely due to a lack of attention from and respect for the United States. We all recognize that the world order put together by figures such as Churchill and FDR during and after World War II could not survive without change, and a great deal of change has been accommodated over the years. But pressure for realistic accommodation has sometimes diluted a focus on the greater good in favor of attempts to misuse or circumvent multilateral institutions that have served us well. Some of this is due to ego, some to ignorance leading to predictable mistakes, some to budget priorities, and some to bad faith. We need not sort all of that out for our purposes.

We acknowledge that, depending on one's politics, these developments could be viewed as including things like the United States' recent nationalistic tendency to bash NATO and the UK's troubled exit from the EU.

Peter replied, "Rightly or wrongly, we believe that although the United States has been part of the solution for the most part after World War II, it has become an element of the problem in recent years. We each have our burdens to bear, a former President who got along with our Prime Minster perhaps too well, and of course, Ukraine. I understand Ukraine is off the table except perhaps for cocktail chatter, which is always the holiest, and at the same time, the most meaningless form of conversation. Regardless, we believe the US can—over time and with proven good works—once again assume a constructive leadership role in the world.

Salt replied: "We do not presume that the role played by the United States during the Cold War can be re-established, nor could that be sold in the United States. But we think it is in the interest of most of the world for the United States to become again more constructively engaged. We need to trade isolationism for what some refer to as inclusive multilateralism. We seek the input of carefully selected allies as to what role makes sense for America, what the barriers are, and whether these allies might be willing— over time—to be openly supportive.

"Our new President seeks to restore some elements of democratic world order, but the President is painfully aware of the recent behavior of the United States and, indeed, the events of January 6. He understands that he is well-known and respected as a Senator but is a new and untested player on the world scene. Given the extraordinary things going on in the world these days, the President is not in a position to go very far out on a limb here. In other words, the President is willing to take the risk of leadership if others support the United States in such a role, but not the risk of being stabbed in the back or accused of folly. And, of course, this can't be viewed as a power grab by the United States because it is not that—though many will refuse to accept that proposition.

"Put another way; we are here in a first meeting of this type to learn whether there are shared concerns on the part of the UK, and—if there is interest in joining in efforts to rebuild genuine multilateralism—how to prioritize efforts and issues and what role the United States should play over time.

Not to put too fine a point on it, but if we can't identify shared concerns and willingness to participate between the United States and the UK, there's not much sense in pursuing this further with others. This is not to attempt to put undue pressure on the UK, but we do need to understand whether others think we're just plain nuts to try to put Humpty Dumpty back together when we know we were involved in pushing poor Humpty off the wall."

Salt paused. Peter Banks smiled. Everyone was speechless for a few moments. Peter finally broke the silence. "Well, I wasn't sure what to expect, but it was not this. The proposition is unusual, to say the least, and the whole subject is more than slightly above our pay grades. To put it in military terms, this is something that needs to be discussed with generals, and we are privates. I think it would be a mistake for us to respond at all right now. We have this group on our side of the table available through tomorrow. Rather than formulating a response on an off-the-cuff basis, I suggest we pause and allow our groups to talk among ourselves and perhaps a few others. We could then reassemble in the morning for an initial response and decide what else, if anything, makes sense at this time. It may be that we just can't deal with this at all in a short time frame. What you have outlined is not unambitious, to say the least. In any event, we hope you can join a few of us for a private dinner this evening here in Whitehall."

"That is more than reasonable," said Salt. "But I'm a little concerned that I have not stated our case either fully or very well."

"I think we get enough of it," said Peter. "You were more than articulate. And besides, this is the type of topic that you talk about initially for either forty minutes or forty hours. We don't have time for the forty-hour version."

"When should we return?"

"Let's aim for 4:30 pm in case we have some questions, but we'll have dinner, which I am told is at 6:00 pm following cocktails."

Chapter 29

London: Further Reflections

As Salt and Louise were leaving, walking down the steps in front of the British Foreign and Commonwealth Office, Salt opened up and said, chuckling, "I'm pretty sure we were just thrown out of the British Foreign and Commonwealth Office on our asses, but I can't tell whether they were horrified or laughing. But it was all very polite. How the hell am I going to explain this to the President and Stuart Bacon?"

"Don't worry about what you'll need to say to the President," said Louise. "If this is not going anywhere, Stuart will blame you in absentia, and you won't get a chance to explain anything to the President. But I'm not sure the Brits won't experiment, at least a little bit. Though they will likely want it in small bites and be able to maintain at all times plausible deniability."

At the appointed hour in the morning, Salt and Louise arrived back at the Foreign and Commonwealth Office and met again with Peter Banks and the team. They were all in stiff upper lip mode and difficult to read.

After niceties, Peter Banks opened the discussion. "First," Banks said, "we appreciate very much your visit and the interesting concept underlying the discussion. As you can understand, at this point, we're not high enough in the food chain to do more than listen and react, and this group could not sign up for anything. In addition to getting others involved, there needs to be meat on the bones here. However, in principle, we are supportive to some undefined extent and, subject to some reasonable conditions, willing to continue discussions."

"Well," Salt said, laughing, "that has to be a finalist for the most caveats of all time. Want to add any more?"

Banks also quietly laughed, saying, "I knew you would get the message."

"Okay," said Salt, "what are the conditions?" Peter responded: "In no particular order:

"Until we advise to the contrary, the UK is not to be referred to as being involved, much less supportive. To be frank, we were burned more than once by your prior administration, and it will take time to restore trust if it can be restored at all. This will take actual experience. No amount of talk will get there.

"You may disclose discretely to a preapproved list of governments that we have discussed the subject and are willing to think about it, but no more than that.

"We have to agree to some core foundational elements that give the discussion more substance. This is essential. We're out if we can't identify shared goals at the outset.

"We need to be kept up to date on discussions with others. We don't want veto power over who you talk to or daily updates, but we need veto power over who you talk to about us being possibly involved and how.

"We have the right to withdraw from the discussions at any time and for any reason."

Salt looked at Louise for silent assent and got it, so he responded. "Those are all fair enough and agreed to," said Salt. "I share the trust issues myself. In response to your need for more substance, let me summarize a few of the points we discussed with the President and Stuart Bacon. I need to emphasize that these are both partial and preliminary." At that point, Salt, in effect, converted much of the Napkin B content into guiding principles and goals, reading slowly off his list so the Brits could take notes:

- good faith attempts for the United States to rejoin Paris Climate Accord
- good faith attempts for the United States to rejoin Trans-Pacific Partnership
- much more limited and targeted use of tariffs and unilateral economic sanctions
- strong and collaborative support of NATO, not to foreclose continued pressure on member state defense spending
- approach to North Korea to be closely coordinated with allies, especially South Korea and Japan
- a new approach to Iran to be closely coordinated with allies, particularly parties to the Iranian Joint Comprehensive Plan of Action that our prior president abandoned
- a thoughtful and collaborative approach to Ukraine's challenges

- The United States stays out of Brexit and related issues (other than US-UK trade treaty discussions)—those are for the UK and the EU to resolve

~*~*~*~

Salt went on to emphasize that the Evans administration was in the process of knocking off priority actions that had been on the Salt/Louise issues list. For example:

- The US has rejoined the Paris Climate Treaty
- The US has not joined the Trans-Pacific Partnership yet, but the US/UK/AU submarine treaty is in place
- NATO is stronger than ever

The US is playing a lead role in Ukraine

Salt concluded by saying that a few other items did not make this short list but were important. These included the US relationship with the WTO and WHO. He also emphasized that the United States was glad to entertain suggestions from the UK.

"An interesting list," said Peter. "But back to the issue of why are you here, rather than your secretary of state, and why me and my team rather than our foreign secretary?"

Salt took a deep breath and responded, "I have the same question at some level. As we discussed this morning, we must acknowledge that the United States has suffered significantly diminished credibility around the world, whether dealing with friends or foes. We are viewed as volatile, xenophobic, isolationist, unreliable, and untrustworthy. The lack of trust is a deep and serious problem. We have reluctantly concluded that people viewed as political appointees or otherwise closely allied with the new administration will not be as effective as such persons have been in the past, no matter who they are. What they say to others in the world will be treated as more blah, blah, blah. And what they say will stand only for as long as that person is around, at best. The goal is to get these topics more fully into the hands of smart, trusted, and apolitical senior career diplomats who can work on this in the background without being forced prematurely to disclose the nature and status of the project. We report to Stuart Bacon and the President.

"As to why you and your team," Salt continued, "my understanding is that Stuart and your foreign secretary agreed on the composition of the teams. I don't know what the specs were."

"Well, your candor is valued if that is what this is," Peter responded. "We need to have more time to discuss this among ourselves this afternoon. Please come back again later this afternoon, when we can have dinner here and, I dare say, a gin and tonic or two. I don't anticipate being able to have much in the way of further substantive discussions this evening, but perhaps we can chart the next steps."

As Peter was walking Salt and Louise out, he pulled them aside and spoke quietly. "I don't want to overdo this, but you need to understand that the moment you walked in the front door today, you were probably identified as persons of possible interest to Russian intelligence. It is not something to be proud of, as we think that label applies to just about anyone who comes through the front door until proven to be not of much interest."

Peter reminded them that the UK had recent experience in dealing with Russia acting covertly and aggressively within the UK's borders. In 2018, the Russian military intelligence service poisoned a former Russian spy who lived in a small English town and his daughter with the weapons-grade nerve agent Novick. If what Salt and Louise were proposing gained momentum, it would be of interest to the Russians, Peter emphasized, and Salt and Louise should be careful.

"Thanks, I guess," said Louise. "And here I expected our food for thought to come this evening."

As Salt and Louise left the building, Salt looked at her and asked, "Was that for real?"

"Time will tell," said Salt. "If you don't mind, I need to take a quiet walk and think about things. Why don't we meet in the hotel lobby at about 4:30 pm?

"Fine by me," said Louise.

It was a typically gray and damp winter day in London, but not raining. Salt took a long walk around the nearby areas of London. Since they were in the neighborhood, he walked slowly by Westminster Abbey and Parliament and even got nearly as far as Buckingham Palace. As he walked, he decided he might as well be optimistic and think about what he would say to the Foreign and Commonwealth Office Brits about the next steps. He pulled out of his suit coat pocket his wrinkled version of Napkin B from their discussion with Stuart and the President. He read it again:

- Stuart Bacon is secretary of state.
- Pepper reports directly to Bacon and President Evans, including reasonable direct access to Evans.
- In G-7 and other selected countries, a direct contact in the US embassy, acceptable to Pepper, will be established, with such contacts reporting solely to Pepper and the secretary of state with respect to this project; the project is not to be shared with political appointees.
- Good faith attempts to rejoin Paris Climate Accord.
- Good faith attempts to rejoin TPP.
- Much more limited and targeted use of tariffs except where agreed by the G-7 or another grouping of similar interests.
- Strong support of NATO, not to foreclose pressure on member state defense spending.
- The approach to North Korea is to be closely coordinated with allies, especially South Korea and Japan.
- Approach to Iran to be closely coordinated with allied parties to the Iran nuclear treaty the US withdrew from (Joint Comprehensive Plan of Action), and stay out of wars in the Middle East.
- Commitment to strengthen senior professional staffing at State Department.
- The rapid movement toward renewed New START talks without requiring China to participate.
- Ukraine.

He mentally added the WHO and global health issues to his version of the list. He also realized that he had thrown the New START treaty and Ukraine back into the mix.

He recalled that the President had said that the list was for discussion and not sharing. He also said the new administration could not yet live with comprehensive immigration reform. After thinking more about it, he decided he would talk to Louise about orally walking the Brits through appropriate items—assuming they had any interest.

Chapter 30

London: Evening with the Brits
[February 23, 2021]

Upon arrival at the hotel, they went to the bar. They drank water this time.

Louise said she had discussed the security of the bar with Ed Jordan of the embassy, who felt it was pretty safe until they had reason to believe someone was focusing on them.

"Well—what do you think?" asked Salt.

Louise responded, "I guess it's about what we should have expected in an optimistic case, based on the reaction you got from your Canadian friend. I think we need to start somewhere, and the UK is the right place for that. Peter Banks seems like a decent enough and straightforward guy. And, of course, the Brits have their own issues, so there is a limit on how much bashing they can dish out to us. We need to think about the next steps. It feels to me like we need to pick one or two matters to focus on and hopefully start building credibility."

"Agreed," said Salt. "Let's think about that while we freshen up for dinner."

When they met in the hotel lobby, Louise looked like a different person. Until then, Salt had seen Louise only in a black pantsuit and white blouse. Now she was wearing a striking dress—not quite what Salt would call a cocktail dress but very tastefully colorful and snazzy just the same. And she had done things with her hair. "I'm not sure what the rules are these days," said Salt, "but I hope I won't offend you if I say you look lovely. My only question is whether your gun fits in that small handbag."

"No offense, and thank you," said Louise, "and the gun fits." She continued, "I hope I won't offend you, Salt, but is that the same shirt and tie you had on this afternoon?"

"Yes," said Salt. "What about it?"

Louise frowned and asked, "Do you have a clean shirt in your room?" "Yes," said Salt again.

"Okay," Louise said. "You go up and put on the most heavily starched, clean white shirt you have with you. While you do that, I'm going around the corner to a men's store I saw this afternoon to get you a new tie. You have five minutes. Get going."

Eight minutes later, Louise was helping Salt with his new, dressier tie. "There," she said. "Now, you look like someone who has been to London before."

"Thanks," murmured Salt as they climbed into a cab. "Now, what do you think about where things stand now?"

Louise responded, "You're right; we need to have a very short list of goals. It needs to be something that will garner the UK's attention for other reasons. And it needs to be something that we think we can quickly make progress on. We need an early-stage win if at all possible."

"Completely agree," said Salt. "Let's see what they come up with."

They arrived back at the Foreign and Commonwealth Office and were met by Peter Banks's young male assistant, who was the essence of propriety and care while he took their temperatures. He followed all of the relevant protocols carefully. They were taken to another very formal and ornate meeting room with silk wall coverings and huge glass chande- liers. The Foreign and Commonwealth team was assembling and having their traditional gin and tonic while maintaining social distance foregoing masks. The conversation was light and stayed that way through a tradi- tional British dinner of lamb or Dover sole, touching upon subjects such as the Royals, COVID-19 and the failure of both countries to handle it well, US state and local politics, comparisons of the House of Commons and the US Congress, developments in Hong Kong and elsewhere in Asia, the last-second avoidance of a no-deal Brexit with the completion at the end of December of the UK-EU trade treaty, and the Black Lives Matter movement in the United States and the UK, including the significant demonstrations in London. Over dessert and coffee and tea, they debated whether Winston Churchill was a racist. That discussion continued later and required an after-dinner cordial.

Peter led off for the Brits after dessert, gaining attention by stand- ing and carefully pinging his empty glass. "Salt and Louise, we have been thinking about our earlier discussion. We are not backing away from what we said, but we feel honor bound to emphasize how difficult this will be. It is possible to destroy a country's reputation in a very short period of time based on a few issues. It is much more difficult to restore mutual trust and confidence, and the restoration efforts need to focus on issues important to both of us. Progress on petty issues won't cut it. The more we think about it, the more we think this effort is what you Yanks call a very heavy lift that will take a long time. If we proceed, we need to manage the expectations of our respective leaders."

Louise spoke up, agreeing with Peter's overview. Continuing, she explained, "Peter, we think we need to identify one or two matters that are important enough to generate the needed level of attention, are in the land of the doable and are not so complicated that it's likely to take years to develop trust around those matters."

"Do you have anything in mind?" asked Peter.

"We have a couple of items to bounce off of you," Louise responded.

Salt was pleased that Louise was stepping up and taking the initiative, and he was impressed and kept his mouth shut.

Louise continued. "The post-Brexit US-UK trade negotiations are stalled on several fronts. Let's pick two of those issues for our working group to focus on. In addition, let's focus on one or two elements of the Ukraine relationship. Now that the United States has a new administration that believes Ukraine should be recognized and new complications have not yet surfaced, it should be easier to make progress between our countries and then with NATO and ultimately Russia."

"Sorry to interrupt," said Peter, "but this is important. We will think about that list, which on its face seems reasonable. The US-UK trade negotiations are front of mind. To be honest, we're concerned about the United States on the trade front. We are all focused on the continuing COVID-19 crisis, whether the two vaccines that are being focused on will work, how fast, and the effects of the continuing recession. Our economists see US manufacturing as being in trouble. And the United States does not have left many domestic tools to deal with these issues. You have used up most of your dry powder in the form of monetary and fiscal stimuli, and it could be tempting to blame Brexit and Europe and impose more tariffs. Europe and we would view that as a form of economic warfare. Some of us are also concerned that the supply chain lessons of the COVID-19 experience and the survival of some of the America-first themes will cause the US private sector to embrace near-shoring and invest heavily in new facilities. That could involve the use of robotics and artificial intelligence to insulate manufacturing from labor costs and make it financially feasible to move more manufacturing back to the United States."

"Fair enough," replied Salt. "But let's not forget the role of the UK and Brexit in terms of fragmenting trade and breaching alliances. We are also a bit unnerved by your politics, including your prime minister, who does not seem to have the right temperament to manage a country, and the leader of the pro-Brexit movement. We just don't know much about the new head of your Labour Party. There is quite a thick and unpredictable stew cooking in the UK as well as in the United States."

Louise leaned in. "All of us involved in this process will have to be assessing whether we think the European Union will survive the combined effect of Brexit, COVID-19, the recession, and the rise of the right around the world."

Peter concurred. "Unfortunately, all of that does have to be on our radar." Smiling, he added, "I guess you Yanks should know a leader not qualified to run a country when you see one.

Who could forget the July 2018 show in Helsinki?"

Peter continued, "Returning to your list, we would have liked to add reinstating the Paris Climate Accord and the JCPOA treaty with Iran and others, but we think those are too ambitious in all kinds of ways. And the United States is not in a position to take a lead role in those. In any event, we need to define the parameters of our target issues in more detail and make sure we have a shared understanding of what would constitute a mutual win on those issues for our working group. Let's see if we can achieve that definition over the next week or so."

"Thanks, Peter," said Salt. "We hear you on the target issues. We will need to discuss these with Stuart tomorrow, and he will no doubt need to consult, but we will do that and revert. Hopefully, we can achieve a mutual understanding soon and also agree on who should be involved. Another topic we might put on the short list is managing global pandemics, the role of the WHO, the role of China vis-à-vis the WHO, and what else might be needed to support the WHO. In any event, thanks for your time and thoughts today, not to mention dinner."

"You're most welcome, Salt and Louise. Let us know how Stuart reacts to what we have discussed and when you think we might kick things off. I think we have some of the same domestic attitudes and challenges surrounding these topics. In that regard, history can be both interesting and illuminating, and I double-checked a couple of items late this afternoon. On August 30, 2013, our House of Commons refused to support our Prime Minister's request for authority to intervene in the Syrian civil war to respond to, among other things, the use of chemical weapons. That rejection was a first of sorts and a surprise. Two weeks later, President Obama's efforts to obtain US Congressional approval for that effort suffered the same fate. However, a deal with Russia salvaged a joint effort to remove chemical weapons. Then almost three years later, on June 23, 2016, the British people approved Brexit and, in effect, more isolation. Later in the same year, the citizens of the United States elected President Pope, who became a fan of Brexit and the kinds of things it stood for, including America first, which really meant America first, last, and always.

So there is an extent to which the British people and Parliament can be leading indicators of what the United States is going to do—a barometer of sorts. We need to learn from that phenomenon.

"By the way, remember to also be alert when you leave tonight. I doubt you have attracted much unwanted external attention yet, but it pays to be careful." Peter then smiled and added, "By the way, if, as North Americans, you can develop an answer to how you solve a problem like Prince Harry, that would be a bonus. We're actually fond of the young man and his wife."

Salt and Louise intentionally started to walk back to the hotel rather than looking for a cab. After ten minutes or so, Louise asked Salt, "Does it feel to you like someone is following us?"

It was dark, of course, but they were in the well-lit Whitehall area of London. Salt looked around and said, "I don't see anything unusual."

Louise quietly laughed. "It is very unlikely that you would see someone in a situation like this. Anyone who is any good would stay out of the line of sight. You have to almost feel them."

"So you feel something is amiss?" Salt asked.

"Not certain of it," said Louise. "But I just have a sense that there is someone out there watching us. Maybe what Peter said is giving me the willies. Let's grab that cab." And they did.

After arriving at the hotel, they went to Salt's room and sent an encrypted message to Stuart, asking for a window of time to talk the following day. They each had a drink from the minibar and chatted for a few minutes.

Salt went into thoughtful mode and commented, "Thanks for your help today. You were on point and effective. Well done. And then, if I may say so, in addition to gaining their attention with what you said, you nearly destroyed their concentration level with your striking looks. As the Brits would say, 'Bloody hell!' And remind me what I owe you for the new tie."

"Thanks, Salt," said Louise. "I think we can make a good team if we work at it."

And they were off to bed.

Chapter 31

Off-Ramp: Middle Eastern Diversion

[February 24, 2021]

S alt climbed out of bed at about six thirty on Wednesday morning and checked the shoe phone for emails from the United States. Nothing yet. Even though it was the middle of the night in Washington, he had been hoping to get some guidance on the shortlist to be proposed to Peter and his team before they lost another day. He got dressed and went to the coffee shop in the lobby for breakfast. Louise was there, back in her black pantsuit attire.

"Hope you slept well last night," she said.

Salt responded, "It took me a while at first, but then I went into a good, deep sleep. I think the jet lag has worn off. How did you sleep?"

"Fine, thanks—though, like you, it took a while to get to sleep. Too much on my mind."

They then turned to the short list of post-Brexit US-UK trade issues that could be focused on with the Brits as the trial run for the relationship-building exercise. There were so many—virtually all potential trade issues between the two nations—that they decided it made more sense to defer to Peter and Stuart and their teams; they were better positioned to identify the items that were both urgent and important for the UK, and they would have a better idea of what would be relatively easy to fix. These discussions were not starting without any prior back–and–forth. Maybe they needed to get a short list from the Brits and then consult about priorities with the right players in the United States.

Louise then effectively pointed out that, although the team had not yet rung up a long list of achievements, the US as a whole was knocking things off the group's list before it even got off the ground.

Salt picked up the necessaries from the bakery and, before he forgot and just to further complicate things, upon his return to the table, asked Louise if they could have a quiet dinner in the DC area on Sunday evening to give them time to prepare for the Monday afternoon meeting with Stuart and the team that had been confirmed. Louise said Sunday dinner would work.

_~*~*~*~_

They also discussed a short list of Ukrainian issues and decided they would propose some things to Stuart. They didn't discuss or comment on Salt's late addition of managing global health issues. Louise did not want to touch that item.

They then turned briefly to what the next geographical target should be. France? Germany? Someplace more exotic?

As they were finishing breakfast, Salt and Louise got email messages on their shoe phones instructing them to get to a secure location where they could talk on a landline with a speakerphone. And sooner rather than later. They called Ed Jordan at the embassy and made the necessary arrangements. They then grabbed a cab and got to the US embassy by 10:30 a.m. London time—or 5:30 a.m. in Washington. Ed Jordan settled them in a secure conference room in the embassy and then graciously departed.

At 10:45 a.m. London time, the phone rang. It was Stuart and a group of about five others who were huddled around a phone. Turned out the group in the United States was in the Situation Room in the basement of the White House.

Stuart opened the call. "We're very eager to hear how things have been going in London, but we need to shift gears to look at an even higher priority.

"You two are generally aware of the JCPOA treaty with Iran and others. And we will give you a full debrief later. As you'll recall, the treaty was signed in Vienna in July 2015 by the five permanent members of the UN Security Council (China, France, Russia, the UK, and the United States), Germany, the European Union, and Iran. President Pope withdrew the United States from the treaty in May 2018. The treaty limped along until 2020, when things deteriorated, including the breakout of hostilities at varying levels among Iran, Iraq, the United States, and others. Apart from relatively minor skirmishes and continuing confusion, nothing significant happened during the balance of 2020 and the US election process. But Iran had a serious bout with the coronavirus and blamed the United States and its sanctions regime for Iran not receiving more aid and assistance to deal with the pandemic.

"President Evans campaigned on the basis that something like the JCPOA should be brought back to life. Now that President Evans is in place, Iran has just gone to Germany to say they are willing to talk, but it must be fast and secure, nonpublic. We realize this is beyond your remit, but we would like you to help launch this. And soon."

"How soon is soon?" asked Louise. "Tomorrow," said Stuart.

Salt protested, "But we're greenhorns in this and relatively uninformed about the people and the details of how we got here. We would be in over our heads on the first day. And more important, there are really good people available at State and other places who could run circles around us."

"You'll have to run fast," acknowledged Stuart, "but you can do it. And this is just the first step. We need to keep this very quiet, so we must first field a very small and minimally recognizable team. That would be you two plus Gretchen Grant of the State Department, who was involved in the details of the JCPOA but not in a highly visible way. Maybe one or two Germans know her. Gretchen is getting on a flight to Berlin this evening, arriving in the morning. Step one is to meet in Berlin with the Germans, who have perhaps maintained the best relationship with Iran. We would like that to happen tomorrow, but in the real world, it will need to be on Friday. We envision a first meeting with the Iranians next week, with dates and locations to be determined. Are you in?"

"What do we do with the Brits if we start focusing on this rather than what we discussed with them?" Salt asked.

Stuart was forceful. "We tell them the truth. We say you have been diverted for a few days and that, meanwhile, we in Washington are studying the results of your discussions in London so we can get back to them soon.

We cannot and will not hang them out to dry. That effort is too important." "Holy shit, Stuart." Salt sighed. "You know we didn't sign up for this."

"Admitted," said Stuart, "but life sometimes presents unanticipated and important challenges."

"Okay, let's cut to the chase and stop wasting time," Louise said, entering the fray. "Assuming we mix well with the Germans and Gretchen, we'll help get it launched."

Salt's mouth dropped wide open. He was obviously becoming agitated, and the control freak in him came to the surface. "What the fuck, boys and girls. Are you all out of your Goddamned minds? Jesus H. Christ, what is going on here?"

Stuart started to respond, but Louise cut him off. "Look, Salt; you're a Boy Scout with patriotic tendencies and smart. You're eventually going to agree to do this, so let's save fifteen minutes of histrionics and start learning about this cluster. This has about the same chance of success as the half-baked shit we threw at the Brits yesterday. At your age, a good failure or two won't hurt your résumé. My diplomatic/intelligence career, on the other hand, will be baked to a crisp. In other words, get over it."

A few moments of silence followed. Salt frowned and said, "I'm listening."

"Good," responded Stuart. "I'm turning you over to Walter Williams, who has shifted back and forth between State and the CIA in recent years but has remained focused on the issues surrounding the JCPOA and Iran. Like Gretchen, he is one of our best and most knowledgeable. Thanks, all."

Stuart jumped off the call, and Walter joined and introduced himself. Unlike Louise, Walter did not have street experience, but he was obviously plenty smart and knowledgeable.

Walter suggested, "Let's begin at the beginning." And he did.

Chapter 32

Iranian Backgrounder I;
Tracks in the Snow

[February 24-25, 2021]

As Walter explained, the rich history of Persia goes back essentially to the beginning of time. In the 600s, the schism between the Shia and the Sunni Muslim sects in what is now Syria developed, ostensibly over different views as to who was able to interpret the Koran, descendants of Muhammad or a broader group. Persia (named Iran in 1935) is more of the Shia persuasion, with a limited view of who can interpret the Koran. What is now Iraq housed both persuasions, though Saddam Hussein was a Sunni. Some of the larger and more oil-rich countries in the Gulf area are also more of the Sunni persuasion. One need not have a degree in Middle Eastern history to conclude that the Shia/Sunni schism is deep and most likely forever lasting and must be respected. It won't go away in our time.

Even these introductory remarks generated questions, which Walter dealt with nimbly and patiently. The Shia-Sunni relationship and which branch of the Muslim faith dominated and where were of particular interest.

After dealing with Q and A, Walter deftly skipped forward through several centuries and many important developments. Iran was neutral in World War II but was occupied by the UK and Russia. In 1953, a military coup backed by the United States and the UK overthrew an anti-Western government. Thus entered the Shah of Iran, who, with his family, remained in control for many years. But in 1979, the Iranian revolution took place, the Shah was overthrown, and Ayatollah Khomeini established a strong Shiite regime in the form of the Islamic Republic. The year 1979 also witnessed the US-Iran hostage crisis, which lasted 444 days, ending in 1981 on the day Ronald Reagan was inaugurated.

Walter reminded them that since at least 1980, the Assad regime in Syria and Hezbollah in Lebanon, both Shia in persuasion, have been supported by Iran. The Iranian support of Assad has been particularly strong since 2011. The fierce Iran-Iraq war took place from 1980 to 1988, beginning with an Iraqi invasion of Iran in 1980.

Iran stayed on the sidelines for the most part during the height of the Gulf War (Operation Desert Shield) between 1990 and early 1991, following Iraq's invasion of Kuwait and the subsequent US-led invasion of Iraq (Operation Desert Storm) in 1991.

After dealing with several questions, Walter took a breath and continued, "Iran has been directly involved in many skirmishes with the United States of varying strength over the past decade or so. These have included a variety of incidents involving the United States and Iraq, and, to a lesser extent, Israel. There has also been domestic unrest in Iran from time to time, as the Iranian population does not uniformly support what amounts to a theocracy plagued with allegations of fraud and corruption. There was significant domestic unrest in Iran during 2009 and 2010. In 2014, Iran intervened in the Yemen Civil War, which is ongoing."

Walter reminded them that the situation between the United States and Iran had become tenser in 2019, with Iran launching periodic rocket attacks into Iraq, an attack on the US embassy in Baghdad in January 2020, and what some refer to as the assassination by the United States of the prominent Iranian military leader and folk hero, General Qassim Soleimani, commander of Iranian Forces (including the Quds Force of the Islamic Revolutionary Guards Corps), in a January 3, 2020, drone attack near the Baghdad airport. In conclusion, Walter explained, "Ever since that event, it is fair to say that Iran, Iraq, and the United States have had an even more troubled relationship. By the end of the first quarter of 2020, it became clear that Iran would not move in the direction of serious discussions with the United States or its allies until the US presidential elections had been held.

There have been no significant developments since. The coronavirus pandemic added significantly to Iran's internal issues and popular unrest."

After answering a host of questions, Walter called a time-out, saying, "I think that's what I was supposed to cover today. We think it would be helpful for you to meet up with Gretchen Grant in Berlin tomorrow and also let us try to set up a meeting with the Germans for Friday. We were hoping to aim for Thursday, but Gretchen will be jet-lagged, and we think it makes sense for you two and Gretchen to have some time together in Berlin tomorrow evening before meeting with the Germans on Friday.

"By the way," Walter added, "Gretchen is a serious player here. She knows her stuff. She was not prominent during the 2014–2015 discussions with Iran, but she was there and has been closely following Iran ever since. And she is well respected by the Germans."

"Thanks, Walter," said Salt. "You know, a reasonable helping of history is a good thing. I used to work with a very wise man who said that, when evaluating people, it's important to follow 'tracks in the snow.' In other words, you can tell a lot about where a person, a nation, or a group is headed by understanding where they came from and what direction they are going. Following the trajectory of tracks in the snow is not foolproof, but it is a good start. Thus the importance of history. Something that not all political leaders understand. So, thanks."

At the completion of Walter's presentation and their questions and related discussion, it was four o'clock on Wednesday afternoon in London. Walter hung up. It had been a long call and a long day without a lunch break.

After Walter hung up, Salt turned to Louise. "Who is this guy Walter, and does he know his stuff? He seems to know not only facts but how they fit together and influence events."

"You're right," said Louise. "He's bounced between the Agency and State, not because he's a problem but because he's brilliant. He's African American, smart as hell, works like a dog, keeps up to date, may have a photographic memory, and is reliable. He may have a little nerd in him and will never operate in the field, but nobody cares."

"Good," Salt said. "Let's make sure he stays on the team.".

Chapter 33

Walk in the Park, Talk, and More

[February 24, 2021]

There was just a bit of daylight left on a cold but not very damp London evening. Salt turned to Louise and said, "I think I need to find a protein bar and take a walk in Hyde Park and noodle about all of this."

Louise responded, "You take your walk. I need to take a run. How about if we meet in the hotel lobby in two hours? Your job is to talk to the concierge and get a reservation for six thirty or seven at a decent Indian restaurant within walking distance of the hotel. Indian food is typically very good in London. Your other job is to watch your back while taking your walk and be aware of anyone tailing you. I'll call Stuart's assistant and get us on a flight to Berlin in the morning and in a hotel tomorrow evening."

"Yes, ma'am," Salt responded, "though I think the risk of me being followed is overblown."

"Better safe than sorry," said Louise. "See you in two hours."

They both needed a break, and as they thought about things, no firm conclusions were reached while either walking or running. Salt thought about whether he should fly to Berlin in the morning, bag this whole operation, and head back to the United States and the farm near Carterville. This effort was headed in a much different direction than he was led to believe at the outset.

Salt's interest was in solving trade issues in a fashion that would help ordinary Americans—like those in and around Carterville—and honoring Meredith by trying to improve global responses to health issues. He was essentially a free trader at heart. He believed trying to provide artificial protection or impose artificial restrictions on businesses and industries was a mistake. Over the long haul, they had to be able to compete.

But a lot of government assistance was being doled out all around the world in an effort to stem the recession. And even Salt was in favor of steps to ensure things like a level playing field, appropriate intellectual property protections, and incubation of new businesses. These kinds of issues were capable of inspiring Salt to become involved in a mission. Meeting with the Brits to discuss US-UK free trade agreements, which would inevitably affect US-EU trade agreements, also grabbed his attention. Of course, the elephant in this room was China, and improving that very complicated and troubled trade relationship (or was it a war?), including the Huawei controversy, could have a huge impact back home. That was the sort of thing for which Salt would defer retirement.

Dealing with Iran did not promise to materially improve trade issues in the United States. The United States was essentially energy independent, and the Iran situation was a mess that really went back centuries. Iran was certainly very important, but this wasn't going to morph into Salt's sweet spot, and he was not happy about being pushed in this direction. He was concerned that he was getting pulled into inside the Beltway chaos when he really wanted to be focused on helping those outside the Beltway.

Salt eventually talked himself into thinking that one more day would not be such a big deal, though he was still peeved about how he was getting volunteered for things without any prior notice or discussion. Hell, he wasn't even on the payroll yet. He needed to figure out what his ejection mechanism would be. As he brooded, he blamed Stuart for the most part, though Louise was no help. But Salt also admitted to himself that there was more to Louise than he had originally thought.

While mulling over these issues, he ate his protein bar to carry him over to dinner. He didn't notice any tail but reminded himself that he probably would not recognize a tail unless they carried a sign saying, "It's me."

Salt and Louise met in the hotel lobby at six thirty and reported on their assignments. Louise had flight arrangements, and Salt had the Indian dinner reservation. They walked quietly over to the restaurant and immediately noticed the staff's compliance with mask and distancing requirements when they entered.

After being seated and ordering drinks and appetizers, Salt started the discussion. "So, Louise, tell me what you think about all of this and what it means to you. What do you want to get out of this?"

"Well, that's a complicated set of questions," Louise responded, "and I thought about them on my run this afternoon. As we discussed at Helen's Place in Carterville—which seems like a very long time ago—I'm eager to get closer to the diplomatic corps in some way, so this is a massive opportunity for me if we can pull it off at any appreciable level. I understand that you and I are at different places in our lives and that I'm being selfish and using you to some extent, but it's also true that you're uncertain about what you want to do. Are you really ready for retirement in the country? You're a thoughtful guy and a patriot in your own way, but you'll never go out and drive a tractor. I doubt you're ready to hang 'em up and down deep, and so do you. I think you would go nuts."

Salt responded instinctively. "I didn't realize that you're a shrink as well as one of what my new barber calls pointy-headed members of the Deep State. But I'll admit that you're not too wrong. I'm struggling and willing to concede that to you. The stakes are very high in this particular game. To say the least, we're not the most likely duo to pull this off, and if there were not a need for virtual anonymity, we would not be sitting here. For me, it's a conundrum. If we do this, we cannot screw it up. Who needs that kind of pressure?"

"The pressure is real, I admit," said Louise, "but think how cool it would be to play even a small role in beginning to restore the United States to a place of genuine respect, influence, and moderation in the world, including in the health care arena. At some level, we're all in this to be able to do some good. Let's just do the best we can."

Louise wanted to pause the conversation and give her comments time to sink in. She said, "Excuse me, I need to visit the ladies' water closet. Think about what we might be able to achieve, and maybe we'll even enjoy working with each other. You're not as much of a dinosaur as either of us thought." Then she was gone.

After Louise returned, they moved on to lighter conversation, finished dinner, and Salt paid the check.

As they started to walk toward the hotel, Louise asked, "Did you see those two guys in the shadows as we left the restaurant? They were just standing there when we came out of the restaurant, but now they're walking about sixty yards behind us. Let's split up. I'll take that cab over there, and you walk back. Let's see what they do."

The two men stopped and talked quietly as Louise and Salt split up. There being no other cabs handy, they turned to follow Salt. But they kept to themselves as Salt neared the hotel. Salt now admitted to himself that Louise was right about a possible tail. But what to do about it? Nothing, Salt concluded, other than being aware and careful. Besides, they would be in Berlin by early afternoon tomorrow.

After reaching the hotel, Salt and Louise met up in the hotel bar again, and Salt disclosed his agreement with Louise regarding the tail. They agreed they would mention it to Stuart on the next call that offered an opportunity. After one glass of wine, Louise abruptly stood up and kissed Salt on the head and, after looking back at Salt on her way out of the bar, went to her room without saying another word. After Louise was gone, Salt wondered what that meant and how in the hell he was going to get to sleep after that kind of teaser.

They both went to bed thinking about things.

About an hour after they left the bar, Louise used a gizmo to pick the electronic lock on Salt's door and walked in. She still looked fabulous and was wearing very little. Without saying a word, she climbed into bed with Salt, and they became better acquainted. Louise was gone when Salt woke up on Thursday morning.

After sitting up on the edge of the bed the next morning, Salt wondered if what had happened the night before was just a dream. It was a hell of a dream, if that's what it was. But there was a psychological complication. Salt started feeling guilty as if he were cheating on his wife.

She had passed away nine months ago, but Salt remained intensely loyal to her memory, and he missed her daily. Salt honestly believed he needed to move on with his life, and that was what his wife would want. But there was still that uneasy feeling.

Salt and Louise met up in the lobby. They were both quiet when leaving the hotel in a cab, then at the airport, and on the plane. There was no sign of the tail—if there was one. But Louise said she felt it in her bones.

Chapter 34

Berlin Bearings

[February 25, 2021]

Since Brexit had not yet been fully implemented, they didn't need visas or other new travel documentation for Heathrow flights to Berlin. They did need their COVID-19 test certificates. The flight was not very long, and it was surprisingly crowded, with most of the passengers wearing masks, so there was no serious talk. They grabbed a cab at the Berlin airport and, at Louise's insistence, continued to be careful about what they said in public places and in the cab. Someone had trained her well.

On the way from the airport to downtown Berlin, Salt was reminded of how interesting and diverse Berlin was and its complicated history. Berlin had the feel of a much newer city than many other European capitals, and much of it actually was newer. It suffered serious damage during World War II and was then hampered by being an island inside East Germany, with the city itself being divided by the wall from 1961 to 1989. After the October 3, 1990, reunification, there was massive investment in East Germany and East Berlin, resulting in newer buildings being of a different architectural species than in Paris or much of London.

There remained in the city other evidence of its past. This included wonderful museums, Checkpoint Charlie, the Brandenburg Gate, and remnants of the Berlin Wall, which stirred the memories of those old enough to remember President Reagan saying to Mikhail Gorbachev in 1987 in a speech at the Brandenburg Gate, "Tear down this wall." And there were a number of thoughtful memorials demonstrating a deep national awareness of the Holocaust.

Louise and Salt found the Novatel hotel near the Foreign Office, checked in, and grabbed some lunch while waiting for Gretchen. In 2000, the Foreign Office had moved from Bonn, the capital of West Germany, before the reunification. Their meeting on Friday morning was going to be at the Federal Foreign Office, housed in a modern building at Werderscher Market, not far from the Spree River in the Berlin area that housed several museums and government buildings.

Another recent change involved the government. After 16 years at the helm, Angela Merkel stepped aside as the German Chancellor. Germany has as many as 38 parties. To replace Ms. Merkel, the conservative CDU/CSU and the Christian Democrats, both center-right parties, formed a coalition party. With significant EU experience, Olaf Scholz was named Chancellor, and Anja Besecke became the foreign minister, the first woman to hold that position.

Salt and Louise waited in the coffee shop for Gretchen Grant to arrive. She had landed in Berlin that morning on a typically delayed commercial red- eye flight from DC, waited forever on checked luggage, and then took a short nap when she arrived at the hotel. "How about a backgrounder on Gretchen?" Salt asked Louise while they were waiting.

"Top-notch," Louise said. "She will never carry a weapon in the field, but she can use her considerable people skills in almost any situation. She speaks two or three languages, has good judgment, and knows everyone in the Agency and State. She's always in demand. And she's a nice person to boot."

"But can she spot tails?" asked Stuart, only half kidding.

"Sure, and she could track you without any difficulty," smiled Louise. "That works for me," said Salt. "I guess I have to give Stuart credit. He's given me the all-stars to work with. He must think I need good help, and he would be right."

Gretchen joined them at 3:00 p.m. She was a bit taller and heavier than Louise, less athletic looking, had very curly, longish, dark hair, and was attractive. It took only sixty seconds to figure out that she was very smart, and German was one of her languages.

They had a coffee in a quiet corner of the coffee shop and then adjourned to Salt's room for a more detailed chat and update.

"Well," said Salt, "this should be interesting. This will be a much different meeting than what we had in London. In this case, the Iranians contacted the Germans in an apparent effort to open things up. That means that Anja Besecke, the new German federal minister for foreign affairs, is aware and will be involved at some level. At a minimum, we will be outranked. We can be sure that Stuart has spoken with the minister. I expect the minister to show up at some point in these meetings. We are to ask for a Martin Weber, who seems to be a troubleshooter of sorts for the minister and was involved in the JPCOA negotiations."

"I know him," said Gretchen. "He was involved on the fringes of the JCPOA and is smart and a bit hard to take. He's very linear in his thinking and will want to take the lead. I suggest we listen for the most part, express our willingness to play ball, talk about the next steps, and let Stuart or the President arm wrestle with Martin and the minister about who takes the lead on this. My understanding is that Walter Williams will join us by phone tomorrow and remind us of the background so we can be sure we're all singing from the same hymnal.

"And by the way," Gretchen said, "the word is that by the end of the day today in the United States, the President will send to the Senate Stuart Bacon's nomination to be secretary of state."

Salt said, "Shit. I knew this was coming but was not aware of the timing. Stuart must have a senior role in the new administration, but in the short run, he'll be diverted by preparing for Senate confirmation hearings and very hard to get hold of.

We need to remember that, net, net, Stuart's nomination is a good thing over the long haul. We'll just have to put up with logistical issues in the short run, and there will be a higher risk of leaks than if you were not with the project. Nothing is simple."

Gretchen gave to each Salt and Louise copies of the detailed background briefing package that had been promised. "Something to keep you from being bored this evening before we meet with the Germans tomorrow morning," she said. They agreed that Gretchen would take it easy for the evening and that Salt and Louise would each have room service and study the briefing packages Gretchen had hauled over on the plane in her carry-on baggage.

Chapter 35

Initial Team Thinking
[February 26, 2021]

T hey met for coffee on Friday morning and then headed for the Foreign Office. On the way over, Louise told Gretchen about the possibility of tails. "Interesting," commented Gretchen. "I really had not anticipated that.

Goodness."

Martin Weber greeted them at the Foreign Office, took their temperatures, provided masks, and escorted them to an interior and modern conference room with no windows, gray walls, white counters, and glass tables. Nothing on the walls. The room felt cold and sterile, but any room that modern had to be very secure. Weber introduced three other members of the German team, two men and a woman, and said that Foreign Minister Besecke would likely briefly join later.

Salt introduced Walter Williams, who had joined by a secure landline from Washington, where it was the middle of the night. Salt explained that he wasn't sure who had arranged for Walter to join the session, but all agreed that ensuring the group had a common set of background facts in mind was a good idea. Salt asked Walter to provide the Reader's Digest condensed version. It was, after all, Friday in Berlin, and there would be limits on attention spans.

Walter gave an overview of his background and reminded them that the Joint Comprehensive Plan of Action, or the JCPOA (what most people call the "Iran nuclear deal"), was signed in July 2015 after nearly two years of negotiations. The parties were Iran and the five permanent members of the UN Security Council (China, France, Russia, the UK, and the United States), plus Germany and the European Union—an unwieldy group if there ever was one. The agreement was preceded by years of smaller group negotiations, starting in 2003. The United States refused to participate in those discussions.

Walter continued, "The agreement was imperfect, as President Pope used to clarify. But in many respects, it was remarkable. Just getting those parties together and agreeing on anything for fifteen years was a minor miracle."

"The treaty covered—and we gave Gretchen some written background on this to share with you: (1) nuclear capability, including an inventory of enriched uranium and centrifuges and inspections by the International Atomic Energy Agency; (2) early stage exemptions from the nuclear provisions that allowed for the loosening of certain economic sanctions; and (3) broader relief from economic sanctions over time.

"The JCPOA was controversial in the United States at the time of and following its adoption in 2015. The Obama administration was supportive of the agreement, but President Pope campaigned against the agreement in the 2016 presidential election. As you know, President Evans was a supporter of the principles behind the agreement during the negotiations and the 2020 campaign but didn't endorse the agreement as such."

Martin asked pointedly, "Can you please remind us of when the United States dropped out of the treaty?"

Walter answered, "President Pope withdrew from the agreement on May 8, 2018, and at the same time imposed harsher economic sanctions on Iran. The withdrawal was as controversial as entering into the agreement in the first place. Our understanding is that US allies were at first dumbfounded, then mad as hell. The other parties tried to hold the agreement together, but it fell into disrepair, pending the outcome of the US 2020 election. The difficulty of reinstating the treaty was also heightened by Iran's involvement in various hostilities in Iraq, Syria, Yemen, and Lebanon during 2020 and the COVID-19 pandemic. And, of course, the status of the treaty was affected by geopolitical developments involving the United States, Russia, and China. This subject is a very complicated web."

Salt noted to himself that Walter was doing a nice job of providing a balanced recounting of the relevant history. There was very little pro-American bending of the facts. That was important for developing some credibility. The Germans recognized the same thing and did not present unbalanced questions or comments. The repartee was very civil.

Walter continued, "The current state of play is that, as a practical matter, the treaty is dead. The Evans administration has signaled interest in fixing the treaty, but Iran's demands have been too high so far. There are a number of parties who want the agreement to be improved and brought back to life. Moreover, the possible use of Iran's petroleum reserves to offset the loss of supplies from Ukraine could be a great development but is likely a pipedream (no pun intended). That won't happen without a strong signal of serious interest from the United States and Iran. Given the challenges associated with the United States, China, and Russia at the present time, the initial feeling is that it makes more sense for the United States and Iran, and perhaps Germany, to talk among themselves and make progress before bringing together a collection of other parties to the table, which at the present time would sort of resemble the bar scene in the first Star Wars movie. As evidenced by the initial contact here, Germany could probably be the most helpful of the non-US parties to the deal. But we need to keep in mind that the Russians and Iranians are in constant dialogue."

Walter concluded, "So, that is the JCPOA for smart people, as opposed to dummies. A full briefing would take days, and we don't have days. And we frankly doubt that you need to be prepared for substantive discussions."

The group in Germany collectively thanked Walter, who then signed off. They took a break for the lunch of salads, small sandwiches, and crisps that had been brought in. All things considered, the mood was surprisingly relaxed. Salt wondered if the Germans were having a hard time taking this seriously.

During lunch, Martin Weber recommended that, at any meeting held during the next week to ten days, there should be no reason to try to make substantive progress. The agenda would be whether the United States and Iran were serious about talking, who should be involved, and the logistics associated with what would need to be secret negotiations if at all possible.

Louise commented, "It feels to me like there's a one-day get-acquainted session with enough substance that we can get useful sounding on the level of Iran's interest in meaningful discussions."

Others agreed with that shorthand overview.

Chapter 36

German Minister Cameo

[February 26, 2021]

After lunch, Martin asked the American team, "Where do you think we go from here?" At that moment, Foreign Minister Anja Besecke walked in and joined the meeting. "Perfect timing," said Martin, "as we were just starting to talk about what we want to do with this opportunity—if it is, in fact, an opportunity."

Salt suggested that it would be helpful to discuss again exactly what the Iranians had said to Martin and his team when they recently inquired about resuming discussions. "That's fair," said Minister Besecke in perfect English, "but before we get into that, who are you, Salt? We've got very senior people here in the Ministry who have been involved with the US on a variety of matters, and I've been banging around the diplomatic world for quite a while and, no offense, you suddenly appear out of nowhere on behalf of President Evans and Stuart Bacon, talking about some very important stuff."

"Sorry, I thought Stuart had given you a backgrounder," replied Salt. "He did," responded Minister Besecke, "but you know Stuart; he tends to move through things quickly on a once-over-light basis."

"Well," said Salt, "I'm actually not the most qualified person for what I'm doing here, and I might not be qualified at all, but that's also the reason I'm here. Nobody in the world would guess that I'm up to serious diplomatic stuff, and nobody would confuse me with a decision-maker. The likelihood of the media or others thinking I'm doing something newsworthy is low. I guess, in some respects, I'm the personification of expectations management. But I'm supported by two great emerging diplomats, Louise and Gretchen, as well as Walter, and I'm smart enough not to commit diplomatic suicide. I know that my foot does not belong in my mouth.

And I'm not here because I made large political contributions to anyone. I'm essentially apolitical but committed to finding the middle ground in nearly all of what I do. There can't be excessive winners and losers in what we do—an approach the last US administration rejected."

Salt went on to provide a bit more background on his career at Treasury, State, and law firm. Minister Besecke and the others listened intently.

Salt continued, "I may as well be completely candid about our mission here. When we left the United States early this week, we were to visit with close allies, including Germany, about how to repair and enhance diplomatic relations with key allies and others worldwide. Germany was at the top of the list, and we want and need to talk with you about Germany, the EU, NATO, Ukraine, and the region more generally, and global health issues. But you folks received the call from Iran, and we had to divert. That does not mean we're not vitally interested in the Germany-Europe discussions. Indeed, we would characterize those topics as both urgent and important."

When Salt was done, the Minister said, "Well, thanks for that last bit. It helps provide context for how you were pulled into these discussions. You're an unconventional choice for all of this, but you are on an unconventional mission. So maybe you are perfect. Just please keep in mind that Germany's credibility—not to mention our gas supply--is also at stake in this enterprise, and it must be said that our experience with your last administration taints our reaction to you. To be candid, we have been double-crossed by the United States too often; we will be careful here. The lack of trust is palpable throughout Germany. Not only will our diplomats be concerned about collaboration with the United States, but so will the general public. We must not be seen as being very committed to anything. Please understand that this is not personal—at least not yet." And only then did Minister Besecke smile.

"I get it," said Salt. "And I appreciate your candor. We may actually be able to get along."

"Good," said Minister Besecke. "You may speak with Martin as if you were talking to me, and I expect him to keep me fully up to date. Carry on." And she left.

Salt was unsure what to make of the discussion with the Minister, who seemed reasonable and was surprisingly direct and informal. Clearly, the Minister did not want to have her fingerprints on this escapade, and she felt strongly enough about that to cede control to someone who probably should not be in the lead. The posture of things could not be better for the Germans. They had plausible deniability and someone to blame if things headed south. No guts, no glory, thought Salt.

Chapter 37
Berlin: Next Steps
[February 26, 2021]

Salt pretended that he had not sorted things out in his own mind. "Damn," he said. "We didn't get into the next step with the Minister before she left."

"Right," said Martin. "There are two reasons for that. First, she thinks you might be okay if a strange choice. For now, you get the benefit of the doubt. Second, in any event, she wants plausible personal deniability. You have just cleaned up after some recent elections and are facing the midterms. President Pope, who we have no comfort with, finished an election in the United States and is already fighting the next. Here we are dealing with a new government that does not yet have the gravitas of former Chancellor Merkel. However, he emphasized that a strong coalition backs the Government, and Germans, as much as anyone, understand the implications of Ukraine, including how to heat homes next winter. So, bottom line, as you Americans say, we are both a little bit at loose ends in terms of oversight. We had best not screw things up."

With that, they took a fifteen-minute break, with each team going to its corner of the large room. Salt explained his situational analysis, and the others concurred. Like it or not, the US contingent was going to lead the meeting with Iran.

They resumed with Martin returning to the question of what happened next and Salt returning to the question of what the Iranians had said.

"Okay," said Martin, "I'll go first. I was in the room, and they said very little. There were only two of them. They said that, with the change of US administrations, it seemed like a logical moment to consider resuming discussions. Still, they had not had much comfortable contact with the new US administration. Since they know some of us, they decided to ask for our thoughts." Martin reviewed some of the dialogue from the meeting.

The Germans asked if the Iranians had any proposals, especially on nuclear issues. The answer was no. The Germans also asked what the Iranian goals would be for any discussions, and the answer was speedy relief from economic sanctions, which were creating domestic instability and worsening the dire COVID-19 conditions. The German team responded that talking about sanctions relief without nuclear issues being on the table was a non-starter. At a minimum, there would need to be simultaneous progress, and the Germans said the allies and other parties might require progress on nuclear issues before any relief could be had. The Iranians expressed disappointment with that news, but in truth, they knew that would be the answer.

"In other words," concluded Salt, "on the surface, the meeting was a waste of time, but it was still a signal that Iran has domestic unrest issues over the effects of sanctions and the coronavirus and wants to be in a room with us."

"That's a bit oversimplified but right," said Martin.

Louise observed, "What this means is that a first meeting involving the United States is necessary but will end up being a nothing sandwich. And realistically, we will not have any proposals on the table. This feels like we will be wasting time and money on another exercise that is probably something we need to do but hard to get excited about in a positive way."

Gretchen asked, "Are we saying that we're willing to have a meeting so long as we don't offer or give up anything and use it to try to smoke out some further information from them?"

"I think so," said Salt. "What's your take, Martin?"

Martin stated, "We are in agreement, but I need to try to catch the Minister before she leaves. Why don't we leave the conference room for an hour so you can try to reach the United States, and we'll touch base with the Minister? By the way, what would we propose for a meeting place? Berlin? Vienna? Geneva?"

Salt thought for a few moments. "Those are all fine, but they're venues for serious discussions. I'm not sure we're ready for a prime-time location where a sophisticated press might notice us. I would try Prague.

It's a great city and has a lower profile than the others. If we get a meeting arranged, I will try to get the use of a meeting room in the Zofin Palace on the river just south of the Old Town area in Prague."

"Works for me," said Martin. "We'll check back with you in an hour."

Since she was more of a regular at State, Gretchen made the calls to try to catch up with Stuart in the United States. Calls to his shoe phone were not answered, which wasn't a surprise, and they had no idea who Stuart was closeted with, though most likely it involved the Senate confirmation process. They called Walter, brought him up to date, and asked him to try to find Stuart and get a green light.

After reconvening, they advised Martin of the state of play with Stuart, and Martin had good news—Minister Besecke was okay with the plan with several conditions. First, it had to stay secret. If at any time the cover was blown, the Germans would cease talking and deny that there had been any recent conversations. Second, she wanted to formulate the allies' position on uranium enrichment that could be used as vague teasers with the Iranians, but it had to be a hard ask. Finally, before going into serious discussions, it would be necessary to get back relevant hostages. The team needed to identify what that meant.

The teams agreed to caucus among themselves around these assignments on Saturday and meet again on Sunday at one in the afternoon to understand the status, build talking points, and be prepared for a meeting with the Iranians as early as possible next week. Since he had been involved in the last discussions with the Iranians, it was agreed that the US team would ask Martin to make the call to suggest a meeting during the next week. Those with assignments went off to attend to them.

Thirty minutes later, Martin opened a panel on one wall of the conference room that hid a bar, and they went informal on bar snacks, spirits, and German beer. Later, Gretchen, Louise, and Salt agreed to have a nonbusiness dinner and meet at one o'clock on Saturday afternoon to formulate ideas for discussions with their new German friends on Sunday afternoon—unless things got shot down (literally or figuratively) in the meantime.

Berlin was hopping that Friday night, not paying much attention to social distancing and masks, the US team did have to wait for a table in a trendy restaurant, but they survived and enjoyed the seafood. Salt thought This is not *Carterville.*

They went to their rooms immediately after getting back to the hotel. That evening, after getting ready for bed, Salt shaved and knocked on Louise's door down the hallway. She welcomed him in. Once again, nothing was said.

Chapter 38

Berlin: Game Plans Emerge
[February 27, 2021]

S aturday was a busy day but not as crammed as the prior week had been. Salt worked out and took a walk, Louise did a serious workout and run, and Gretchen caught up on other things that had been on her plate before being volunteered for this unusual gig.

The team gathered at one o'clock in Salt's room and discussed the overall state of play and approaches to the meeting with the Iranians. Being the new player on the team, Gretchen led off and commented that the Minister did not even attempt to hide her view that the US players were an unconventional and motley crew, and of course, it was hard to disagree with that assessment. Salt was pleased that the interaction among the US team members was healthy without the common hierarchy in such efforts. Gretchen and Louise were straightforward, noting for Salt's sake that they— more than Salt—would need to be careful and duck when the blame started to be thrown around, as it almost certainly would.

During the discussion, Martin called and said he had spoken with the Iranians, and there was tentative agreement on a very clandestine meeting in Prague on the following Wednesday.

This was going to be a preliminary meeting. To some extent, there was nothing to prepare for, as nothing would be agreed to. The key thing was to listen so as to be able to unpack what was being communicated rather than being distracted by what was said.

Key parameters to the discussion had to include (1) the hostage point made by Minister Besecke, (2) Iran ceasing entirely an increasing level of cyberwarfare, (3) reinstatement of nuclear provisions with clear milestones that were a bit tougher than in the JCPOA and also at least as verifiable as the measures included in the first deal, (4) a lifting of sanctions consistent with Iran's behavior vis a vis Ukraine that would take place over time and could not be characterized as a giveaway, (5) cessation of terrorist support by Iran, (6) some emergency COVID-19 assistance to Iran and (7) hostages. None of this would be easy. This was particularly true as to nuclear capability, as it had become clear that Iran had exceeded the level of enriched uranium allowed by the JCPOA by early 2020. This wasn't a case of stopping enrichment at a current level but rather retreating from the current state of play.

They developed their outline, put it in an email with the bullet points to be reviewed by Walter and Stuart before sharing it with the Germans, and then hit send. Walter reacted with a few comments later in the day.

Before breaking up, they discussed among themselves whether Salt and Louise had been tailed. Louise believed they had been tailed in London, and her educated guess was that the tails were Russian. Neither Salt nor Gretchen had a good reason to disagree. It could have been almost anyone, including the Germans, Iraqis, Turks, or Iranians. Whoever it was, they were good. The likelihood of an incident seemed low, but the interest level would change dramatically if and when it became apparent that the US team would be in discussions with the Iranians.

Chapter 39

Berlin: Straight Talk

[February 28, 2021]

G retchen had made arrangements to catch up with an old friend for dinner on Sunday. That left Louise and Salt to fend for themselves. This had the potential to be awkward. Louise asked shyly, "Do you have other plans, want to be alone, or would you like to have dinner together?"

"If you don't have other plans, I have had more than enough dinners with myself over the years. Let's have the concierge try to find us a place that's relatively quiet and nearby, with quiet being more important than nearby," suggested Salt.

"Good," said Louise. "Why don't you deal with the concierge, pick someplace, and just let me know what time and if there's a dress code."

"Done."

They met in the lobby at 6:30. Salt had worn jeans earlier in the day, but he was wearing a sport coat and trousers now. Louise had been in workout clothes earlier in the day and had not changed into one of her black pantsuits. She was still in a pantsuit, but it looked much different than the other versions. Salt wondered what her secret was in terms of packing.

They got to the restaurant, ordered a bottle of good red wine, and waited for each other to break the silence.

"Okay," said Salt, "I'll go first." He spoke quietly and carefully. "I'm sorry and disappointed in myself that I may have taken advantage of you on this trip. I have never done anything like that before, and it won't happen again. I never cheated on my wife while traveling—or otherwise—and I'm not a one- night stand kind of guy.

And that includes women who are almost young enough to be my daughter. You're smart, pretty even when wearing a black pantsuit, and apparently not in a relationship, so you're very attractive in various ways.

173

You need to be careful as well. We may need to report this to someone in the chain of command so they can get rid of me, though I'm technically a consultant who can be fired anytime. If you're uncomfortable, I'll leave Berlin now and report why to Stuart. If you can stand it, I think we should wait a few days to get this first Iranian meeting behind us. I can then disappear without any awkwardness."

"Shhhheeesh," Louise responded in a heated tone. "First, I can take care of myself. If you were stupid enough to try to force me into something—and I know you would never do that—you would end up needing medical care. I have skills you have not yet seen. Get over that. Second, I think I was the first violator here, and I'm sorry about that—or maybe not. Third, although I try not to look like it, my age starts with the number five. Fourth, my guess is that until a few days ago, neither of us had slept with a member of the opposite sex for nearly a year. That's not good. Finally, as I have said before, you are a Boy Scout, but there is nothing inherently wrong with Boy Scouts. You know the Boy Scout motto is 'be prepared.' That's good advice for dealing with me. And the first time I crawled into bed with you, you were prepared.

"Look," she continued, "I'm not suggesting that I'm falling in love with you or anything like that—who knows how you deal with that— but I think I could enjoy your company outside of working together, especially if you got used to black pantsuits for me and better ties for yourself. And God knows we could use some stress relief. I suggest that we not get hung up on this, impose on each other, or let whatever it is we have to interfere with the mission. In other words, let's see how this develops and, in the meantime, get over it."

"That sounds like a great resolution for the time being." Salt smiled. "Thanks."

"See?" said Louise. "You actually can smile."

They went on to enjoy a good dinner and a discussion about things other than the mission. When they got back to the hotel, it was awkward. They were silent in the elevator and while walking to their rooms. Louise finally said as she got to her door, "You have ten minutes to knock on my door. After that, I'm going to sleep."

Salt knocked.

Chapter 40

On to Prague

[March 1, 2021]

O n Sunday, after coffee, working out, more coffee, and break-fast, the US team got together and walked over to the German Foreign Office.

"There it is again," said Louise. "What?" asked Gretchen.

"The feeling that we're being watched," responded Louise. "I wonder if Tweedledee and Tweedledum are back with us."

Nobody was stupid enough to stop and look, but the group picked up the pace more or less automatically. As they walked over to the German Foreign Office, Salt commented that even he felt it now and that his guess was they were Russians or someone working for them. He wondered out loud what had tipped them off, but maybe it was just standard operating procedure, as Peter Banks had suggested in London. In any event, there were no incidents on the walk over.

Martin Weber let them in and guided them to the same conference room they had been in on Friday. "Welcome again," said Martin, "and thanks for your suggestions. We have spoken with Minister Besecke, and she is satisfied with the overall direction. It must be said, however, that she is not optimistic about anything coming of this. Frankly, if she thought this initiative—or even this meeting—was going to have any positive results, she might have wanted to lead the mission herself. In that connection, and no offense intended, she is a bit concerned that we are sending to this first meeting people who do not have enough stature, such that there is a risk that the Iranians will be offended."

Salt said, "Well, we were pretty transparent about that with you and Minister Besecke, as well as with Stuart, when we said we had similar con-cerns, but there is also the significant risk of this getting into the media if any outsiders notice and take the initiative seriously. Gretchen will try to reach Stuart and run this by him once more, but I doubt there will be a change in the game plan."

"Fine," responded Martin. "In that case, we're glad for you to be the primary spokesperson, Salt." Salt smiled as he felt a little like the donkey in a pin-the-tail-on-the-donkey game, but a further debate over whether this would work at all was not to be gained.

They turned to the working draft of the bullet points that outlined the messages to be delivered but not handed out. None of them would be easy. The US-German team would acknowledge a need to continue to ease some sanctions and provide some COVID-19 relief, but they were not willing to follow the course of action followed by President Pope in dealing with North Korea. There needed to be actual verifiable progress on the nuclear side of things before there would be material sanctions movement. Or—since it might be easier and demonstrate mutual good faith—there could be some minor measure of relief in the event of hostage releases or a verified reduction of sponsored terrorist activity. Getting out of the cyberwarfare business would also have value. And, recognizing the serious nature of the impact of sanctions, the allies would be willing to move the talks along quickly.

After a couple of hours of discussion, they decided there was nothing further to game play, and they broke up.

As they were walking out of the Foreign Office, Salt asked Gretchen to try to track down Stuart or, if he wasn't responding, Walter, who might be able to reach Stuart and tell Stuart again that the Germans were not happy with the greenhorn nature of the team, especially Salt.

On the way back to the hotel, they had the same feeling about being tailed. Salt laughed quietly and suggested, a bit tongue in cheek, that the CIA might be following them. All agreed that anything was possible as they made dinner plans.

After dinner, when they were back at the hotel and Gretchen had gotten off the elevator on a lower floor, Salt said to Louise, "I doubt I'm in a position to meet later. I have a text from Stuart saying he wants to talk to me this evening and will call sometime in the next hour or so."

Louise said, "Hmm, that should be interesting. Good luck, and get some rest. Text me a quick summary when you're done with the call."

A few minutes later, after Salt was settled in his room, his shoe phone rang. It was Stuart. "Walter has brought me up to date, including the disparaging comments by Besecke. She needs to get over it, but more important, so do you. Do not—I repeat, do not—continue suggesting that you are not the right guy for this. You are there on the ground and need to take charge. You're the right guy for two reasons. You are, in fact, the right guy. And you have been sold as the right guy. We all know you don't care about your neck. But my neck is out there on this, and so are Louise's and Gretchen's. Use your Monday to clear your head and do something like go to a couple of the great museums there in Berlin. And get yourself to Prague early, so there's no hassle."

Stuart seemingly spoke without taking a breath, and it was clear that Salt was to listen and not talk very much, if at all. Stuart also explained that, although it was not certain that one would be needed (Louise spoke Arabic), State was sending from Baghdad, an interpreter for the meeting. Salt and the team should brief her or him.

"Okay—I get the message," said Salt. "We can talk about the long term after this week. By the way, has anyone mentioned to you these two guys who may have been tailing us in London and here in Berlin?"

"Yeah," responded Stuart. "If you're being tailed, it's not us. Maybe we need to think about giving you some protection, but that wouldn't be very low profile. We've told Louise to be careful and ready. Everyone is trying to figure out our new foreign policy; it's not surprising that someone would be curious about what you're up to. It may be nothing, but you can't be too careful these days. Good luck." Stuart hung up.

Salt texted Louise, "No change in plans," and then texted both Louise and Gretchen about working out in the morning before breakfast, having someone get them on a flight to Prague on Monday night or early Tuesday, and rooms at the Hilton near Old Town in Prague for them and the interpreter, and getting together with the interpreter in Prague on Tuesday. For once, he was able to go to sleep quickly.

Monday was actually relaxing. Salt briefed Gretchen and Louise about his listening session with Stuart during breakfast. By midmorning, they were booked on an evening flight to Prague and ready to burn some time museum hopping and shopping. It was a break they all needed.

The flight to Prague, as was the short cab ride downtown, was uneventful. In the cab, Salt explained to Louise and Gretchen that Prague was one of his favorite cities in the world. Prague had avoided much damage during World War II and while part of the Soviet bloc, and had a lovely and large Old Town area, complete with cobblestone streets, a number of shops that sold Czech glassware of all kinds, a wonderful town square, and an amazing astronomical clock dating from the 1550s, and outside tables for those who want to sample Czech beer and food. It seemed full of cheerful young people. The Charles Bridge crossed the river near Old Town, and on the opposite side of the river, the foot traffic followed a pedestrian street that led up a hill to a medieval castle. Salt once had a colleague who had traveled a great deal and described Prague as the "best museum-quality city" in Europe. Salt agreed. If one had to be someplace in Europe, Prague was a good place—even though it was cold in early March.

The scene in the Town Square was inviting enough that they decided to stop for a bite to eat and a beer while sitting at one of the outdoor tables. Just after the food was delivered, a shot rang out. "Sniper" yelled Louise while she turned the table over on its side to give them at least some modest cover. The first shot had ricocheted off the sidewalk, giving a flesh wound to one of the servers. Louise had her gun out but really had no discernable target. Then another shot rang out. With the team flat on the ground, the bullet went through the table. "Up and out of here," yelled Louise, who thought she had an idea of where the shots had come from.

She stood up and walked toward that spot, looking a bit like a thin version of Clint Eastwood, getting off six shots and then running like hell in a much different direction from the rest of the team. While running, she tore off and tossed the black coat of her pantsuit, leaving her white shirt as a top. She knew that Salt had stayed at the edge of the square to make sure she got out of the square, which had turned into bedlam.

Chapter 41

Facing the Iranian Front
[March 2, 2021]

Tuesday was a relaxing day in terms of meetings. They stayed inside the hotel. But Salt was on edge, constantly playing through his mind possible scenarios for the meeting with the Iranians. It was good that he didn't have to concentrate on anything else. He expected the other team members to be similarly distracted, but they were leaving him alone. The weather wasn't too bad, so they got together mid-afternoon, walked through Old Town, browsed in a couple of the crystal shops, and hiked across the Charles Bridge and up to the castle and back. They noted that seemingly everyone was wearing a mask. There was no sign of a shooter or Tweedledee and Tweedledum. They could be anywhere, but Louise felt pretty sure they were gone and no longer in Prague.

The group caught up late in the afternoon with the interpreter, who turned out to be a UK citizen whose family had moved from Baghdad before Iraq invaded Kuwait and was thoroughly English. She was smart and would be very good if needed.

They had arranged for a private room in the hotel for dinner with the small German team, consisting of Martin Weber and two others. They had considered getting a room in the US or German embassy for dinner, but that could have been a low-profile breaker.

The dinner discussion initially did not include anything of substance. They seemed to be as ready as they could be. But Salt then broke the boredom by saying, "I'd like to share something I've been thinking about all day. It's probably crazy, but just in case . . .

If you were looking at the world from space, you would see that (1) the Ukraine war is likely to be a long-term disaster, don't focus on solving that; (2) the world needs agricultural products and maybe some petroleum from Ukraine; and (3) Ukraine and Russia have nuclear power plants that are ticking time bombs. Indeed, northern Ukraine is the home of the infamous Chernobyl plant that suffered a serious incident in 1986; Europe's largest plant, the Zaporizhshia Nuclear Power Plant with 15 reactors, and a number of other nuclear plants, located mostly in southeast Ukraine, these are danger zones; the Russians use the Ukraine plants as 'cover' because the Ukrainians cannot safely shoot into the plant; (4) the US, France, the UK, and Ukraine have people and technology that could significantly reduce the nuclear risks associated with the plants in Iran; (5) Iran has petroleum that Europe needs, and Iran also needs to diversify its energy sourcing; and (6) Iran's economy is melting down and needs to be able to trade more freely." These conditions, summarized in a rough drawing Salt had concocted (see page 220), contribute to meaningful domestic unrest.

The meeting on the following morning was at the Zofin Palace, which was built in 1836–37 and was an amazing neo-renaissance building on an island in the Vltava River just south of Old Town. The city of Prague now owned it. It was quite lovely both inside and out, but not what one would call a tourist attraction. It is used for cultural events and as a conference center. The US team had arranged for the use of an obscure but very classy conference room on the mezzanine level with a view of the river.

The US and German teams walked from the hotel to the meeting and arrived around 10:15 a.m. The Iranian team, consisting of three members plus an interpreter, arrived promptly at 10:30 a.m. The leader of the Iranian team was Ashkan Gilani. The Germans knew a bit about him from previous discussions and gave Salt a heads-up that Gilani could attend the meeting. Gretchen had also done some homework on him. Gilani was a low profile in Iran but would not have been selected if the leadership of Iran did not trust him.

After donning their masks and engaging in the mandatory introductions and pleasantries, the teams sat down in a socially distanced pattern for discussions. Gilani spoke first. "Our team is fluent in English, and I assume the German team is as well. Therefore, I propose to hold the meeting in English, with help from the interpreters as needed."

"Agreed," said Salt.

Gilani continued, "Before we start, we have one question. No offense intended, but who are you, Mr. Pepper? We have no record of you being in prior meetings with either Iranians or Iraqis, and we need to understand your role here."

Keeping in mind Stuart's admonition from the Monday night call, Salt responded, "Surely you do not think the United States would send to a meeting someone the new administration does not have confidence in. At least, to some extent, you asked for this meeting because there is a new US administration. In that context, you should expect to see new people. That does not mean they are ignorant or not empowered. However, we accept your question as well-intentioned, if slightly insulting. The answer to your question is that I am a duly authorized representative of the United States with authority to speak on behalf of the secretary of state designate Stuart Bacon."

"Thank you," said Gilani. "As I said, we meant no offense. You must understand that we have to wonder if you are a new version of, or how you compare to, the last president's so-called personal lawyer, Mr. Rubin."

Salt smiled. "I'll have to give you points on that one, Ashkan. But I will readily admit that I don't compare to Mr. Rubin."

Gilani clearly understood both the obvious and nonobvious content of that reply. He continued, "Well if you have questions about our bona fides, we are glad to answer your questions."

"Thanks," said Salt, "but that is not necessary, as we have done our homework before arriving. And we understand that while our governments in the United States and Germany may be in various stages of transition, yours may be as well."

That jab resulted in the silent treatment for a few moments, with members of the Iranian delegation looking at one another with raised eyebrows.

Salt decided to break the ice: "Your government asked for this meeting. Perhaps it would be helpful for you to explain why."

"It is really quite simple," responded Gilani. "The current state of relations between Iran, on the one hand, and the United States and its allies, on the other, is not a basis for peace. We agreed to a comprehensive treaty in 2015 only to have, shall we say, an impulsive US president unilaterally drop out of the agreement at a time when all concerned agreed that Iran was in compliance with its obligations under what you call the JCPOA. This was a massive insult to all parties involved, especially Iran. It is understandable, therefore, that Iran has backed away from the JCPOA, and unless it can be fixed, we will ignore it."

Salt responded, "As I am sure you are aware, the new US government disagrees with a number of the actions taken by the Pope administration and has already communicated through appropriate channels its desire to rejoin the treaty. Of course, the US knows that you have already backed away from the 2015 agreement, as you are well above the JCPOA-enriched uranium limits as we sit here today, perhaps by a factor of 10. And we are aware of the explosion that took place in one of your nuclear facilities on July 2,000. .”

"Perhaps," said Gilani. "You also know that we could have taken much more aggressive actions in response to US provocations but decided not to do so before understanding more about the US attitude and plan."

Then Gilani sat back and said in perfect, unaccented English, "Look— we do not understand much about you or the new administration. But we can't wait long for progress in the US-Europe-Iran relationship. And we cannot engage in substantive discussions at all until we have meaningful relief from the ridiculous economic sanctions the United States has in place against Iran and its leading citizens. Truly, if a weapon of mass destruction has been detonated, it is the US sanctions. They have caused severe and unwarranted harm to Iranian citizens, especially with the effects of COVID-19.

You know from your satellite surveillance that we are digging trenches to serve as graves for the poor souls who die from the disease. You need to understand the seriousness of the situation. It is criminal. America must also call off its Israeli dogs who regularly bomb our people."

Salt was quiet for a moment and then responded. "We designed the sanctions to work well and have effects proportionate to the actions of Iran vis-à-vis Iraq, nuclear capabilities, terrorist support, cybercrime, and other issues of concern. Our satellite surveillance also shows that Iran is active in Syria, Yemen, and Iraq. You complain about Israel and refer to us as criminals while you inflict an incredible level of despair in places like Syria and Yemen. The whole world knows what you are up to in Venezuela. And as you know, we made humanitarian exceptions to the sanctions in relation to COVID-19. I'm a person who searches for the middle ground, but there can be no discussion of sanctions relief without material progress on these related issues. That is the substantive position of the United States because it is right, and you also need to understand the US political limitations on what it can agree to. The new administration will not follow the North Korea discussion model embraced by the prior administration here."

Gilani frowned. "Perhaps we need to meet separately in the room next door to discuss things among ourselves. Do you assure me that there are no listening devices in that room?"

Salt responded, "I'm sure it is wired for something, but we're not a party to that and have no listening capability in that room. And the national government of the Czech Republic does not know we are here."

With that, the teams separated for discussions among themselves, which ended up going through the consumption of sandwiches that arrived during those discussions.

They reconvened at 1:00 p.m. Gilani opened. "We may be at an impasse for today. We have told you that we need up-front sanctions relief before we can participate in substantive discussions. Could you please give us an overview of what you need if we are to achieve that?"

Salt responded without hesitating. "Certainly, and not necessarily in priority order: (1) release of all hostages with ties to the parties to the JCPOA; (2) cessation of state-sponsored cyberattacks; (3) reinstatement of nuclear limitations with a longer term, lower levels of the enriched product than called for by the JCPOA, and higher levels of verifiability; and (4) cessation of support of terrorist organizations and activities."

Gilani reacted immediately: "But this is ridiculous. You walk away from a treaty and then demand that your position be improved from what it was under the treaty to reinstate it. And you dare to do that after depriving our people of help from the coronavirus. How typical of America."

"I'm sorry you feel that way, especially given the COVID-19 assistance we have provided," said Salt. "Perhaps we need to think about these issues and resume discussions at another time, but soon."

"Well, in that case, we have found one thing we agree on today," Gilani responded as he packed up his papers and then left with his team.

After the Iranians left, the Americans and the Germans took a few minutes to compare notes, with all agreeing that the meeting was about what should have been expected in the first meeting. Martin Weber would report back to Minister Besecke, and the Americans would report back to Stuart Bacon. The Germans would get on an evening flight to Berlin. The American team was stuck in Prague for the evening and would take a morning flight back to Washington with a connection through Frankfurt.

After the German team departed, the Americans spent time in the Palace conference room, agreeing on the message to go back to Stuart. Basically, the results were not surprising, there was no real harm (or good) done, and the next steps, if any, would depend on what the Iranians came back with. Salt said he was still thinking about exposing his "big picture" thinking with Stuart, but the phone was not the right vehicle. For a deal to happen, there needs to be something in it for everyone.

The American team then packed their papers and started to walk along the river back to Old Town and the hotel. As they were walking, a young athletic male wearing a stocking cap and a mask ran up behind

Louise and grabbed her bag with her papers in it. She knew immediately that she had a crisis on her hands; it would be a disaster if a foreign power got possession of her copious notes and other materials in her bag. Her black pantsuit wasn't an issue, but Louise did not have on the right shoes for a chase in a rough cobblestone area, though she took off like a bolt of lightning after the guy, pulling her pistol out of her small handbag as she ran. As she neared the guy, she started yelling at him, and the crowd on the sidewalk started to rush off the river side of the sidewalk and get out of the way. Louise started yelling in Arabic without success. She hollered again in English, and the guy didn't stop. Louise was losing a shoe and about to lose ground. Having no choice, she fired her pistol once into the air and hollered one more time, this time yelling, "Stohp!" with a Russian accent. Taking advantage of the parting of the crowd, Louise stopped and took aim. The guy must have seen Louise take aim. He wisely dropped the bag and took off. It was not clear whether the Russian "Stohp" or the pistol did the trick. But he didn't look back and kept going.

Louise picked up her bag, and the team hustled off into a crowded, narrow, cobblestone side street, broke up, and kept going. The combination of the cobblestone pavement that was impossible to run on in street shoes, the density of the crown, and the fact that they hardly looked like terror or crime risks allowed them, to quickly get lost in the crowd. They each kept to themselves; the last thing they could do was draw attention to themselves or report something to the local police.

At the hotel, Louise confirmed that she had recovered all her papers. They discussed whether this was a local hit, the work of the tails who had picked them up in London and Berlin, or someone new ordered in from Moscow or Tehran. Salt agreed with Louise that they maybe had more surveillance than the team thought. And it could be that the Iranians had leaked the meeting, either purposely or inadvertently. The guy who grabbed Louise's bag was a new player; Tweedledee and Tweedledum were much more subtle and of a different persuasion.

Louise deposited her bag at the hotel desk to be put in the safe, Gretchen called and gave an update to Walter, who would, in turn, update Stuart, and the team headed out for another walk around Old Town, a stiff drink, and a decent dinner.

The next morning, Thursday, Gretchen attended to some sightseeing, and Salt and Louise took off on the long flight, connecting through Frankfurt, and arrived at Dulles International around 10:00 p.m. without incident. They were in coach again and were not able to talk much through their masks during the flight, but both had plenty to think about. They knew Stuart was occupied on Friday with Senate confirmation hearing preparation. They had tentatively scheduled a meeting with Stuart on Monday afternoon. Salt and Louise parted ways after landing. Salt found his car in the long-term parking lot at Dulles and headed for Carterville with a plan to take Friday off. He and Louise would touch base sometime over the weekend.

Chapter 42

Back Down on the Farm

[March 9, 2021]

It was sort of good to be home, but Salt had to ask himself whether the farm was really home—and what was he going to do with all the damn moving boxes? They didn't seem to be disappearing on their own.

Salt slept in on Friday morning, found some instant coffee and very stale rolls that were inedible, took a shower, and made his short-term survival grocery list. Over his lousy cup of coffee, he began to think about what came next. He had been too tired on the plane back to the United States to think seriously about such things and had focused instead on watching a series of bad movies. It was hard work to try to think cogently about complex issues.

The issues included: (1) did Salt want to retire?; (2) if so, where?; (3) if not, what would he do?; (4) was Stuart interested in having him continue on something?; (5) if so, what?; (6) what about Louise?; and (7) what about Margie? This was complicated—lots of interdependent and moving pieces.

Salt thought about all of these issues but did not resolve any of them, in part because he was still in transition in terms of losing his wife and moving and retiring and so on, and he wasn't really aware of what Stuart had in mind for him (though the library of books Stuart gave them was not very subtle). His first efforts had not had dazzling results; maybe Stuart was no longer relevant. Salt decided that he needed to continue to think about things and reassess as the number of uncertainties decreased. Or was that just an excuse for avoiding the whole can of worms?

Late in the morning, he went to the grocery and returned to the farm to make himself a ham sandwich for lunch. He then forced himself to work on more boxes for the rest of the afternoon.

He made himself another ham sandwich for dinner, had a drink, watched a western movie that didn't make him think, and went to bed.

On Saturday, he slept in again, showered, and moved around a few more boxes, pretending it represented meaningful progress. The coronavirus– shortened football season was over, and he wasn't a big fan of basketball on TV, so nothing on TV represented a compelling diversion. Since he was bored and listless, he talked himself into needing to get his hair trimmed again. He called Georgie's and got a number.

He had some time to kill, so he called his tenant, Jack Davis, to see how things were going. It had only been a couple of weeks since he last spoke with Jack. Salt just wanted to let Jack know he was interested. Jack answered the phone.

"Hi, Jack," Salt said. "I've been out of town and just thought I would check-in. How are things going?"

"No news here," responded Jack. "I'm still thinking about what, if anything, to plant. Am I better off taking whatever the government will give me to leave the ground fallow, or should I plant something? You know, the biggest factor in the market is China. We're still waiting to see the end of the so-called China trade war that President Pope was going to resolve before he got distracted by the damn impeachment mess, and then both the Chinese and we had to focus on the damned coronavirus pandemic. Then our elections took precedence. As a result, nothing is resolved. Meanwhile, the farmers of America are feeling like pawns. President Evans needs to get a move on."

Jack said, Salt, "I have some grain in storage that I'll have to sell at some point. I don't know what to do or when. I'll need money if I decide to plant in the spring, but as I say, I don't know what to plant—or if. I hope you'll continue to be patient and that someone in DC understands that many of us are hanging on by our fingernails."

"That's easy," said Salt. "Do what makes the most sense for you and your family, and we'll work things out when things start to look up."

Just before hanging up, Jack inserted another new element for Salt to consider, "I've been thinking about this for a while now, Salt, and I finally concluded that I am going to join the Daughters and Sons of Liberty. You may not have heard of them, but I thought you should know."

Salt reacted, "Oh, I know of them, and I don't have any objections at this point, and since we don't even have a lease right now, we'll just add this to the handshake deal."

Jack was sincere when he said, "thanks."

While he was dealing with these types of issues, he decided to have a follow-up with Dr. Sherman. He had available a slot in the late afternoon on Tuesday.

Chapter 43

Dr. Sherman's Two Cents Worth

[March 9, 2021]

S
alt sat down in front of Dr. Sherman's desk and opened up and
explained that he had been thinking more about his maze of relationships and wondered if Dr. Sherman had any thoughts.

"I do," said Dr. Sherman, "but are you sure you want to cloud your
mind with more outsider input? You probably know the right answer; you
just don't like it."

"In your case, yes," responded Salt. "We don't know each other very
well, but I trust you to tell me what you really think, based on your good
common sense and years of counseling. So I'm ready. I know you are blunt. "

"OK," said Dr. Sherman, "here goes. Cases like yours are neither new
nor profound. Lots of people have issues like this when dealing with grief.
You want to be able to fix with a band-aid what actually requires time
and major surgery. You had a special relationship with Meredith; there is
nobody quite like her on a shelf somewhere, or anywhere for that matter.
You need to settle in, rip off the band-aid, and deal with major surgery in
terms of your personal life. The worst case is a mistake of omission, not a
mistake of commission.

To complicate things, you have met two attractive, smart, and interested women very early in the grief process. There is no reason not to have
friends like these, but, my God, they are very different people. You sure
have covered a wide range of possibilities in your early days of being single.
In one sense, that is lucky, but you have to be honest with yourself and
them. If you want to screw your life up, you are free to do that until the
Supreme Court takes that right away from us.

You're ready for and need deep friendships. Build them up, but manage everyone's expectations at the same time. If they are not willing to be
"managed" in that sense, they will float away.

So the diagnosis is that you are a nut case. You have good reason to be. But do not make it worse! The prescription is what we have been talking about. You need to simplify your life and heal from a deep wound before making life decisions, and it would be horribly unfair to these two very different but great women to go too far, too fast."

Salt was quiet for a moment and then said quietly. "Well, that's good advice. I had hoped you would come out differently, but it seems that we are in violent agreement. Truth be told, we are in the process of implementing that approach in both cases. That may not involve a strict "hands-off" regime.

Dr. Sherman just shrugged his shoulders.

Chapter 44

Salt and the DSOL

[March 9, 2021]

Salt was not done with Dr. Sherman. "Okay," said Salt, "ready for the next one?"

"You mean the cockamamie idea that involves you working for the government and something loosely affiliated with the DSOL at the same time?" Dr. Sherman finished, "I had hoped the government threw you out of something when you asked about what I call the 'double deal.'"

Salt winced and acknowledged: "Well, the truth is that we are a long way from having something concrete to propose. Right now, it is a nothing burger. Some of the working group share your views." Dr. Sherman rolled his eyes back into his head. "Others are more entrepreneurial, "commented Salt. "Probably a majority is against it."

Dr. Sherman said dryly, "Great government at work. They don't like it but will not interpose an objection right now." Doctor Sherman shook his head and muttered, "Jesus Christ, you've got to be kidding. And I thought they would make this easy for me. Turns out they are gutless wonders. Well, you're already leaning toward doing this. I can comment on this and other cases and even arrange for some demonstrations. Let the record show," said Dr. Sherman, "I don't vote on whether we actively promote these deals, and I would not. But I can at least decide if someone or something is worthy of consideration. You'd be surprised at how often we do these dog and pony shows. But we use someone's legal skills to make sure they acknowledge being fully advised of the conflict-of-interest issues.

Chapter 45

Georgie's: Progress toward the Middle

[March 9, 2021]

S alt did not really need a trim, but he did not feel like spending the entire day alone either. Besides, he was wondering if anything had come of his political football game. When Salt called and asked for a number, Georgie estimated that Salt's number would be called around 4:15 p.m., so Salt decided to be safe, and headed for Georgie's a bit early. When Salt walked into the shop, he noticed that the excess chairs were still stacked in the corner to allow for social distancing, and all of the barbers and most of the customers were wearing masks. All eyes were focused on the TV. "What's on?" asked Salt.

"You mean you don't know, pointy-head?" asked Georgie in his more sarcastic tone. "Hell, man, this is Atlantic Coast Conference—we call it ACC—basketball territory, and Virginia is playing North Carolina. Kindly get the hell out of my line of sight so I can watch the game out of the side of my eye without butchering my current customer. I need to multitask if I'm ever going to get to you."

"Okay, okay, sorry," responded Salt. "Who are you rooting for?" "Anyone other than Duke and North Carolina, and at the top of the favorites list around here is Virginia," explained Georgie.

"You're a pretty big guy," commented Georgie. "Did you play basketball when you were in high school here?"

"Sort of," responded Salt. "I was on the team but didn't play much." "Sorry," said Georgie, "but now I have to ask. How much is not much?"

"Little enough that one day when the coach was in a foul mood, he told me I should just stop practicing and do squats instead."

"What did that mean?" asked Georgie.

Salt smiled. "He was telling me in his own code that the only action I was going to see was getting up off the bench at time-outs and the end of quarters and then sitting back down, so I might as well do something relevant like squats."

Several in the barbershop stifled laughs.

"Don't worry," said Salt. "I'm over it and have to laugh at myself. By the way, how is my political football game going?"

"See for yourself," said Georgie. "Take down some of the new notices and see what your bulletin board looks like."

Salt did as instructed and was pleased with what he uncovered. True to the understanding, Georgie had handed out pushpins and asked customers to place a pin on the corkboard—as if it were an illustration of a football field—to represent the player's political views. Most of the pins were between the thirty-five-yard lines. There were a few in the extremes (what you might call the red zones or even the end zones), and a few, like Salt, were right on or very close to the fifty-yard line.

"We played honest," said Georgie. "We did not look when customers put their pins on the bulletin board—well, not much anyhow—and we didn't give anyone shit about where they placed their pins. It was better than a news poll. No margin of error."

"That's right," commented Homer, the other male barber. "We kept Georgie on the straight and narrow here. And you were right; most people are looking for the middle ground and are not extremists."

"Most people," piped up Don, the retired guy, hunter, and NRA and SOL member, "would be the operative phrase. That's me in the right end zone and proud to be there—and I'm not alone, you will notice."

"That's great," commented Salt. "The point of this exercise is that there is a wide spectrum of political views, and if you want to get anything done, you'll likely need a mix of support from both sides of the fifty-yard line. We don't have to agree on everything, but we should where there is common ground between the thirty-five and forty-yard lines."

"I'll admit that it was sort of interesting," said Georgie, "and Homer, Ellen, and I decided we would leave the bulletin board up for another couple of weeks before taking it down. But now the question is, what will your pointy- headed friends do with all of this post-election goodwill? Best they do not piss it away."

"I would be very surprised if they didn't understand that," said Salt, hoping to himself that the new administration could deliver.

Georgie finished with his customer and said to Salt, "Okay, you're up.

Ready to lower your ears."

"I just need a trim," said Salt. "I'm not sure, but I may be going on a business trip and thought I should get less shaggy in case I need to go. Besides, I wanted to see whether you had destroyed the political football game."

As Georgie was finishing up, Salt said, "So now that I'm a regular here, do I qualify for the Hair-i-Care program?"

"Well, we have a new application form," said Georgie. "Take a look while I'm finishing your trim." Georgie handed Salt the new form, which included the following questions:

Hair-i-Care Application

Name:_____

1. Are you a woman or a male with black or brown skin? If so, stop here. You qualify.
2. Are you seventy or older?
3. Have you had five of your last six haircuts here?
4. Did you participate in our political football game?
5. Have you volunteered anywhere during the past two months?
6. If you are a male and you used our restroom for #1, did you lift the seat during the recent mid-term elections?
7. If so, was your aim good enough to hit the hole?
8. Were you left or right of center?

"Well, I guess I don't qualify," said Salt.

"Right," said Georgie, "but keep working on it. Someday you'll get there."

"How many do you have to get right?" Salt asked.

"Depends," said Georgie. "On what?" asked Salt.

"A lot of things," said Georgie, "including what kind of mood I'm in. So stop acting like one of those liberal media reporters on cable news always asking way too many stupid questions."

"Got it," said Salt. He shut up. The ACC basketball game was over, leaving most in a bad mood since North Carolina had overcome a stingy Virginia defense and won. The shop began to empty out about the same time Georgie was done with Salt. As he was leaving, Salt asked for a hint on item eight of the Hair-i-Care questions.

"No way," responded Georgie. "You're a pointy-headed member of the Deep State from Washington, DC; you are a primo leak risk."

Salt smiled, paid Georgie, and left.

Chapter 46

Suits Salt

[March 9, 2021]

Having talked to Jack Davis and Dr. Sherman, been to the grocery, had his haircut, and not be eager to return to a lonely and messy farmhouse, Salt decided to take a chance and call Margie Hatcher. She answered the phone, and Salt explained that he had been unexpectedly out of town and felt he owed her a call. He screwed up his courage and asked if she had time for dinner on Sunday night.

She was committed to a church meeting on Sunday evening but said, "If you don't have other plans, rather than wrestle boxes around your farmhouse tonight, why don't you drop over in an hour or so, and I'll add an extra helping to what I'm cooking, and you can join me here? All you have to do is drop by the bakery in town and get a couple of cupcakes for dessert. And maybe you can find a bottle of white wine at the grocery that would work for you."

"That sounds great," said Salt, "but I'm not very dressed up." "Neither am I," said Margie, "so come as you are."

Salt had time before the bakery and grocery closed to stop by Roy's clothing store. Roy was there—without any help or customers—and looking a bit lonely. "Roy," said Salt, "I need to see your dressiest suits in my size. I may be going to some meetings with some fancy dressers and need to measure up."

"As you can guess," said Roy, "we don't have people who need to dress like that very often, but you're a pretty common size, and we have more in that range than in other sizes. Let's see what I have to add to the navy blue suit you bought last time."

Roy brought two chalk-striped suits off the rack, one gray and one very dark blue. "These are pretty formal," said Roy. "You'll need some quality white shirts and good ties with these."

Salt stopped himself from responding to Roy for a few seconds. He wasn't sure what had come over him. Here he was buying suits for the job with Stuart in DC before he had decided to take the job—scary. Regardless, he responded, "Fine, let me have both suits, and let's pick out some shirts and ties. And good news, Roy: I don't need the alterations to be done today this time."

"Great," said Roy. "I don't mind telling you that things have been a bit slow, what with the layoffs at the manufacturing plants and the distribution center out on Route 81. I hope the new president gets moving on the trade issues, morphing viruses, monkeypox, and more testing before we all go broke."

"Amen," said Salt.

As Salt walked to his car, he wondered again what the hell he was doing. He had just gotten a haircut and bought two suits because he might be going to meetings with fancy dressers. He did that without knowing where Stuart's head was—or his own, for that matter. And then, he agreed to have dinner with Margie without resolving Louise's situation. This did not feel like life simplification.

When Salt arrived at Margie's, she was not dressed to the nines but once again looked very attractive. She was not wearing a black pantsuit. Salt thought to himself that she had been a comfortable and helpful companion at their one dinner and on the few other occasions when they had interacted. That actually meant something.

The discussion over dinner was low-key and unobtrusive. As they finished dinner and the wine, Salt said, "It's good to be back. I just wish the boxes were not waiting for me. My trip was unexpected and got in the way of really moving in."

"Was your trip business or pleasure?" Margie asked.

"Definitely business. I had to go to Europe for a couple of meetings."

"And here I thought you were retired." Margie smiled.

"Fair point," said Salt. But he had to stretch when he continued, "These were sort of follow-on meetings that related to some of what I had done years ago when I was still with the government and then in my law practice. Pretty boring trade stuff."

Margie took that statement as a hint that the subjects of the trip were actually not very boring and that Salt wasn't going to say much more.

"Out of curiosity," Margie asked, "how would you grade President Evans so far?"

"Well," said Salt, "that's a good and fair question. But I think it's too early to tell. There's a lot on the president's plate, and it will likely be a while before we can give the new administration a grade. They have brought in some good people from a pretty broad political spectrum, and that's encouraging."

Salt needed to change the subject, so he asked, "So, how are things with you and Carterville?"

"I'm fine," Margie responded, "but I'm not so sure about Carterville. There have been more layoffs, and the manufacturing slump continues; the downtown stores feel empty, I'm told the real estate market is slow, notwithstanding the low-interest rates (which we all know cannot stay this low), and the college is worried about losing even more students over the continuing coronavirus cases and the economy."

"I noticed that Roy's clothing store and the bakery seemed to be pretty empty for a Saturday afternoon," commented Salt.

"You are no doubt right," said Margie, "though a good percentage of the men around here were almost certainly glued to the ACC basketball game this afternoon."

Salt left at 9:45 p.m. after helping with the dishes. There were no awkward moments, though Salt realized that he had finally really noticed Margie and recognized her for the very nice person she was. He made a note to himself to be careful. He didn't need more complications. The world had enough.

Chapter 47

Rough Seas in DC
[March 10, 2021]

T he next day, Salt drove to DC for his dinner meeting with Louise at a quiet restaurant in the Tysons area in Northern Virginia, near McLean. During dinner, he explained to Louise why he did not want to be trapped in the Iran mess. At the core of his reasoning was the fact that even though there was only a 5% chance of anything coming out of Iran, it could become consuming—and for a long time. Salt was at the point in his life when he wanted to be able to set his own priorities and focus on those. If he wanted to be working on others' priorities, he would have stayed with the law firm.

The Iran situation was tantalizing as a challenge and could achieve much good if successful, but success was a long shot, and it was a foreign relations issue with less domestic impact than others. Salt explained to Louise the inside/outside the Beltway dichotomy that Salt had focused on during his walk in Hyde Park and was driving him. And then there was his desire to do something on the global health front.

Louise listened politely and then took her turn. "That's all well and good for you, Salt, but frankly, it's cockeyed and selfish. Where your head is here is all about you. Sure, your new friends in the middle of nowhere in rural Virginia have a role in your thinking, but the reality is that your focus is all about you. That might be understandable and acceptable if you had a snowball's chance of being in the right place at the right time again, but be realistic. So you would like to solve the China trade issues. Great. Just take a number behind Nixon, Kissinger, and a hundred others, dead and alive. The Chinese are wise, patient, and controlling. Some good can come from effective dialogue, but you're not positioned anywhere or with anyone in China. Hell, there are some who think that China is seriously thinking about invading Taiwan.

The stakes are too high for someone with your background. Those in front of you with deep ties into the Deep State will wipe you away. Somehow, you have lucked into potentially being in a lead role with the UK and maybe the EU on trade issues and at the table with Iran. What in God's name makes you think you can replicate that position with trade partners and enemies in Asia? Or do more good? Really?"

Louise had just warmed up. "And then there are others you have conveniently forgotten. Gretchen and I, and to a lesser extent Walter, are willing to put our careers on the line to try to make you look good. Sure, we think we can get something out of it for ourselves, but we can also go down with an aged greenhorn. We have our own balancing act to perform. And your self-centeredness makes a difficult situation much harder."

Salt was taken aback by the vitriol. He had to admit that she had scored a few valid points, but he was nonetheless hurt. And then he blurted out the worst thing that could have passed through his lips: "Is this why you picked the lock to my room in London—to get more control over me?"

She stood up and said, "I can't believe you're enough of a moron to even think that, much less actually say it. Have a good night, Pops." She walked out of the restaurant before the main course was served.

Salt sat alone and picked from both plates but focused more on his cocktail.

Regardless of how good or harmless his intent might have been, he had screwed up big-time. He was sure that Louise was enough of a pro that she would show up at the meeting with Stuart. To not show would be a career- limiting gesture. But she would say very little—at least at first.

Salt decided to think more about it in the morning but felt that he would most likely just see what Stuart and Louise had to say and where the chips would fall. And he had to tell them about Alexander Hamilton and his crew. He shuttered at the thought. Besides, he had no choice, and there was that nagging grain of truth in what Louise had said. Damn.

Chapter 48

Confession: Good for the Soul and the Mission

[March 12, 2021]

This time, the meeting with Stuart was at the State Department. When Salt arrived at Stuart's office at two o'clock on Friday afternoon, he was shown into the elegant waiting room outside Stuart's huge suite of conference rooms and his office. The scene was the real deal. Dark wood, huge rooms, many original oil paintings, heavy wood furniture, mostly antique, and interesting items from abroad are on display. It was a bit like a museum and dripped importance.

Louise was already there in the waiting area. To his surprise, so was Gretchen. Salt had not heard from Louise that morning, and neither Louise nor Gretchen said a word when he arrived. Salt managed only a polite "Good afternoon." This had the makings of an awkward meeting. No, a disastrous meeting.

Stuart called in Salt and Louise but not Gretchen, who may have been there for the moral support of Louise.

Salt seized the initiative. "Thanks for making time for us today, Stuart. We appreciate it."

"My pleasure," said Stuart. "We owe you two a big debt of gratitude for taking on some interesting situations without much prep time. You should know that we have heard from the Brits and the Germans, and both groups were very complimentary of how you handled yourselves despite being in very tough and unique situations. Both groups are doubtful that we can accomplish much over the long term, but they are fully prepared to undertake reasonable efforts to make what you talked about happen.

"The Germans, of course, are focused on the Iranian situation, which is complex, to say the least. They have not heard back from the Iranians and may not. You were a little curt with them, Salt, but nobody second-guesses how your team handled things. It seemed pitch-perfect. It is possible that the Germans or we will need to call about a follow-up meeting rather than wait for the Iranians to call back. If we ever get beyond first base, the US and German teams would have to be repopulated with more experienced hands, but we would like you to continue there and with the Brits in the short run. But we all need to remember that all of Europe is rightfully worried about how they are going to heat their homes this winter.

The implications of Ukraine are far wider than could have been foreseen. You know how Americans react to high gasoline prices—how would things be if there were only half as much gasoline?" Or how would we deal with famine in this country if we have an even worse drought?"

"Thanks for the feedback, Stuart," said Salt. "As you know, neither Louise nor I signed up for these kinds of gigs at the outset. I'm not aware of what Gretchen thinks about all of this. However, if you think we made progress, I'm willing to help get these initiatives moving forward, at least past the six to nine-month launch phase. I may have an opportunity in a private/government sector gig that could be useful as a cover. But it would not take all of my time. I can delay a final decision for a few months. If what we want to do is working, I'll commit to this 100%. But after all, Stuart, there is no commitment to me in this; I have no idea what I would be paid, and I could end up being a handy scapegoat. Louise should also be protected—do not underestimate how good she is, and a very quick study. "

Louise went white as a sheet, and Stuart went red as a red pepper. "You must be shitting me, Salt, because if you're not, I must be shitting myself." He was just warming up.

After Salt could get a word in, he said, "Look, I knew you'd be pissed. Around here, I am an apple in a sea of State Department and US Aid and CIA oranges. If I—no, we—can pull this off, it is only because Agent 99 here is pretty amazing.

I would like to try to make the double-dip work, and I have told the other party very little of what we're doing, even though they seem to have understood that the US gets first dibs on my time. I have told them the same thing as I have told you; I respected the chain of command structure by not telling Louise first. That was extremely difficult for me, and I am sure hurtful to her. You need to know Stuart that I have been very impressed with the team you have me working with. Together, we may be short on relevant experience, but Louise and Gretchen are both smart, streetwise, and resourceful. I don't speak for them, and I strongly urge you to talk to them, or at least Louise, separately from me."

"I'm glad to do that, and there's no time like the present," said Stuart. "There are two other things you need to be aware of, Stuart," said Salt.

"Holy Shit," roared Stuart. "Now there is a third shit missile about to hit me."

In a jittery but calming voice—very hard to do, by the way—Salt went on: "First, for a variety of important reasons, if and when it becomes possible, I really would like to have a hand in things related to global health care and Asia. For reasons I would be glad to discuss further with you, this is personal and real. The rationale for the healthcare interest is obvious, as we discussed when we met with President Evans. As to Asia, for today, it is enough that I tell you that one of the things our diplomacy needs to display is an appreciation of the interests of all Americans, including small businesses and farms. Not all of our trade issues are in the nature of the Huawei matter. Our people need to think we are worried about them as well as our multinationals. There is a connection between foreign affairs and ordinary citizens. I know you know that. We need to preach it more widely, so more people recognize the connectivity.

"Second, I sincerely apologize, but while we were in Europe, there were a couple of times when Louise and I were under stress and working closely together. Louise is not only very smart but attractive to boot. And I like her a lot. Nature took its course, and because of my stupidity, things happened.

Those things did not, and will not, in my judgment, interfere with our working together or separately on this mission. It is not clear to me what will happen with the relationship. Indeed, it may be over. But I need to be straight with you on this: what happened, happened. And, of course, Louise needs to be heard on this."

"Thanks for your candor, Salt," said Stuart, still trying to shake off the other news, "but what the hell were you thinking?"

Salt knew Stuart did not really expect a response to that, so he stood up, shrugged his shoulders, and headed for the door to leave Stuart's office. Stuart roared loud enough to stop Salt before he got to the door. "I just want to make sure I have this straight. All you want is (1) the ability to work on a colossal project for us and our major allies and on a part-time basis with someone in the private sector who might have conflicts with us, (2) ignore the fact that some would call you a walking EEOC charge, and (3) be able to dictate your future assignments. Anything else?

"Well," murmured Salt in his most quiet voice, "pay and admin." He smiled, turned on his heels, and practically ran out of the office.

Stuart then opened up on Louise. "Okay, Agent 99—what's your take on all of this messiness?"

Louise sat up and strongly stated, "I'm very interested in staying on this team and working on this initiative. I believe in the mission and think— at least for a while longer—it makes sense to keep the team together. I agree with Salt about the messiness and uncertainty about where that's going, and you need to know that everything was consensual and at least as much my fault as Salt's. The part-time bit and deal with the private sector I know nothing about. I almost fell out of my chair when he mentioned that. But it has to have come to him—he was not marketing himself, had no idea what he wanted to do, and was not looking for anything. He does not even have a resume. It is probably fair to pay him something, though that is a close call today, and he has got to have some admin support somewhere."

"Ugh," muttered Stuart. "Can I assume no embarrassing texts or emails will appear at a Congressional hearing someday?"

"None," said Louise. "We're smarter than that."

Stuart stopped talking and sat at his desk, thinking. He asked a question once in a while. One of those was, "can you work with this guy, and can he work with you? There is a ton of baggage here."

Louise took a deep breath and said, "Well, this is a lot more baggage than I anticipated, but I can make it work if he can."

Stuart was clearly not a happy camper but looked up and said, "Okay— you and Salt need to get yourselves down to HR, get this disclosed and papered, and do whatever else needs to be done. If we can get this by the HR types, we will continue the team starting a month from now. Tell HR we need to figure out a payment amount; he gets half of that for the next thirty days. For the next thirty days, your job is to find out everything about the other party that could be a stopper. This is over if Salt or the other party does not cooperate. Got that? Over. Dead."

Then he asked," Is Gretchen aware of this, and where is her head?"

"She and I talked at length this morning about everything I knew then, and she is on board," said Louise.

"Okay. Catch up with Gretchen and share the new stuff. As to Salt, take him by the ear, and get this straightened out with HR. And send in Gretchen." Stuart looked back down at his desk; the meeting was over.

As Louise was walking out of Stuart's office, she turned around and said to him, "You know, Stuart, it should not be a crime to be human and care for someone, especially if those involved are lonely adults, so long as the caring is not unwelcome."

Stuart looked up and added, "And so long as it does not interfere with the mission."

"Goes without saying," said Louise as she turned back around.

Then Stuart got in his final jabs. "Remember two more things. This guy is almost old enough to be your father, and he is still a head case dealing with the death of his wife. He's not ready to deal with this rationally."

Louise finished walking out without responding to Stuart, but she said to herself as she finished walking out, "maybe not yet."

In thirty seconds, Gretchen appeared. Before she could sit down, Stuart asked, "Are you aware of what's been going on, and are you nonetheless interested in staying on the team?"

"Yes, sir," responded Gretchen.

"Okay, good," said Stuart. "Were you involved in anything inappropriate on this mission?"

"No, sir," responded Gretchen.

Stuart sighed and said, "Very good, and thank you. Now get going and make sure the other two don't screw this up. They may need a witness down in HR."

Stuart thought for a few minutes and then called in his assistant and asked him to set up a meeting with Salt, Louise, Gretchen, and Walter in two weeks to get the Iran situation on the President's agenda as soon as possible. He did not think these folks could help in Ukraine, where our best and brightest were already fully engaged. However, there were many issues in many places, and he asked his assistant to give each team member a beach book bag full of books on Turkey, Greece, Syria, Iran, and the Soviet satellite countries.

Stuart silently hoped that some of the inherited crises and dysfunction would soon abate. That would be a good thing. But until then, there was a mountain of issues to attend to. And he needed good help, even if they came with a few warts.

Chapter 49

Daughters and Sons of Liberty and Friends

Having received as much of a blessing as he was ever going to receive from Stuart, Salt called Hamilton and set up a meeting for a few days later. He used those days to empty a few more moving boxes (he noticed that he was throwing out more as time passed). He also spent a lot of time thinking about what he would propose to Hamilton. He had never put together a "business plan" of any sort, and he readily concluded that it would be wrong-headed to go further than an outline of possibilities. The good thing: there was no agreement yet on any level, or even what he would be, so he did not have to worry about lost income, being fired, or reputational damage, for that matter.

Hamilton had given him the names of a few people who he thought could be helpful: a three-star general; well-respected former EPA and FEMA officials; a known Army corps of engineers official; a former energy company executive; a person with nuclear clean-up experience; and a small team with infrastructure, urban renewal, and low-income housing finance expertise. Somewhat to Salt's surprise, all of these folks extended themselves to be available to chat with Salt. It became clear that Hamilton was well-connected in a broad range of relevant disciplines. Salt also knew that Hamilton's choice of this group reflected where he wanted to go with the project.

In thinking, along with Louise, about what Salt began to call the Capital Area Sons of Liberty, later changed by Louise to "Daughters and Sons of Liberty," Salt immediately realized that he had to break down the efforts into several related categories with geography and expertise being the initial organizational guideposts.

From a geographical standpoint, for starters, there would be US and Central/Eastern Europe. The disciplines pursued would be different in the geographical areas, with a focus on where the public sector needed a boost from the private sector.

In the US, for example, areas of focus might include urban renewal (not including things like bridges, which are the responsibility of the government sector), things like multifamily and single-family housing, certain aspects of curriculum delivery, where appropriate stronger virtual vocational training, should be a focus, and the like. These efforts would require, in many cases, a combination of public and private sector funding, with the private sector financing in several forms, including donated equity or deeply subordinated debt, equity provided as a match to public funds (e.g., $1 of private money for every $3 of public funding, and construction financing provided as a bridge to conventional permanent funding. DSOL Hamilton Funds, LLC would play major roles in the initial stages of some of these efforts. Reverend Sherman would be on the boards of the entities focused on the US (he had not yet been asked), as would others who would understand the mission and provide both skills and diversity.

The Central and Eastern Europe activities would initially be focused on developing and implementing a "Marshall Plan" for the post-war region. Of course, a major element of the plan assumed that Ukraine would win the war. First things first. The Russians should be happy to take a rebuild off their balance sheet. The types of projects would need to be prioritized carefully so the return (broadly defined) would provide the needed bang for the buck. The post-Soviet experience in Central Europe would provide guidance. The program would need to include a major dose of privatization.

In assessing how potentially interested parties could be decent fits for inclusion and incentivized, Salt spent some time thinking about what he and Louise had learned and talked about in Europe a few weeks ago. There were a multitude of reciprocal national fixes and opportunities—if one could ignore history and the politics of things. As shown in the rough diagram on page 220, Ukraine needs to be rebuilt, be able to get its foodstuffs to markets and solve major safety issues at nuclear facilities. If the plants could be operated safely under an international commission, they might provide non- carbon-producing energy.

Diagram

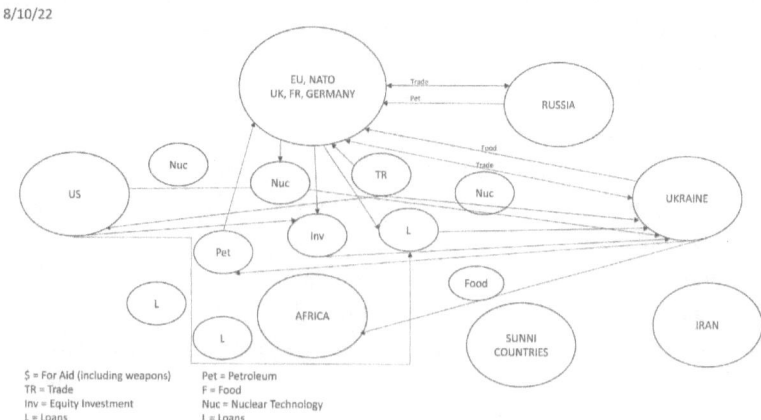

$ = For Aid (including weapons)	Pet = Petroleum
TR = Trade	F = Food
Inv = Equity Investment	Nuc = Nuclear Technology
L = Loans	L = Loans

nother major need was a secure energy source to replace the Russian supply chain in Europe. In all of their thinking, Salt and Louise assumed that Russia would not want to, or be allowed to, participate. The major immediate need of the Ukrainian allies was access to a secure supply of energy. Ukraine might respond to some of that need, but it would not be enough. Iran could help if it wanted to, and it could use financial assistance, including from the likes of the ECB and the World Bank. Risky and bold but not as crazy as it first seems. The Iranian people would likely be enthusiastic. But both Iran and other parties had to come back to the table. Perhaps it would be wise for Iran to be part of a larger solution set than be alone on the outside of major global developments that would affect Iran whether or not they played with the major democracies on critical issues.

The issue was how to get in place the necessary treaties. But that might be a bridge too long to cross. Perhaps as an interim step, temporary progress could be achieved by "executive orders" enforced by the US,

NATO, and EU. Sophisticated players would scoff at the notion of doing something as sweeping as this without a formal treaty. But why spend two years on a treaty that history teaches us can, in many cases will be abandoned without much in the way of consequences. There might come a day when the Sunni nations could participate, for they are clearly part of the regional solution, but, again, at this point, Iraq and Saudi Arabia would be kept informed and not counted on as active at the front end.

Hamilton asked a number of questions along the way, became quiet at the end of Salt's presentation, and then made his first comments; "Well, I asked for something ambitious, and you have delivered. It may reflect a lot more imagination than realism, but none of this is pretty, and sometimes you come to a fork in the road.

"By the way," Hamilton emphasized, "I assume Louise is involved here and supportive."

"Yes. She thinks it might be so nutty that elements of it could work."

"OK," said Hamilton, "I need to run this by some of the types of people we said we would need. That takes about a week. You guys (1) turn this into some kind of presentation that suggests we have a clue, (2) talk to your buddy in Germany (I think Martin is his name), and do it on the basis that makes him limit how far up the chain he has to go, we aren't asking Germany to do anything yet, and (3) discuss with Martin whether you or he should make the first call to Iran about this if we get that far. My preference is you, Salt.

Hamilton said he would talk to Doctor Sherman and let him and "Samuel" chat with the local DSOL." We need to understand what anyone doing a thorough diligence review of Dr. Sherman would find. The core local team will need some coaching. All other locals need to be out of the picture for a couple of months in terms of further developments until we see if this has any legs. We definitely need to manage expectations."

"How about our government?" asked Salt, "They will need to be updated at all times. They will also want assurances that if we go or make commitments to Iran, and then things get iffy, we will not walk out of our understandings Afghanistan style."

Finally, Hamilton reminded Salt that he needed to see his updated file.

And Salt responded in kind," Right, and I need to see yours, as well."

Hamilton concluded with a stern reminder to Salt that none of this reduced his commitments to Stuart and the US. This also applied to Louise since she would have to pick up part of the load.

Salt commented that he was fascinated and excited about the possibility of making a difference in this kind of undertaking and said to himself that he was scared to death that if kicked off, it could fail.

Then again, he had retired . . . and was happiest in the middle of things.

Epilogue

Despite being hot under the collar, Stuart suggested that Salt and Louise disappear for a week or so, and then find some good old GSA (Government Services Administration) space and furnishings for a temporary office.

So they took advantage of a short break in the action for some time off in the sun at some good dive sites in the Red Sea. They did not travel as a married couple, but ended up spending a lot of time together.

During the course of the trip Salt thought from time to time about how this would go down with Margie. But that was a negotiation that would have to wait for another day.

Salt and Louise were both experienced divers, but they were cautious in approach and took a "refresher" course with two blonde and tanned Canadian dive masters who would take them out to dive sites by boat, and who were of course nicknamed Barbie and Ken. As they neared the first dive site, an old small freighter in about 60 feet of water, they started to pull on their gear. The male dive master, Ken, hollered "hold off there. The water is nearly 90 degrees Fahrenheit, so unless you want to come out as red as a cooked lobster, just put on a T-shirt and go down to 50 feet or so and hope you can find some cooler patches of water. You'll also notice that there are fewer fish than five years ago; they've gone deeper in search of more moderate temperatures."

"How about the coral in this area?" asked Salt. "Same story," said Ken. "We see it every day, so it is not as obvious to us. But if you have not been here for a few years you will notice that it is much more bleached out." "That's a real shame," commented Salt. "But nothing compares to the devastation in Maui as a result of the lightning fires they recently experienced. They managed to get in three dives before having to hightail it to the airport.

They were both quiet in thought as the plane took off for Washington. Louise finally asked whether Salt had a clue as to what was next for them.

211

Salt responded, "Well, funny you should ask. I did not want to spoil your last day of diving, but Stuart gave me some hints when he called this morning. You may want to order another gin and tonic for this."

"Great" said Louise, "10 to 1 its nothing good."

Salt just shook his head and started to explain, "You are aware of oncoming trials of President Pope and others in New York, DC, Georgia and Florida. Heaven only knows which comes first. It would be far from ideal for any of those to overlap with the 2024 primaries (pretty likely) or the major party conventions. Imagine a world in which Pope is the winner through the primaries and has the most votes leaning his way going into the conventions, but is then convicted of something serious and wins the popular vote by a hair. That's when the litigation fiesta really begins.

Pope will use every trick in the book to get past the primaries and trials— at least his—so they follow the November 2024 election. Just for grins, insert a deadlocked convention somewhere in the middle and things not going so well in Ukraine. This would be an invitation for a repeat of January 6 sponsored by your friendly non- democratic authoritarian government."

Louise's only comment: "No thanks. And by the way, what the hell does this have to do with us and what we're supposed to be doing? And what about our election laws?"

"Fair questions. On elections laws, we have to comply. Full stop. Don't ask me where your paycheck is coming from because I don't know. Second, recall that we were brought in under Stuart's request to help the government understand how deep a diplomatic hole had been dug during the Pope administration.

We went on what amounted to a listening tour and then got pulled in prematurely to discussions with Iran, which may have, by the way, contributed to the recent release of some of the U.S. hostages held in Iran. Who knows? In any event, our unfinished business in that mission had to do with trying to understand why our citizens and those of other countries were so negative about the United States.

Strangely enough there are lots of alienated citizens in the U.S. who have similar feelings about their country. It is mind-blowing that after two impeachments, more indictments than you can count on your fingers, Pope still appears to have a commanding lead in the polls and could be re- elected.

So our last assignment involves trying to understand both U.S. and non-U.S. attitudes toward our country. This assignment is essentially the same job as our first adventure, but is focused on trying to attain a pre-convention understanding of how anyone could be so negative about our country as to even think about voting for Pope.

So pack your gear and look alive. The stakes are higher than many think. "Saw that movie," said Louise, "Once was enough." She then got a call saying team meetings would begin in DC first thing in the morning.

JAMES J. MAIWURM
1429 Harvest Crossing Drive McLean, VA 22101
Phone: (202) 256-6669
E-mail: james.maiwurm@gmail.com

SELECTED PRIZES/HONORS:

- Distinguished Alumni Award - College of Wooster 2024
- Chair Emeritus (Retired), Squire Patton Boggs (US) LLP
- Director: Sandy Spring Bancorp, Inc. (NASDAQ: SASR) [until 2021]; prior Advisory service on two other public company and several private company advisory boards
- Foundation Boards: Lewinsville Pres. Church (Chair) & Squire Patton Boggs Foundations

Non-Profit boards; prior service on other non-profit boards (College of Wooster and others)

EXPERIENCE OVERVIEW:

An unusual combination of legal, management/board, leadership, and international experience:

- Chair/Global CEO of top 25 global legal practice with 1500 lawyers and 44 offices in 21 countries; led transformational combinations with 475 lawyers from UK/Western European firms, 80 lawyers from Australian firms, and 300 lawyers from US-based firms with offices in the Middle East, as well as other growth initiatives around the world, including Asia
- Named by Law 360 as one of the ten most innovative law firm managing partners in 2012
- Significant experience in leading and growing international service businesses
- Service as Chairman and CEO of publicly-held 1300-employee international professional services (engineering) firm; led the restructuring of the business
- Advisor to senior management and boards of directors on matters such as governance and disclosure issues, development of acquisition strategies and structures, and dealing with financing sources

- Service on boards and advisory boards of publicly- and privately-held businesses and non-profit organizations
- More than 40 years as a transactional lawyer, representing a diverse range of businesses, from entrepreneurial start-ups to Fortune 50 companies, in private equity transactions, public offerings, and domestic and crossborder acquisitions, dispositions, financings, and joint ventures

SELECTED PUBLICATIONS/ARTICLES

- "Beachlead Aqusitions: Creating Waves in the Marketplace," 38 Business Lawyer 419 (1983) (co-author with James M. Tobin)
- "Annual Disclosure in a Declining Economy – Some Year–End Reminders," 5 Insights 1 (1991)
- "The ABC's of ESG," National Law Review (January2023);(https//www./lexology.com/library/detail.aspx?g=1549d836-385f-4667-85c8-https58f0712246cf12246cf)
- Inheritance of Crises and Dysfunction, James J. Maiwurm (2002 (1st Ed.) and 2024

SELECTED RECOGNITIONS/PRIZES

- Award for best senior undergraduate history student
- Phi Beta Kappa
- East Ohio Gas Scholarship Award
- George F. Baker Scholar
- Best Brief Award in Michigan Law School Moot Court Competition
- Who's Who Lifetime Achievement Award

AUTHOR
Books

- Inheritance of Crises and Dysfunction (novel) (2024)

SELECTED SPEAKING PRESENTATIONS

Panelist, "Marketing Through Mergers: Strategy, Integration & Business Development Opportunities Pre- & Post- Acquisition," 23rd Annual Marketing Partner Forum (Thomson Reuters) (January 2016), Orlando, Florida

Panelist, "Current Trends in the Legal Profession," 2015 Latin America Legal Executive Briefing (Thomson Reuters) (November 2015), Buenos Aires, Argentina

Panelist, "Global Law Firm Developments," Canadian Managing Partner Roundtable (Hildebrandt Consulting LLC) (October 2015), Sonoma, California

Panelist, "The Changing Legal Profession," 2014 Latin America Legal Executive Briefing (Thomson Reuters) (November 2014), Buenos Aires, Argentina

Panelist, "Law Firm Mergers: What Law Firm Leaders Should Know," 19th Annual Law Firm Leaders Forum, The Changing Model; How the Radical Changes in Legal Service Are Reshaping Law Firm Organization & Practices (Thomson Reuters Legal Executive Institute) (November 2014), New York, New York

Panelist, "International Structures and Governance Options," Global Law Firm Leaders Conference (Sandpipers Partners LLC) (September 2014), London, England

Panelist, "Law Firm of 2020," 2014 Legal Executive Briefing (Thomson Reuters) (May 2014), Pebble Beach, California

Panelist, "The State of the Legal Profession: A Global Perspective," 2013 Asia Pacific Legal Executive Briefing (Thomson Reuters) (March 2013) Shanghai, China

EXECUTIVE LEADERSHIP EXPERIENCE:

JANUARY 2011 TO DECEMBER 31, 2014:
    Chair of Global Board and Global CEO
    Squire Patton Boggs LLP (AU, UK, and US)

SEPTEMBER 2009 TO DECEMBER 2010:
    Chair of Firm and Management Committee
    Squire Sanders (US) LLP

MAY 2003 TO SEPTEMBER 2009:
  Firmwide Managing Partner (COO)
  Member of Management Committee (2006 to 2009)
  Squire, Sanders & Dempsey L.L.P.

FEBRUARY 2001 TO MAY 2003:
  Managing Partner
  Washington, D.C., and Northern Virginia Offices
  Squire, Sanders & Dempsey L.L.P.

APRIL 1999 TO DECEMBER 2000:
  Chairman, President and CEO
  Kaiser Group International, Inc. (formerly ICF Kaiser International, Inc.)
  Fairfax, Virginia

BOARD SERVICE:
  Corporate:

Kaiser Group Holdings, Inc./Kaiser Group International, Inc.
  (NYSE/NASDAQ)
  (Global engineering services provider)
  1999 -2005 (Chair)

Kaiser-Hill Company, LLC joint venture)
  (DOE contractor under $4 billion Rocky Flats closure contract)
  1999 -2005 (Chair, 1999-2000)

Workflow Management, Inc. (NASDAQ: NMS)
  (Integrated business graphics arts and consumables services, opera
  tions and fulfillment provider)
  1999 -2004 (Chair of Special Committee of the Board of Directors)

TRAX International Corporation
  (ESOP-owned government services provider) (Board, 2000- 2005,
  Advisory Board, 2015-2019)
  Sandy Spring Bancorp, Inc. (bank holding company; NASDAQ:
  SASR) (Board and Audit and Risk Committees, 2015-2021)
  HBR Consulting, LLC (Advisory Board, 2016-2019)

Non-Profit:

Mason Festival of the Arts Board (Chair)
2007 - 2009

Board of Advisors to the College of Visual and Performing Arts
George Mason University
2003 - 2009

The Tower Club Board of Governors
2003 - 2009

Davis Memorial Goodwill Industries, Inc.
1998 - 2003

Technology Resource Alliance
1995 - 1999

Century Club of George Mason University, Inc.
1994 - 94, 1997 - 98

Squire Patton Boggs Foundation
2014 - 2024

American Red Cross, National Capital Region
2016 - 2018

College of Wooster (Board of Trustees and Alumni Board)
2016 - 2020

Lewinsville Presbyterian Church Foundation (Chair)
2020 - 2025

ACTIVITIES:

Commission on the Future of the Arts in Fairfax County, Virginia
(2007 - 2008)
Founding Chair, Grubstake Breakfast Venture Capital Forum
(1990- 1995)

Founding Chair, Technology Resource Alliance (sponsored by George Mason University and Virginia Center for Innovative Technology) (1995 -1999)

BAR ADMISSIONS:

District of Columbia and Virginia

EDUCATION:

B.A., College of Wooster, Ohio (1971), Phi Beta Kappa, George F. Baker Scholar
J.D., University of Michigan Law School, cum laude (1974) National Institute for Trial Advocacy

PERSONAL:

Married (50 years), Wendy S. Maiwurm (retired medical social worker; grief counselor). Children: James G. and Michelle K.
Born December 5, 1948
Author: Inheritance of Crises and Dysfunction (2024)

SELECTED BUSINESS ACCOMPLISHMENTS:
Squire Patton Boggs (including predecessors, e.g., Squire, Sanders & Dempsey L.L.P.)

- During the first year as Chairman accomplished a combination with 475 lawyers UK based firm with offices in Western Europe; during the second year, led a combination with 80 lawyer firm based in Western Australia and other growth in Asia Pacific; and Singapore during the fourth year, led combination with 300 lawyer firm based in the US with offices in the Middle East
- Served as first firmwide Managing Partner (COO) for 800+ lawyer global law firm
- Reorganized and enhanced the performance of the administrative group
- Assisted in efforts to increase profitability
- Initiated industry/sector focus and client service team concept

- Extensive interaction with US and non-US offices, practices, and issues

Kaiser Group International, Inc.

- Provided stabilizing leadership to troubled Kaiser Group International, Inc.; inspired confidence of concerned clients and joint venture partners and disenchanted professional employees
- Established action-oriented turnaround mentality, flattened management structure, implemented focused redefinition and marketing of lines of business, led efforts to achieve necessary $20 million cost reduction
- Secured new and existing business and resolved client issues in Australia, the Philippines, the Czech Republic, and throughout the United States
- Negotiated and managed major asset dispositions and resolution of third-party claims; orchestrated restructuring of $140 million of debt
- Led joint venture efforts to obtain a new $4 billion government contract
- Built effective relationships with divergent constituencies: directors, noteholders, stockholders, employees, joint venture partners, clients, and outside advisors

LEGAL PRACTICES
Litigation 1974 -1986
Corporate 1986 - 2023

Areas of Legal Practice Emphasis:

- Capital formation and securities transactions, including private equity transactions and public offerings, and private placements of equity and debt securities
- Merger, acquisition, and divestiture transactions involving North, Central, and South American, European, and Pacific Rim interests and operations, including private equity investments, leveraged buyouts, and tender offers
- Domestic and international joint ventures and strategic alliances

- Financial workouts, including debt restructurings and recapitalizations
- General corporate, governance, and securities counseling, review of disclosure issues, proxy contests, development of acquisition strategies, dealing with financing sources, and advising boards of directors

www.ingramcontent.com/pod-product-compliance
Lightning Source LLC
Chambersburg PA
CBHW030447250626
47154CB00003BA/1167